Chronicle of the Seven Sorrows

Chronicle of the Seven Sorrows

by Patrick Chamoiseau

(Chronique des sept misères)

Translated and with an afterword by Linda Coverdale

Foreword by Édouard Glissant

UNIVERSITY OF NEBRASKA PRESS : LINCOLN

Publication of this translation
was assisted by grants from the
French Ministry of Culture –
National Center for the Book &
from the National Endowment
for the Arts. ❦

Library of Congress
Cataloging-in-Publication Data
Chamoiseau, Patrick.
[Chronique des sept misères.
English] Chronicle
of the seven sorrows – Chronique
des sept misères /
Patrick Chamoiseau: translated
with an afterword
by Linda Coverdale; foreword by
Édouard Glissant.
p. cm. I S B N 0-8032-1495-2
(cloth: alk. paper)
1. Fort-de-France (Martinique) –
Fiction.
I. Coverdale, Linda. I I. Title.
P Q 3949.2.C 45C 4613
1999 843–dc21 99-18845 C I P

THIRD PRINTING: 2000

Contents

A Word Scratcher

FULFILLING its splendid promise, the Francophone literature of the Antilles is coming into its own. Pouring forth at an ever-increasing pace, this literature lays claim to the diversity of our cultural heritage, our quest for a historical past that even yesterday was denied us, a perilous advance into the comforts and pitfalls of the modern world, and the adventure of a new form of expression arising from the confluence of several languages. The Antilles and the Caribbean shed a penetrating light on the dizzying evolution of our global village.

Patrick Chamoiseau belongs to a generation that did not thrill to the noble generalities of Négritude but focused instead on the particulars of West Indian reality. The particulars? One should say, rather, the inextricable mass of experience, a questioning of the wellsprings of language and history, the groundwork on what I have called our *antillanité*, that Caribbeanness so much in evidence and so imperiled.

No wonder that Chamoiseau's first published novel, this *Chronicle of the Seven Sorrows*, plunges us into the world of the "djobbers" of Martinique. For West Indian cities in the making, the "djob" – a method of cartage or transport and, in a wider sense, an "odd job" that is free-form and created afresh each day – has been the driving force of a subsistence economy that was already the rule in the countryside and that is a mode of survival. The art of survival is the painful and joyful talent of those who live in underdeveloped countries. The djob (a word adopted from English, as if the better to emphasize this difference) marks the "industrialized" stage of this art. The djobber has his secret, which is to invent life at every bend in the road. He crafts his rhetoric with a code reserved solely for its practitioners but with an exuberance that splatters far and wide. His speech exalts an optimism that in its daily throbbing pulse almost becomes a kind of wizardry. The market, his natural habitat, is altogether the prodigious belly of the world.

The descriptive art best suited to the exploration of such a universe must go beyond appearances and decipher the underlying and unimaginable wanderlust that gives rhythm to the workings of life. Here we find once more what Jacques-Stephen Alexis, for one, and Alejo Carpentier, for another, have called magical realism: the ferment of a literature of the baroque, outstanding examples of which have come to us from South America.

But the djobbers are disappearing, eliminated by the proliferation of supermarkets, by the explosion of massive and passive consumption that no longer even allows a man to rustle up some work or strive to keep it going day after day, if only in this constantly aborted form. That, according to economists, is the chief mystery of a society exploited by its own comforts, exhausted by surfeit, mired in the malaise of civilization. And so the djobber now seems to us like an indomitable rebel whose babbling shadow gives voice to our unconscious and whose *geste*[1] (whose pathetic flailing) evokes questions that speak to all of us.

Savoring the felicities of expression in the stories Chamoiseau tells, we take pleasure in a technique that is instructive yet robustly entertaining and that stands up nicely to such wear and tear. His narrative unfolds like a novel of suspense, skirting endless catastrophe, with a stream of solutions bursting with humor and extravagant high spirits. I recognize here the masterly delivery of Creole storytellers, whose words must wait breathlessly upon their fellows, whose "punch lines" astonish and enlighten. This style of writing was reaffirmed in Patrick Chamoiseau's second novel, *Solibo Magnifique*.

Such a practice hinges on the encounter – only yesterday denaturing – between French and Creole. West Indian writers will be reproached by some for "enriching" the French language to the detriment of Creole or its requisite defense and criticized by others for perverting that same French, for introducing within it the hidden fault of a wild and unprecedented diversity. Complaints that converge in the same sterile convention. Languages have no a priori, as they have no superego. The encounter between French and Creole was denaturing because oppression was then the order of the day. But it is precisely the literary use of languages that makes possible their liberation within us, and while they are never innocent in practice, at least nowadays we can affirm that their usage could never be unequivocal. We are in the throes of a passion for multilingualism. This passion does not mean at all that we should blend one language into another, on the contrary. The very profusion of all the languages around us demands still more, in exactingness and imagination, of whoever wishes to appeal to the inner poetics of one among them.

With these considerations – more thoughts in passing than scholarly reflections – we have not lost sight of Chamoiseau's flair for the novel, however. He himself informs us that in the multilingual world of the Caribbean, he sees himself as a "*marqueur de paroles*," [2] a "*Chamgibier*" or "*oiseau de Cham*," [3] listening to a distant voice whose echo hovers over the scenes of our collective memory and guides our future. This is an acknowledgment that he walks that line between the spoken and written word, one of the crucial perspectives in literature today.

To preserve or promote the blossoming of the Creole language in the Antilles, while differentiating it from a gallicized patois, is to defend that borderline valiantly. Another approach is to *inform* French with the inventions of Creole: this serves both languages well without bastardizing either one. As we read Chamoiseau, his wealth of linguistic finds, which are often and ingenuously rooted in what are clearly literal transpositions, gives us exceptional pleasure. The same pleasure we take in the works of Alejo Carpentier, in the dexterous twists and turns of Lezama Lima, in the Creole texts of the Haitian Franketienne, in the dub poetry [4] of Michael Smith and the poets of Jamaica.

And so, collectively, we can express our Caribbean reality. If the heroes of whom we dream (whom we dream up?) all meet at these crossroads of poverty, storytelling, and enlightenment, it is because the same song of light and shadow wells up from our Americas. Here Patrick Chamoiseau presents us with a remarkable version of this song, one faithful to its complex harmonies and sparkling with a very personal inspiration. Enjoy his performance.

Édouard Glissant

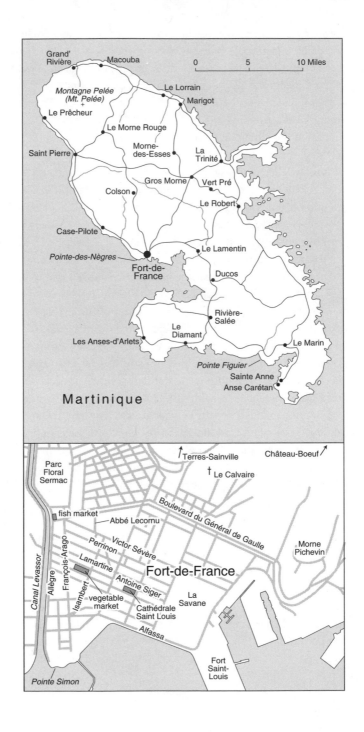

Martinique

Grand' Rivière
Macouba
10 Miles
0 5

Montagne Pelée
(Mt. Pelée)
+
Le Prêcheur
Le Lorrain
Marigot

Le Morne Rouge
Morne-des-Esses
La Trinité

Saint Pierre
Gros Morne
Vert Pré

Colson
Le Robert

Case-Pilote

Pointe-des-Nègres
Fort-de-France
Le Lamentin

Ducos

Rivière-Salée

Le Diamant
Les Anses-d'Arlets

Le Marin

Pointe Figuier
Sainte Anne
Anse Carétan

Parc Floral Sermac
↑ Terres-Sainville
Château-Boeuf ↗

† Le Calvaire

fish market
Abbé Lecornu
Boulevard du Général de Gaulle

Victor Sévère
Perrinon
Morne Pichevin

Canal Levassor
Allègre
François-Arago
Lamartine
Antoine Siger
Fort-de-France

Isambert
vegetable market
La Savane

Cathédrale Saint Louis

Alfassa

Pointe Simon
Fort Saint-Louis

Chronicle of the Seven Sorrows

To the Crow,
who gave me writing.

To Tio-tio,
who gave me the essential thing.

To Ninotte,
my mother,
who gave me everything.

P C

1 Inspiration

. . . History is fissured by histories that cast away upon irremediable shores those who never had time to see themselves through the tangle of tropical vines.

Édouard Glissant, *Caribbean Discourse*

LADIES AND GENTLEMEN here present, the three markets of Fort-de-France (meat, fish, vegetables) were, for us djobbers, the compass of our lives. A kind of sky, horizon, fate, within which we scrabbled life out of poverty.

As we reveal to you who we were, you'll hear no windy boasting: the story of nameless men offers only a single sweetness, that of words, so we'll taste but sparingly of pride. Possessing simply our wheelbarrows and our skill with them, we did not farm, or fish, or bring anything to market. And unlike the railings, the corrugated iron of the roofs, or the cement of the stalls, our participation in market life had none of the comfortable certitude of indispensability.

Just when a vendor's baskets became too heavy for her, the djobbers appeared, at first to lend a friendly hand, later to help out every day in exchange for a little something at the end of the afternoon. Soon this settled into a savvy system, and its rules of procedure were passed along. However could we know who our forefathers were? They had certainly – like many others who were doubtless more talented – left plantation mud behind to tackle life on city sidewalks less likely to trip them up. Surely, during their wandering in exile, they fell into the habit of lollygagging around places humming with life and the reassuring atmosphere of their native countryside: the markets. People noticed their burly arms. Their brawny thighs. People turned to them for such and such a service, this or that message to be hustled over to so-and-so, thanks a lot . . . People called for them to come control the oxen, catch the pigs, budge stubborn donkeys. Our fathers were self-made and we inherited their know-how, the imperceptible something that yet set us apart already from oafish black men whose only industrious activity was the beating of their hearts.

Lugging the vendors' baskets of wares to be spread out on madras cloths, fetching the women smallchange, doing them little favors for a few sous – that was the cream of the djob, our livelihood.

But we were so footloose that our presence there was almost imperial among those who, tied to their stalls, had to pluck so many of poverty's feathers to take a bite out of life. Days spent among these baskets of vegetables were less than glorious, and no eye twinkled with exaltation, but here, time after time, dire want confronted its finest adversaries.

Well, the finest one of all for all time was Pipi, master-djobber, king of the wheelbarrow, the darling of the young vendors and a son to all the old ones. He was a big calabash, embracing within himself both flower and fruit, and just as a single mango bespeaks the essence of the tree, what he was, we were. So, *manmaye ho!*[5] Talking about ourselves makes it inevitable and only right that we should tell you about him . . .

To start off, let's take the beginning, that means his mother, the woman we'll call Mam⁶ Elo, who will become the indisputable queen of *macadam*. She was neither ugly nor pretty, and there was really nothing special about this placid, tidy black woman. She was the ninth of her father's daughters. After waiting hopefully all night before the door to the bedroom where his wife Fanotte had mired herself in the throes of childbirth, the unfortunate man had cried out in rage and disappointment, "Yin ki fanm, fanm ki an tÿou mwen!" (I'm up to my neck in nothing but women!)

In spite of the little bottle of holy water and the impaled toads, fate had sent him another girl. In despair, he vanished for six whole days into the backwoods.

The poor man was a mason, earning good money but not enough to feed his wife and eight daughters, so he also raised sheep, pigs, and poultry, selling them now and then to bring in extra money. He owned two milch cows as well and claimed to be an expert on crabs, because every night, accompanied by his eight reluctant daughters, he scoured a mangrove swamp teeming with these crustaceans near the town of Le Robert. Lastly, through some rather mysterious inheritances, he had come into a plot of uncultivated land where he labored mightily to grow yams, tough cabbages, or sweet potatoes. While his days were filled with small masonry jobs in Le Robert or here-and-there in the shacks of Vert-Pré, a large part of his nights was lost in these other chores, hours of feeling lonely – too lonely – among women who didn't care a snip about such things. Muttering at every turn, "Fanm fanm yin ki fanm ki an tÿou mwen!," he imposed upon his clutch of girl-chicks a brutal discipline that his wife Fanotte speedily relaxed as soon as he reached the foot of the morne⁷ where his old mule was waiting for him. As early as five in the morning, the neighbors would hear the booming voice of Félix Soleil (yes, his name was Happy Sunshine) giving strict instructions to his gazelles, winding up with a "Pay attention to me, eh? All right!" Then off he'd go, with his traditional parting shot to his wife, as she handed him his lunch pail of cabbage-avocados-fried-cod: "Bon Fanotte véyé sé ich ou-a!" (Now Fanotte, keep an eye on your children!)

He would hardly have reached the bottom of the hill when his hitherto drooping daughters would bloom like wildflowers, and with their young breasts jiggling beneath their simple cotton shifts, they saluted his departure with energetic grimaces of relief. Fanotte, who also breathed easier, turned a blind eye. But when these monkeyshines were over, the little girls would begin their assorted tasks, anxious to avoid punishment from a green switch on their cringing backs. Alas, since youngsters and responsibility don't mix, Alice and Adèle would prance off to play tag in the weeds they were supposed to pull, pausing in their mad dashes every now and then to delicately pluck a single blade here or there, thus salvaging their consciences for another half hour. Sitting in front of her cutlass on the precise spot where she was to dig holes for yams, Félicité would twist her hair into fresh curl papers. Pauline, for her part, would put on such a nicely ironed dress and such nicely polished shoes that she hardly seemed ready to go foraging for commelina grass in the ravines. Only Armande and Caroline – who were older, I might add – would set seriously to work, one at the bottom of the roof cistern, the other in the slough of the crab-traps, but they found these tasks discouraging because the crabs escaped by the dozens and there was no end of slime in the cistern. As for Jocelyne, after flinging two saucepans of water into the pig pen by way of cleaning it and tossing the porkers and the poultry a few hands of over-ripe bananas, she usually howled her hatred at the sheep and cows, sending them galloping helter-skelter all over the savanna. Our bucolic beauty would dawdle dreamily after them, entranced by the blossoms in the bushes. And Ginette? Arriving late at the market in Le Robert, she would find herself relegated to a sparsely visited corner, where she remained behind her basket of scrawny yams, waiting in a daze of eremitic expectation unbroken by her cries of "Man ni bel yanmes vini ouê mwen!" (I've got some fine yams, come take a look-see!) or those hourly magical incantations intended, according to Fanotte, to attract a brisk business. This seclusion did not prevent the girl from refusing any sale should some good woman happen to ask about her prices, so true is it that the only proper customer to start off an honest day's trade, as Fanotte always said, was a ballsy young man. And so, at around two o'clock, with the market slowing down, there she'd be with a full basket, which she'd sell off dirt cheap at rattling speed. Meanwhile, the mother, Fanotte, a woman crushed and deadened by her husband's authority, was paying no attention to her daughters. She'd sweep her shanty, shake out the straw mattresses, set the laundry washed the previous day out to dry in the fresh air, put the rest of the dirty clothes to soak, cook up a few ti-nains⁸ and a bit of salt meat, then head off to the corrugated tin stand by the side of the highway where she sold spices and blocks of ice. She'd spend her days there, trudging back up the hill every hour to nudge her cooking along and make sure Alice and Adèle hadn't been struck down by a Long-beast⁹ in those rank weeds they were supposed to have yanked up a long time ago. That's how the day went by until the moment Félix Soleil's old mule was heard wheezing on its uphill plod.

The mule was barely tethered before Félix Soleil was tugging a green liana from that snarled growth of bushes we call raziés in Creole hereabouts and stroking it with cement-hardened fingers. Without even pausing at the roadside stand where Fanotte was on the lookout for him, he would bolt toward his hut, seething with anticipated fury, shouting the "Sé fanm-la mi mwen!" (Women here I come!) that sowed indescribable panic among his daughters. Adèle and Alice, still lingering at their games, were usually the first to try out the vine du jour – followed by Ginette, who could never account for how such choice yams could bring in only that's all? in the way of money. Next in line for the plant-of-pain were Caroline (the cistern was still dirty, or not yet full), Pauline (her bundle of commelina grass waved before her like a flag never got her off the hook), Jocelyne (perpetually incapable of explaining clearly where all the cows and sheep had gone), Félicité (Come on now, doesn't take all day to dig one measly yam hole!), and finally Armande, mute under the lash, so exhausted was she from scrambling after scattering crabs, while a sweating Félix Soleil, laying on the now-tattered vine, shrieked out his inability to accept that seventy cages could cough up just fifteen crabs, *tonnan di sô!* [hell's bells!] . . . After everybody had received her share, the mason would sit at his table, where Fanotte would serve him three fingers of rum punch he'd sip at sourly before going off to hunt down sheep and cows and set out the crab-traps again.

So Félix Soleil came to associate women with all the misfortunes of his life, then of the whole world, and soon, of the universe. The time came when his anger went on permanent boil. His terrible voice opened seams in the walls of the shanty, and on certain full-moon nights he could be seen out in his little yard hurling heavenward his *Fanm fanm yin ki fanm ki an tÿou mwen!* It was also around this time that some sympathetic friends explained to him how impossible it was for a guy with all balls in working order to beget only girls and nothing but, so Félix you've got to get one thing straight: Somebody's slapped a hex on you! . . . Félix Soleil instantly declared merciless war on every toad that wandered across a perimeter traced around the shanty with powdered lime. There were just so many of them every night – twice as many when it rained – that he was convinced these beasties (clearly commanded by a spiteful neighbor) were carrying the curse he wanted to dispel. One Friday, as the church in Le Robert was about to close its doors, he filled a flask with precious liquid from the holy-water stoop. That same Friday the thirteenth, he whittled a hundred tiny stakes of hardest *bois-bombe*, sprinkled them with church water, and set about pinning to the ground all toads that came within ten yards of the shanty. Around his house could soon be seen a wriggling mass of these batrachians, shriveled, wormy, dying beneath onslaughts of ants, crucified by the stakes. Every evening, Félix Soleil inspected his victims and dribbled holy water on them from the tip of a bamboo stalk, murmuring what he claimed were all-powerful prayers.

Félix Soleil's little girls became women. One unbelievable day, they found within themselves the courage to tell him to go jump in the river, him and his chickens, his pigs, his sheep, his crabs, and anything else he might want to take along – because we've had it up to here with you! Without a word, the mason put on his burial clothes and went into town to get a cutlass sharpened, then came home brandishing the weapon over his head. The blade sliced the air with a horrible hiss as Félix Soleil gave formal notice to his ingrates: "Bunch of sluts beat it wutless good-fa-nuttens! . . ." He chased them nonstop all the way to Le Robert, where the wretched women escaped with their lives thanks only to the energetic intervention of the gendarmes-on-horseback. After the dispersal of his daughters, the mason plunged into a blissful quietude and seemed content in spite of the cold rage still driving him to skewer foolhardy toads. Some time later, Fanotte became pregnant again. Félix Soleil let out a war cry that could be heard even in La Trinité: "Aaah, koutala aké an ti bolomm!" (This time it's going to be a lil' fellow!)

His anti-toads campaign grew ever more ferocious. They were found transfixed and holy-watered within a radius of over a mile around his home. His suspicions spread to malefic *soficougnan* butterflies, red roaches, walking sticks, earwigs, *mabouya*-lizards tracked down in damp corners, grasshoppers, stinkbugs – to any tiny critters that showed their noses in his vital circle. He'd wrap the lot in rags the priest would fish from the holy-water basin the next morning. When Fanotte began her labor pains, Félix Soleil sent not for Philomène, who had delivered his eight daughters of misfortune, but a midwife from the Coubaril neighborhood who styled herself Sister Sainte-Marie. The aforementioned prided herself on delivering only boys with nice plump plums. It was a long and difficult birth.

"Must be tethered inside her womb," was Sister Sainte-Marie's instant diagnosis.

To break the charm holding back the child, she applied to Fanotte's suffering forehead a handkerchief moistened with the sweat from Félix Soleil's armpits. The front room glowed red in the lamplight, and there the husband waited in the most agonizing anticipation of his life. At the baby's first wail, Félix Soleil flung himself in anguish against the bedroom door.

"Sister Sainte-Marie souplé, esse cé an tigasson?" (please, is it a boychile?) he stammered.

"Sister Sainte-Marie took off out the window," replied Fanotte, " 'cause it's a girl, Félix."

Félix Soleil didn't even want to see the child. He vanished for six days into the woods of Vert-Pré. He was spotted skirting the cane fields in misty drizzles. He was seen running through dense undergrowth, slinking through inaccessible ravines. People thought he was doomed from then on to drift around silk-cotton trees,[10] but he went home in the end, aged by the stubble on his chin, to find Fanotte with her ninth daughter, a charming baby named Héloïse who, heaps of years later, became the queen of macadam at the market in Fort-de-France, and Pipi's mother – Mam Elo, our friend and compeer.

Héloïse did not add one jot to her father's unhappiness. She never tried his temper. Resigned, the mason did not mention crabs, commelina grass, cisterns, or market stalls to his ninth disappointment. He asked her only to look after the sheep and cows, which the little girl loved doing above all else. She felt free on those savannas, where the sun poured out endless crystalline light that sometimes went milky like frosted glass. Despite their delirious profusion, the cabuya plants put on a handsome display of perfumes, hues, undulations. With sheep and cows tagging along, the future Mam Elo investigated the secrets of grassy places where life-and-death struggles pass unnoticed. When it rained, everything melted into another life, with new colors and smells – but a dull serenity returned with the first rays of sunshine. The animals stayed close to Héloïse. They got along perfectly with the little girl, whose every step was an exploration of this natural labyrinth. And so, through a happiness that simply seemed like taking good care of the animals, Héloïse brought her father some peace.

Unlike her sisters, she was able to attend school. This was a new world, outside of reality itself, where she learned to read and write in French, a strange language that astonished her parents. Fanotte demanded on the spot that her daughter speak French to her – where's your manners, girl? Félix Soleil, however, never seemed able to get used to it. He'd certainly heard French before (the gendarmes-on-horseback used it), but he'd never imagined it in his own house. So, rolling his eyes in a big way, he'd mutter his *Fanm fanm yin ki fanm ki an* *tÿou mwen!* every time Héloïse recited some La Fontaine business about a grasshopper gay singing summer away but winding up poor by winter's first roar . . . That's how the future Mam Elo grew up, with a father who was always in a wonder, when he looked at her, over just what misfortune she would bring, and a mother so meek you plain forgot about her. Héloïse often visited her sisters, who had fanned out to Fort-de-France, Le Morne-Rouge, Le Saint-Esprit, Marigot, in huts where, from fear of finding their father again in the guise of a husband or any other kind of man, they lived by themselves. When she couldn't understand the French world at all anymore, Héloïse left school and took charge of the roadside stand, for Fanotte was now wizened and almost blind. As for Félix Soleil, white-haired and wrinkled, he was still *djok*, strong and alert. He no longer worked as a mason because his sight was failing, and he'd sold his livestock when Héloïse (a young woman with titties) could no longer be allowed to roam the savannas. Still keenly interested in crabs, he now devoted all his time to them, stashing them even in the chicken coops. The girl and the two old folks lived off the roadside stand plus the crabs they sold at Pentecost and Easter. Years slipped away like that. Héloïse became a woman for whom no one came courting. Preoccupied with the stand and with Félix Soleil, now half-paralyzed in a rocking chair, she wound up forgetting Fanotte, who lay so discreetly amid the tatters of her straw mattress that when she died, it seemed only prudent to plop the whole thing in the coffin.

Héloïse and her father lived side by side, without speaking to each other. From time to time the virtual spinster was visited by her sisters, who never passed up a chance to persecute their elderly father, pretending to lash him with a liana and crowing in his ears, "Yin ki fanm ki an tÿou'w!?" (So you're up to your neck in nothing but women!?) Félix Soleil did not understand that — or anything else anymore. Lost in contemplation of a colony of crazy ants that had set up housekeeping in his clothing and the dutty folds of his skin, he let all of life glide by in senile indifference. He died one Sunday, without a drum-roll for the occasion (although the ants did beat a retreat), his only viaticum whatever was left in the flask of holy water he'd had time to empty over his head. Héloïse had this cut into a cement slab for him: Here lies Félix Soleil our father, who had nothing but women before and behind him. When they tried to bury him next to his wife, they could find no trace of her despite a thorough search of the cemetery. And so, in desperation, they dressed him in his one and only city suit, with his church flask and sheaves of white arum lilies, and laid him in the ground all by his lonesome.

Now, ladies and gentlemen here present, this is how the *dorlis*,[11] Pipi's father, arrived on the scene. Leaving the cemetery, Héloïse was toddling off toward a fate sealed into spinsterhood, when something clicked in the brain of Anatole-Anatole, the gravedigger's son, who took it into his head to follow her home. Anatole-Anatole was one of those black folks whose parents, or even great-grandparents, had had nothing to do with the least little *béké*[12] or mixed-blood. His skin had thus remained a magisterial black that seemed to soak up the sun forever. The grounds of the cemetery had belonged to his father, a jolly nigger if ever there was one, who had chanced to come into this patch of land shunned even by scrappy weeds. His name was Phosphore, he was an atheist, and he openly mocked the church, the white man's gods, and above all the local priest – whose request for that rocky parcel of land, however, he did not brush off at all.

"If it's for a cemetery, *monsieur l'abbé*, go ahead and take it . . ."

It was too bad, said the priest, that people were being buried near the crucifix at the crossroads, under silk-cotton trees, and even tucked away behind fields, where Our-Lord was obviously too busy to go pick up their souls. Given permission to use the property, the priest posted a sign announcing this new burial ground. He had the remains of graves once scattered all around the countryside moved there posthaste. To amuse himself, black Phospore strolled among the modest mounds of the first tombs to appear on his land, letting out great horselaughs as he read the epitaphs. The priest was upset by this and fenced off the cemetery. Nothing daunted, Phosphore knocked down stakes and barbed wire and continued his amused inspections. The priest ordered him to leave. In reply, Phosphore told God's representative that he could go shit himself because this is my property, even if I did let you put your thingummies here. Shocked, the clergyman grabbed Phosphore by the neck, threw him down, and tried to drag him from that place of eternal rest. Phosphore managed to get up and delivered a flurry of blows to the priest with a green switch. Humiliated, the man of the cloth countered with this devastating move, which still makes us tremble in our shanties: he shook his cassock at his adversary.

Oh sad life of black Phosphore! Gone were his guffaws and the twinkle in his eye, for this deadly gesture condemned him to straggle among the graves. Hovering endlessly like a drunken hummingbird, he never left the cemetery, staying rooted to the spot where fate had thumped him one. His wife Ninon visited every day with calabashes of soups enriched with herbs soothing to the mind. Phosphore now spoke only to invisible people, a sure sign of hopeless madness. Fatigue alone could bring a halt to his meandering among the graves and drop him in the corner of the cemetery where Ninon, resigned at last, had had a small *caye*, or cabin, built for him. Everybody grew so used to his condition that soon no one could imagine him any other way. Every midday, every evening, Ninon brought him fresh food but no longer even tried to speak to him. Phosphore took care of the graves, tidying them, relighting the candles, fixing the bouquets knocked about by the wind. One day, he dug the graves for the latest batch of corpses. On Sunday the new priest, who had often come to bless his predecessor's victim, made the appointment official with an announcement from the pulpit. Black Phosphore thus turned into Phosphore-the-Gravedigger, and that's what he was called. As for Ninon, she was the-gravedigger's-wife from then on, which put a flat halt to the sales of her brooms. Their son, Anatole-Anatole, by virtue of the fundamental truth that a tiger's cubs are not born without claws, became the-little-gravedigger . . . which, my dear, did not leave him much of a choice when he went looking for a profession.

Anatole-Anatole had acquired the habit, moreover, of following his father's endless ambulations around the plot at the back of beyond. He imitated Phosphore's way of walking, the right-left sway of his head. Sometimes Ninon allowed him to spend the night with his father in the little cabin, a reef of life in the ocean of death, and the child would join in listening attentively to the lively sounds simmering up from the tombs. The clods of earth and memorial stones quivered with loves and regrets. The adolescent was astonished at this; Phosphore, gazing upon his son with an eye like a dead moon, murmured to him before plunging back into absence, "Ah, lil' one, what you don't know is lots bigger than you are . . ." Anatole-Anatole preferred the cemetery to the benches in school. He spent more time digging graves with his father and chasing body snatchers and other damned souls on darksome nights than he did reading or writing. Making himself comfortable in his father's hut, Anatole-Anatole took over much of the maintenance of the cemetery, for Phosphore's strength seemed to be waning with age. Their complicity cut them off for good from the rest of the world. On occasion they would leave their graves to drink a rum punch in town. That emptied out not only the sidewalk where they marched along but the unlucky bistro as well, the moment their shadows crossed the threshold. They drank alone, laughing silently, proud of the fear lapping all around them. Down at the other end of the bar, the proprietor, Cécène, would intone spells to ward off contagion from the men of death. After their departure, when the midday crowds poured in, Cécène would solemnly shatter the glasses they had used, sprinkling the shards with dust collected from the thirteenth pew in the church.

So that's how Phosphore and Anatole-Anatole lived their lives. Ninon, seduced by a *couli* [13] from Basse-Pointe (a specialist in bamboo brooms) had packed up her things and decamped without even looking in at the cemetery. She was going to grab fate, she said, by a different end. One Sunday, Phosphore and his son, sitting near a grave, were listening to the secrets of a child who'd been afraid to grow up, when word arrived that Félix Soleil was dead: he had dreamed, rumor had it, of a tenth daughter sent over by Fanotte from the other side, and I'm tell- ing you his heart failed at the news, so he needs his hole in the ground 'cause priest says get-crackin'-burial's-at-five-o'clock. As always, father and son debated where to plant the new arrival.

"I hear you, Papa, but listen: we'll put him near that back wall over there – since he was a mason he'll be able to repair it every now and then . . ."

"Just so, lil' one, but isn't it better to stick him in near his wife Fanotte?"

"Well now, I'd sure enough forgotten her!"

They turned the cemetery upside-down without finding hide or hair of Fanotte. When the funeral procession arrived, the grave was ready, near the wall, the cement tombstone sent by Héloïse that very morning set up at the head . . . Anatole-Anatole was hoisting one end of the coffin on his shoulder when he locked eyes on Héloïse. He'd seen her before without finding her attractive. But on that particular day, bathed in tears, completely drained of the ruddy sap that imparts a healthy glow, she seemed to have entered the realm of the living dead. Because of his deep familiarity with that other world whose frontiers give the human soul serious pause, Anatole-Anatole appreciated everything that brought life and death together. Héloïse belonged to both worlds: she dazzled him. Leaving his father to put the finishing touches on the new grave, he followed her.

Her sisters had gone, and Héloïse was on her lonely way home to the silent shanty when fear struck: one of those men of the night, who lived off the boneyard, was on her heels! . . . Every time she looked back she scared herself even more. Anatole-Anatole was closing in on her. They were leaving the town, and when Héloïse walked past the last shack, she burst into a run on the sun-baked road. Anatole-Anatole kept to his steady pace. When she got home, all in a flutter, Héloïse barricaded herself inside. Sitting down for a moment to calm her heart, she was soon peeking out through the shutters. The road ran along in gentle curves until it reached a slope and seemed to break off. That's where the placid silhouette of her pursuer appeared. Héloïse almost went mad. She beat her fists on her temples and tucked her trembling body away into a corner of the front room. She heard Anatole-Anatole's footsteps halt at the door.

"What you want you mis'rable fiend?" she shrieked. "Scram or I'm tossing holy water on you!"

Anatole-Anatole went away. Seeing him all shredded like a banana leaf in the wind, his father realized that love had delivered its opening punch.

"So she called you a damn devil?" asked Phosphore anxiously. "And she didn't open the door? Fine. Well, lil' one, if it's love trouble, I've got just what you need. I'm going to teach you something . . ."

That evening, Héloïse went to bed a virgin for the last time, because meanwhile, black Phosphore had revealed to his sorrowing son the Method he'd learned from a sepulcher, and had turned him into a *dorlis*. Anatole-Anatole's modus operandi remains unknown. People get lost in conjecture trying to figure out if he used the technique of the toad hidden beneath the bed, the one of the ant that slips through keyholes, or the one of three-steps-forward-three-steps-back that lets you walk through walls. The fact remains that on the evening in question, he found himself in Héloïse's bedroom despite all locks and barricades. Putting his new expertise as a *dorlis* to work, he went inside her without waking her up and spent eight delicious hours on her sleeping body. His grunts, his tears, his quiverings, his *petites morts* in pleasure mingled with the dainty snores of his partner. When the pippiree bird ushered in the dawn, Héloïse discovered she was as bruised as a windfallen fruit. Seeing the bloody stains on her sheets, and feeling her womb still waiting for the satisfaction sleep had denied her, she knew that she had been defiled by the man of death, and she spent the day soaking in a tub of water with a rosary. That night she put a pair of black underpants on backwards, a procedure said to guard against a *dorlis*. It stopped Anatole-Anatole cold. He had returned and was preparing to thrust home when he dissolved into helpless cry-water over this invincible countercharm. He left the hut to go tell his father, who was powerless as well. Coming back to the bedroom, the *dorlis* went around in circles, as doleful as a crab without a hole, until a sudden sunrise gave him that colossal slap reserved for *engagés*[14] surprised by light. Half of Anatole-Anatole's face then turned as white as a Saint-Anthony's candle,[15] and he went bald on one side. After that, he hid his dreadful ugliness under a *bakoua*[16] with a brim that hung down over his ears, and he left the cemetery only at midnight, wreaking havoc among women who slept without protection.

Reassured by the efficacy of her countercharm, Héloïse recovered some of her former serenity and was almost happy. She attributed the cessation of her periods to the ghastly shock she'd endured and devoted herself to selling her spices and blocks of ice. Her womb had awakened, but she did not realize this right away. Neither did she understand when her belly became as curved as a calabash and her breasts as heavy as sacks of salt. Nor did she believe – it was so unimaginable – her most loyal customer, who would often remark during her idle chatter, "Aaah Héloïse, I'm so pleased for you, seeing you're in an interesting condition . . ." One day, Héloïse felt the presence of an alien life in her womb. This unexpected sensation hurled her into the horrible certainty that she was pregnant by Anatole-Anatole, the new champion *dorlis* of the land. Too distraught to try and get rid of the child, she shut herself up in her shanty, hiding her shame from bad-mouf gossip. It was a troglodytic pregnancy in the semidarkness of a locked and shuttered house. Her customers thought she was dead. After prowling around outside, they alerted the police, who broke down the door, flung open the windows, shooed out the proliferative insects, tore apart the spider webs, and exposed the hapless woman to the stares of the crowd. The shock caused her waters to break, and Sister Sainte-Marie was urgently summoned. The child she hauled into this world was a boy.

"You see, Elo, boys I know how to do, I told your father the late Félix so, where's he now poor man to see this, him who thought I was lying?" gloated the midwife. "But what you going to call him, hah?"

"Pierre Philomène," murmured Héloïse.

Sister Sainte-Marie helped the newborn get a good start in life. She rubbed him with lemon, guava, and tamarind leaves twisted together and macerated in white tafia. That would allow him, she said, to go through life with the strength and spirit of those trees. She fed him the soft part of some bread dipped in honey, the secret of all intelligence. Then she swaddled him, propped him up on the straw mattress beside his mother, buried his cord-of-life beneath a young coconut palm, and took herself off, after preparing that sovereign herb tea indispensable to the devastated insides of brand-new mothers.

Sister Sainte-Marie was hardly out the door when Héloïse felt a presence in the bedroom even through her semiconscious fog. The horror was there: sinister, motionless, with the *bakoua*'s brim drooping over both cheeks, Anatole-Anatole gazed at his son. Héloïse clutched the baby close and howled. The *dorlis* hurried away, his heart broken. Héloïse was not to see him again until many years later, in broad daylight, at the vegetable market.

That same birth-day she crammed her belongings into an empty sugar sack and jumped into the cart of a big sweaty *chabin*[17] going down to Fort-de-France. The man thought a gang of zombies was after her and he urged his nags along the rocky road to the city at tip-top speed. Lying exhausted in the cart behind him, with the baby clamped to her chest and the sack under her arm, Héloïse didn't let out one sound during the entire trip. The *chabin* grew increasingly anxious as night fell and was relieved when the outlying houses of the Château-Boeuf neighborhood heralded their arrival in Fort-de-France.

"Halloo back there madame, where is it you're heading?"

"I'll get out here," quickly replied the woman who was already becoming Mam Elo, and who would wander all night long through the most unbelievable city this side of the black man's hell.

She walked straight ahead, trying to look like someone going somewhere. This wasn't her first visit to Fort-de-France. She had often been there before, with Fanotte and Félix Soleil. But this city previously seen while holding her parents' hands now seemed as hard-hearted as a tarted-up negress, a far cry from the peaceful harmony of village life. Héloïse pressed on past clusters of houses kept in line by the straightest of streets. Night washed the brightness out of wooden façades and their shutters thick with dust from the wind off the jetty. Sometimes the streetlights revealed vivid spots of color, and Héloïse sensed a kind of sadness seeping everywhere. The widest streets, which smelled of soggy cardboard and musty cloth, were those where the Syrian merchants had their shops. Other, more austere streets were usually the territory of shabby tailors who labored endlessly sewing things from sacking. In her roving, Héloïse sometimes went along streets edged with bushes that presaged the presence to the north of the forest of La Trace.[18] She saw cats sleeping on low-slung roofs, and passels of stray dogs. Because during the night – Héloïse did not yet know this – the city was invaded by dogs.

(The song of the dogs. At night dogs took over the esplanades, the dead ends, the pavement underneath cars, and the piles of household garbage. They roamed in angry packs along avenues where bits of rubbish danced in the wind from the sea. After scouring the Démosthène Bridge, they would stream down Boulevard du Général-de-Gaulle, then fan out through the neighborhood of Terres-Sainville, winding up in a clump on Place Abbé-Grégoire where they would bark at the church. Then you'd hear them clatter off at a gallop to the Cimetière Trabaut where, if the gate had been left open, they would rumpus around the poor people's graves, knocking over candles, white arum lilies, and little quimbois-maléfiques[19] that disturbed the quiet of the tomb. Nothing escaped this canine rampage, which sent flying even the images of the Holy Virgin in her robes of light or the still more popular ones of Saint Michael striking down an old nigger, pictures that were stuck into the four corners of the graves on palm-leaf crosses. When the dogs arrived to find the gate closed, they ran riot along the outside walls, trying to leap over these whitewashed barriers. Vanquished, they would charge downtown to scatter the Syrians' trash cans and attack night ramblers. At dawn, they crossed the Gueydon Bridge in Indian file and settled down on the right bank of the Canal Levassor. There, in silent little groups, they yawned in boredom, stretched out among the fishing boats. They were rawbony, but speedy enough to evade the lassos of the city sanitation crews. It was a rare dog that still had both eyes. Not one sported an intact tail. Prompted by an ancestral hatred of these creatures once used to track down runaway slaves, we never missed a chance to wield a crowbar, a cutlass, or more often than not, to give a steering wheel a sudden twist. That's why daylight turned the dogs timid, reclusive, left them straining to blend in at the foot of walls, trembling underneath cars, impatient for the night, when they became wild animals again, the enraged members of an enraged horde that seized control of the city, unleashing against shuttered windows the vengeful barking that changed even the most secret dreams into nightmares. *That was the song of the dogs.*)

The fury of these dogs astonished Héloïse when she saw them for the first time down at the far end of a street. She was able to give them the slip. The next ones she ran into were on their own, which made them meek. The night was well advanced. The baby and the sack were growing heavy. Héloïse leaned against a door, which swung partly open on squeaky hinges. Overwhelmed by exhaustion, cradling her baby, she sat down on the first few steps of a staircase leading to an upper floor.

"Well Jesus-Mary-Joseph, my girl, what you doing here? . . ."

Héloïse awakened to see a tall thin woman with the unsmiling face of someone widowed before her time. The person in question was one Madame Paville (the future Odibert, our colleague and friend), who was just leaving for Mass. The devout lady took in the hapless Héloïse, gave her some milk and dry bread, and listened to her troubles.

"Rest your body, I'm going to fix all that when I get back," she declared.

After Mass, she took Héloïse straight off to the Syrian landlord of the neighboring apartments, who had already opened up his store and was busy arranging his rolls of permanent-press polyester and his khaki pants as lovely as certain sins.

"So, Syria, how are you this morning?" asked Mam Paville.

"Aaah Madame Paville, I'm telling you, not bad, not bad, and did you say a prayer for me?"

"Ah Syria, but everyone prays for you already."

Ahmed led them to his shelves, pointing out embroidered shirts, silk ties, plastic tablecloths, velvet rugs with hunting scenes, organdy skirts, vests with fob pockets. He moved confidently through his chaos of fabrics, eager to show them everything. There was not the tiniest speck of dust on those rolls of material piled up to the ceiling, which seemed like cliffs in danger of landslide. "Syria" was from Lebanon. When he'd stepped off the boat, his sole riches had been a wheelbarrow and a few bolts of cloth offered by the local Syro-Lebanese community. Within six years, he had become the owner of a store, an apartment on Rue Blénac, and some small lodgings on Rue François-Arago he was looking to rent. After displaying his treasures, he led Mam Paville and Héloïse behind a stack of packing boxes to his office, where the cash register was. He invited them to take a seat, then sat down himself, with eyes half-closed, hands joined at the fingertips, leaning forward with that saurian attitude he assumed when discussing business.

"So, Madame Paville, who have you brought me here?"

"This is Héloïse Soleil, a friend of mine who's fresh arrived from Vert-Pré with her chile, so I was thinking Syria could let her have one of his apartments . . ."

"Well of course! That's what they're there for! But what's this young lady do?"

"Thing is I only just got here, Monsieur Syria," said Héloïse, "and I haven't found work yet but that won't take long . . ."

"Oh it doesn't matter, I'll let you have the apartment anyway, but the little lady should come in afternoons do a spot of cleaning around here, all right?"

The Queen. That's how Héloïse found somewhere to live in Fort-de-France. She furnished the place through the kindness of a carpenter who lived in the apartment below hers. In the morning, she would sell sandwiches at the markets, then clean Ahmed's store in the late afternoon. Mam Paville, her neighbor, lived with her two sons and her mother, Mama-Doudou [Sweet-

Mama], a stoop-shouldered old woman whose weasel face didn't have one single wrinkle. Although the widow was always

stern and quite distant, taking little further interest in Héloïse, Mama-Doudou, on the other hand, never let an opportunity to visit slip by. She'd sit down with the two boys, rattle on about life and health problems, and bombard Héloïse with advice about the proper way to raise the baby Pierre Philomène, future king of us djobbers.

"But who's his father, huh?" Mama-Doudou asked one day.

Héloïse so dreaded this question that she'd gotten a dozen answers ready. Not a one made it to her lips that day: she could only quiver and sob. Mama-Doudou thought she understood – flap! – and exclaimed, "Ah, he's dead, I know that sorrow, I lived through it for myself and for my daughter . . ."

And she confided to Héloïse the key to their lonelinesses . . .

Back when she was a beautiful *câpresse*,[20] Mama-Doudou had a man, one Hector, part-*couli*-part-black-part-Chinese, the owner of the *Thanks-Be-to-Heaven*, a handsome craft that he took out himself to earn his living as a fisherman. In stormy seas and calm ones, good moon or bad, Hector's boat was always awash with fish.

"But how can anyone on his own catch so many fish, hah?"

This question tormented the markets. Soon tongues were wagging about black magic, pacts with the Devil. So much was said that when the *Thanks-Be-to-Heaven* was lost with all hands one day without warning, no one was surprised: devilish contracts always come to a sad end . . .

With Hector gone, Mama-Doudou found herself a widow with a baby on her hands: Elyette, daughter of the mysterious fisherman. The girl who would grow up to be Mam Paville and then become Odibert the pepper vendor lived with her mother in relatively easy circumstances. Mama-Doudou had saved a great deal during the time when her man was making good money. The one nuisance was that their neighbors would look away whenever they met and cross themselves when they went by, so true is it that the wife and daughter of a devil's debtor could only be in pawn themselves. And thus there grew up around the two women a silence in which the protective gestures of *quimbois* flew fast and furious. Wishing to prove her purity, Mama-Doudou attended Mass every day with her daughter. She volunteered to take care of the hibiscus bushes at the priest's house and the statues in the cathedral, which she polished for hours with woolen rags. No one put on a more spectacular show of faith at the yearly High Mass, at noon Mass, at midnight Mass, at the Mass of the Holy Ghost and all the others, wearing a silver-spangled black veil on her hair. The child who was to become Mam Paville was relentlessly submerged in this extreme devotion. She learned to walk near the altar, spoke her first words beneath the tabernacle, played with the chalice, and nibbled on unconsecrated communion wafers swiped from the sacristy. She quenched her childish thirst in the holy-water basins and learned to read from a missal while fiddling with a rosary. At seventeen, she knew the Confiteors better than anyone else, along with the Sanctuses, Agnus Deis, O salutarises, Pater nosters, Credos, and Glorias. An expert on the Gospels, she was also unbeatable on the correct order of all offertories, thanksgivings, communions, and processions. She was consulted by the young priests and finally entrusted with a catechism class. If she didn't become a nun, it's because fate intervened in the nick of time with the unpardonable bellyblow of love.

The cathedral had emptied out shortly after the six o'clock Mass and was preparing itself, in the meditative silence, for the service at midnight (that vital hour when prayers shoot straight up to the Father without any detours along the way). Mama-Doudou and her daughter had stayed behind, as usual, to sweep between the pews. Barely had the dust been gathered into a pile when Mama-Doudou felt a pain in the small of her back and went to lie down on a bench in the vestry. So the old woman disappeared behind the altar, leaving the future Mam Paville alone, a busy little shadow in the half-light of that holy place. Footsteps were then heard. At first Elyette saw a tall, slim silhouette with a bag slung over its shoulder, crisply outlined by the last rays of sunshine slipping through the door. The stranger knelt and crossed himself awkwardly, and just when he was about to get up, he caught sight of the girl. All the glowing colors from the stained-glass windows seemed to meet in the spot where he was kneeling, and that tipped the balance. Elyette set her eyes on a handsome black man, with his hair cut short at the temples and brushed up nice and high over his forehead, in the English Negro style. Bathed in a tinted aura, his movements took on a solemn majesty and – most importantly – his eyes flashed with the fire of God. Elyette thought she was seeing an angel, a strangely black angel, but . . . whatever else could the good Lord have sent to a little negress like me? . . . That's why she fell over backward between the pews, overcome by this clear sign from Heaven. She came to in the arms of her angel, who was saying, "Ma'am 'scuse me if I made you jump, 'scuse me . . ."

Returning from her little lie-down, Mama-Doudou surprised the couple kneeling side by side, praying together to the Virgin Mary. She found them so well matched that she burst out merrily, "M'sieu what are your intentions, and speak up straight!" Startled, the fellow made a proper mess of declaring his love. Elyette bowed her head in embarrassment and pleasure. The angel's name was Théophile Paville, and he'd come to Fort-de-France from the parish of Gros-Morne to practice his skills as a mechanic. He had a divine gift for fixing absolutely any bike, any warped axle in a gig or cart. Not only that, he'd quickly penetrated the secrets of the new motor cars, thanks to which talent he'd been hired at a garage on Rue François-Arago by a whip-thin *couli*, an affable man despite his loud, vulgar voice.

So Théophile Paville was Ahmed's first tenant, in one of those small, still-vacant apartments smelling of pine and water paint. He and Elyette gave the first life to that dark hallway lined with closed doors. The building was beautiful in those days. Its fine planks were fitted together by a method unknown to the young carpenters of today. Some of the lodgings overlooked the Rue François-Arago, others gave onto the narrow inner courtyard where the kitchens and tubs were located. The solid wood staircase, with its delicately curved handrail, had not yet started creaking, and the one window in the hallway still had its shutters. The garage where Théophile Paville worked was below the apartments on the street side, occupying the ground floor area up to the corner of Rue Lamartine, leaving a cramped space right next to the front door for a joiner's shop perfumed with resin, varnish, sawdust, and ringing until nightfall with the screeches of saw and plane. The sidewalk across the street belonged to the Syrians: shops of enchanting fabrics, not yet enclosed by plate-glass windows and metal shutters. Down the street, at the corner, was the grocery store run by a retired woman who had discovered late in life her knack for the art of selling everything by bushels, pecks, quarts, pints, and half-pints. The young couple made their love début in this setting – which isn't of the slightest importance.

The first baby was not long in coming. Elyette named him Jean, after wavering between Jésus and Saint-Augustin. Elyette's dowry was so handsome that Théophile, watching her wrap up each sou, one after the other, before stuffing them under the mattress, advised her to open a shop . . .

"But a shop selling what?" asked Mam Paville anxiously.

"Whatever you want, long as it sells," replied Théophile.

Neither Elyette nor Mama-Doudou had the tiniest idea what could be sold in a little shop. Time passed. Elyette gave birth to a second boy. It was around then that destiny, in that cruel way it has, decided to whisper a business proposition in her ear.

It happened on a day like any other. Back home from Mass, Mam Paville was feeding her little boys some dry bread soaked in milk when she heard an unusual uproar out in the street. From her window, she saw a crowd gathering in front of the garage where her husband worked. Concerned, she warned her sons they'd be snatched away by the Devil if they didn't stay right by their bowls, and off she rushed down the stairs, bumping into the garage owner at the bottom just as he burst in all sweaty to fetch her. The couli looked as though he'd just been beaned by a coconut: "Mam Paville come quick, some bad luck . . ." Heart pounding, Elyette followed him into the oily cavern and found her husband lying beneath an enormous engine that was crushing his chest. The two grease monkeys, while unable to shift it, were holding it up with all their strength to reduce its weight. Théophile Paville died without opening his eyes, even though burly dockers came running from the jetty and managed to heave aside the murderous motor. The wake was held that very evening. The garage owner had taken care of the administrative formalities during the day. Mam Paville, freshly widowed, revealed in adversity the heart and soul of a *matadora*.[21] Although disfigured by grief, she shed not one tear as she bathed her husband's corpse, bound up his caved-in chest, dressed him in his Sunday best, brushed his hair, crossed his hands over a crucifix, and even succeeded, through love, in transforming the dead man's grimace into a mask of serenity. The coffin was paid for by the garage owner, who felt somehow responsible (the workbench was rotten, I should have replaced it oh la la! . . .) Elyette then discovered all the trappings that surround death, a tremendous business of printed announcements, palls, candles, funeral hangings, hearses, wreaths, artificial flowers. The priest's services for the De profundis. The burial vault and the engraving of the headstone. The black veils to be draped over all the mirrors in the house. The little hats and widow's weeds that had to be obtained from the well-known dressmaker Amédée Balthazar, who specialized in such things. Elyette made her purchases – grimly, bitterly – without thinking about them at the time. Her savings would have melted away if the garage owner, still feeling guilty, hadn't insisted on paying most of the funeral expenses himself. Followed by a throng of people, the hearse went up the street toward the Cimetière Trabaut carrying a hefty load of wreaths, bouquets, purple flowers, and violet ribbons. Théophile, naturally, was reluctant to go. The wheels on the hearse kept skidding even though the engine was running smoothly. At the cemetery, the four pallbearers staggered beneath the coffin, which grew heavier as it approached the grave. This last, by the way, still gaped half-empty even after all its dirt had been piled back in. A light rain restored to family and friends the tears that Théophile was shedding, somewhere, over his fate . . .

This premature widowhood plunged Mam Paville back into religious devotion. No dead man ever had so many Masses and prayers. But the young widow did not lose touch with reality: she had to find a way to feed the children. Using the rest of her savings and the coins the garage owner had presented to her in a cookie tin, she rented premises on Rue Lamartine (not far from the atelier of Adeldade Nicéphore, a consummate gold- smith). When Mama-Doudou, breaking her observant silence, made so bold as to ask what she intended to sell there, the young widow replied with the gravity that would distinguish her forever afterward, "I'm going to sell stuff for funerals . . ."

She contacted a store manager who ran such a business and softened him up by purchasing many artificial flowers, funeral wreaths, and thousands of candles. In this way she obtained the address where he procured his merchandise wholesale, and she sent off a purchase order. Two months later, when her packages arrived, she was able to open the shop of mortuary items where she proceeded to bury that part of her existence not devoted to Masses and prayers. Mama-Doudou raised the children, their mother stepping in only to take them to religious services and other devotional occasions, in the end making altar boys of them the very first chance she got . . .

Mama-Doudou, who no longer remembered what she said, was everlastingly repeating that story to Héloïse, day after day. Listening attentively, Héloïse forgot her own misfortunes, never imagining that providence was saving up for Mam Paville a destiny as a pepper vendor under the name of Odibert. Héloïse escaped from the old woman only when she went out to discover the world that would be hers for the longest season of her life. She was baffled, as one would be at first sight, by the bustling markets where she went to sell her sandwiches. Of course, this was before city hall had tidied things up: meat, fish, and vegetables were still sold all together in happy-go-lucky fashion along the edge of the Canal Levassor or on esplanades where women from the countryside crystallized as if by magic. Everything else, we djobbers included, latched on to these women in a crab-basket atmosphere of seeming chaos. As there weren't any stalls yet, vegetables were displayed on the ground, on madras handkerchiefs or squares of oilcloth. Fish sat around in creels. Hunks of meat were arranged on planks and barrels, fanned by children shooing away flies. The Syrians who hadn't yet opened their own stores trundled among us carts laden with pieces of embroidery, machine-made lace, bolts of cotton or woolen cloth. People came to the markets to do the day's shopping, but above all to sharpen the tongue on disputes and chit-chat, to search for the friend-relative-loved-one who'd vanished around some corner of fate, to spread the news of births and deaths, to dispel the languor of a loneliness, and finally, to consult about one's ailments with the sellers of medicinal herbs and wonder-working seeds. Lost amid the din, for quite some time Héloïse thought she'd stumbled into a riot. Not until much later would she perceive the intangible order in this mayhem.

With a basket on her hip and a tearful little boy clinging to one shoulder, she regularly worked the esplanade that was to become our main vegetable market, managing eventually to inherit a spot from one of the cooks who sold food to the other vendors. From that day on she triumphed through the excellence of her shark *étouffé*, those spicy fritters black folks call *marinades*, and most of all – holy Madonna of Jossaud[22] – her *macadam*, which everyone simply fought over. That's a dish of rice in saffrony yellow sauce and codfish simmered with green peppers. You had to taste that, eyes at half-mast, on a veranda, and let yourself be carried away by those oh-so-slowly savored mouthfuls, oo la la . . .

When Héloïse was just starting out, we djobbers were already there, a lively but scattershot presence, without names or clans. All around the market she was still called Héloïse, for it's only through the respect brought by age and those first wrinkles that her name became Mam Elo. In those days she had the constantly flitting gaze of blackbirds alarmed by an approaching storm. We had a presentiment that something was dogging her, but – far from imagining a *dorlis* – we suspected good old Calamity, which stands in for your guardian angel hereabouts. Her boy went to school and used to join her at noon. He ate with us, listening to the talk with smiles and a sweet disposition, an easygoing child, spontaneous and free. We baptized him "Piphi" at first, from the "Pi" in Pierre and the "Phi" in Philomène, then simply "Pipi," since the niglet found this nickname funnier. That irritated Mam Elo: "I'm telling you his name is Pierre Philomène!" The Queen was closemouthed but always singing beneath her breath in the steam from her cooking pots. Pipi grew up quickly and left school behind to ramble around the markets, studying their subtle operations. In spite of the commotion, everything ran like finest clockwork. Our future king learned that the Caribbean basket was women's business: selling was not work for a man with stones. Women are better at bargaining, weighing out the merchandise, and standing up to haggling. So they are the ones who connect the factories, warehouses, countryside, and seacoasts together, in the heart of the city. Pipi found out that in the hurly-burly of the stalls there existed changeless entities: the *vendors of sweets and seeds* (spices, coffee, coarse salt, cassava, dried vegetables, loaf sugar, bitter chocolate . . .), *bush-medicine women* (selling wild vervain and so forth), and the *odds-and-ends ladies.* These last displayed an astonishing jumble of factory remnants, stockroom rubbish, starch, tallow candles, wax tapers, vinegar, charcoal, lard and margarine, quicklime, varnish, polish, bottles, ropes, pottery, brooms, graters, hellfire tafia, oil, molasses, nails and wire and whatever you want just ask me for it . . .). Then there were the movable feasts: around eleven o'clock every day the *fishwives* appeared, newly supplied from the latest catch, and then, with their seasonal bounty, there were the *fruit and vegetable sellers,* great mistresses of their art. The boy began to notice how wares of the same nature clustered discreetly together, thus allowing the vendors to adjust their prices and bargain with shrewd flexibility, so that their clients might always be allowed the illusion of success. After making his rounds, Pipi would return to the market's lunchspot. There the cooks set their fragrant saucepans over live coals, casting cut-eye looks at Mam Elo's simmering pans of royal *macadam.*

It was Pipi who first discovered Elmire, a *pacotilleuse*[23] whose life had been one voyage after another. In those days, the former traveler displayed a job lot of the world's wonders in her baskets. At the child's pleading, Elmire could talk for hours about each object, conjuring up unknown lands, peoples, and climes. Like Pipi, we'd abandon our wheelbarrows to gather around Elmire at those hours when customers grew rare and the vendors took a load off their feet. Well now, it was at such an hour (the Lord have His mercy!) that the *dorlis* appeared at the entrance to the market, in broadest daylight, spang out in the sunshine, instantly spooking Mam Elo, who spotted him before we did! The Queen spilled the rice she was rinsing and crumpled up – blip! – at the foot of her cooker, while the *engagé* came quietly on. WHAT HORROR, JESUS-MARY-JOSEPH! To see a *dorlis* in the daytime was monstropolous, and what's more, that one, Anatole-Anatole, the corpse-man, was rumored to be among the most fearsome. The vendors crossed themselves. The handful of customers bolted. As for us, open-mouthed and cold-sweaty, we huddled around Elmire. A nasty silence fell upon the market. The *dorlis* walked down the row of cooking stands and came to where Mam Elo lay unconscious. At that moment, Pipi pushed us aside and, stepping resolutely forward, placed his own little body between the terror and his mother. The *dorlis* gazed deep into the child's eyes. Oh, we were imagining a ghastly crash: that glowing red stare hitting those innocent orbs . . . And yet Pipi told us later he'd seen only an ocean of distress, a living suffering.

"Come here, lil' one, and give your papa a kiss," implored the *dorlis*.

The boy didn't hesitate one second. Being fatherless had probably always eaten away at him. Besides, when you meet your own flesh and blood, nothing can stand between you. With what seemed like sobbing emotion, Anatole-Anatole embraced his son for a few moments, or much less, who's to say? Seething feelings can cloud the mind. The *dorlis*, it appears, whispered into Pipi's ear for a long time while his son listened, eyes closed. Before leaving, Anatole-Anatole said to him in a loud voice, "You will learn to speak to the jar, but Beauty will gobble you up . . ."

No one realized at the time that he had foretold Pipi's fate and that no one – not even Mam Elo – would ever again see his hideous form in the light of day. When the queen of *macadam* awoke, she felt strangely relieved. She'd lost that panicky-blackbird look in her eye, while Pipi, alas, driven by storm from the shelter of childhood, began heading out to sea.

Be the son of a *dorlis*? We'd say a big no-thanks to that offer. As for Pipi, he'd taken it badly and was frittering away his days swooping around among the baskets or collapsing into our wheelbarrows. Not wanting to rub pepper in the wound, everyone had buttoned lips on this subject, and if we speak of it today, that's because time has had a chance to put a cool lid on this boiling business. Mam Elo was doing better, and you might have thought her son a carefree soul, but whoever knew how to look could see Pipi sinking a little deeper day by day into a kind of permanent whirlpool carrying him away from us, from life, and impossible-but-true, from himself (Oh deep-sea misery). 35

ROBERT AND WAR

At about that time, there was a trouble-bunch of Germans attacking people in those countries that have four seasons. Even though we didn't have any family over there, a Pétain Maréchal[24] sent us off our very own admiral named Robert,[25] along with some Senegalese and other kinds of soldiers. The Word was that he aimed to seal the country inside an eggshell so he could smother or hatch it as he pleased, regardless of the American embargo. Newspapers and the radio began regularly burning flattery-incense before this Maréchal Pétain, a living god on earth – "We're here in answer to your call, Oh Papa of us all" – who had to be obeyed. People were also talking every which where (in *La Quinzaine impériale, Le Clairon, La Petite-Prairie,* at the scout jamborees, the Mutualist festivals, in songs or poems) about this low-life outlaw named De Gaulle, who could spellbind you just through an English radio broadcast listened to in secret by madmen with the sun in their eyes. Even though we had no stake in this affair, Admiral Robert clapped a shell over the country, and the Americans wrapped it up in a broody blockade. The soldiers began to requisition everything. Finding food in the city required the resourcefulness of Brer Rabbit in those bedtime stories. Fashionable society in Fort-de-France dug up country cousins out in the sticks where the authorities were encouraging victory gardens. It was no longer demeaning to frequent backwoods brothers-in-law, hayseed godchildren, or savanna aunties. Folks set out bright and early for family visits with big bags slung over their shoulders. We'd head out on foot or in cars adapted to run on alcohol. It was around this time that stray dogs and pet cats grew scarce, while mysterious rabbits in tight-closed sacks were sold in the markets for their weight in gold. Those without rustic relations, or those who could not obtain the scanty treasures of the market, now paid slavish and frantic attention to the seafaring fishermen of the Rive-Droite neighborhood. The admiral's Senegalese, fans of fresh fish, procured enough explosives for the sailors to blast whole shoals of blue bonitos. After giving the soldiers their share, the fishermen reigned over a people of starvelings who crawled for the chance to swap coconut oil for some seafood. We djobbers, with our now-useless wheelbarrows, had cudgeled our brains to outwit the famine we could no longer stave off with our poor djobs: we were earning our bread with fermented-orange wine, with sandals cut out of rubber tires purloined from requisitioned military stores, and with many another invention our present-day minds cannot even begin to fathom.

While we were grappling with that life, Pipi, who was adrift inside himself, made the acquaintance of an albino named Gogo, a Doctor of Polishing for all sorts of vehicles, expert in the art of brightening mahogany furniture, aluminum pots, silverware, and certain dentures. A brush, a plastic pail, a series of specialized towels, and a mysterious paste of his own devising were the equipment behind impeccable services famous as far away as the northern neighborhood of Balata. The albino detected such emptiness behind the adolescent's eyelids that he resolved then and there to give him a reason for living by bringing the boy in on his own very latest activity: the "passage." As soon as Admiral Robert began to lay his egg around us, dissidence hatched out. Spurred on by the appeals of Papa-de-Gaulle (one June 24, he spoke to us, yes to us! Directly to us . . .), dozens of fellows struck out across the Martinique Passage towards Free France in risky skiffs, slipping between the sandbars and the admiral's battleships, to brave en masse the crossing to Great Britain's Dominica and the Germans on the far shore. These runs were carried out by a few fishermen from Rive-Droite, Case-Pilote, and Case-Navire, and they enabled up-country patriots to reach the English islands on payment of salt, meat, vegetables, or just plain money. Gogo was one of the few who made these trips without being fishermen themselves. The sea held no secrets for him, so he'd simply borrowed an old tub. Not caring one way or another, Pipi agreed to help out ferrying dissidents to De Gaulle. He never even spoke to Gogo and would hand everything he earned to his mother without a word about his exploits among the battleships. The only person who was able to put a few dents in Pipi's mortuary carapace was Gogo's at-home, one Clarine, an enormous woman with the eyes of an angel. She'd only recently arrived from the countryside, and with her Pipi could chat once more about the heat, the rain, the sharp-set mosquitoes. Even if it was already written in the book of fate, it was too early to say that Clarine would become a mother who'd forget her own child in order to marry a handsome mulatto.[26]

Gogo devoted his nights to dissidence and his days to advancing the frontiers of polishing in the wealthy homes of Fort-de-France. Clarine found the city intimidating and didn't dare leave her room in spite of all her albino's urging. When Gogo and Pipi began spending long hours at dawn dividing up their nightly profits, Gogo asked the adolescent to do him the favor of accompanying Clarine about the city: "Me, I haven't the time, but you do it – after all, she's got to learn people won't eat you alive around here . . ." So Pipi and Clarine grew accustomed to taking long walks together through the rutted streets of Fort-de-France, strolling along the open canals where dragonflies quenched their thirst. The resinous pine of the building façades repelled paint, which peeled off in flakes. Brief rain showers, clearing rapidly, fostered an acrid atmosphere of boiled sadness. At Pipi's side, Clarine began to enjoy padding like a friendly gorilla through the urban uproar. Curious memories would sometimes pop into a fresh compartment in her head, and she recounted them so often to Pipi that he could soon organize them and recite for her the first era of her life . . .

(*Pipi's recital of the life of Clarine, future forgetful mother.* You were born in Le Lamentin, in the neighborhood of Jeanne-d'Arc, with its statue of the warrior maid, its canes, its oxen, its mangoes. Emma, your mother, raised you by herself. The fellow who sent her that nine-month's-delivery package was scratching out a living without her, as far off as the horizon. Despite the defection of this love, Emma pitched right in when her daughter showed up in the middle of the night, turning blue from the umbilical cord in a slip-knot around her neck. Grabbing the fruit of her womb with her own hands, Emma delivered the baby and cut the cord. In the silence and solitude of her shack, she looked after this elephant calf whose corpulence (talk about healthy!) excited the admiration of the neighborhood. She named her Clarine. The child grew up in the sunshine, swaddled in rags and prominently perched on some rocks a few yards from Emma, who toiled away in the sugarcane fields. When Clarine was of an age to go twittering off among the cabuya plants infested with Long-beasts, Emma placed her in the care of a foolhardy *chabin* who one stormy night had met a *matadora* of impossible beauty. Before flying off in a whirlwind of hibiscus, this creature, the last love of his life, had flashed him a diabolical smile that definitely dug a kind of hole in his brain. The besotted *chabin* stayed sitting near his window, jumping at the rustle of leaves or weeping in hopeless waiting for a whirlwind of hibiscus. He supported himself by taking care of the children in the surrounding huts. That's how he came to be in charge of Emma's daughter Clarine until she was nine years old. In exchange Emma brought him some Portuguese yams, two or three sweet potatoes, some cane syrup, or killer tafia. Like all the other children, Clarine never cried with the addlepate-*chabin*. At the weensiest whimper, the man would put a hand on her head and she would sink into a cottony slow motion, playing with her fingers and toes without any more whining. The uncanny power of the elderly sweetheart freed Clarine from earthly realities and bodily frailties, placing her in such an angelic state that at six years old she was still a stranger to speech, and all her life she kept an enchanting gentleness in her eyes. What came next was no help at all. At the age when kiddies go off to school, Emma thought Clarine would be more useful tending the cattle of a M'sieu Pierre, a dusty ole mulatto who taught music at the seminary-college, and who in his idle moments – for a just-in- case – provided himself with a little bovine livestock in the Lamentine savannas. Emma's earnings were four sous a month.

After the almost cataleptic state in which the *chabin* had plunged her, Clarine found herself in a no less anesthetizing situation: the company of five placid cows on a savanna of saw grass. Whenever she felt like singing, her tongue could only imitate the bellowing of the beasts in her care. The poor girl would have remained mute all her life without a surprise attack from fate, which sent her, at the hour when the cows drank from a water hole bleached white by the sun, this extraordinary being: Alphonse Antoinette – well-known local musician, clarinet virtuoso, wizard of the beguine, major of the mazurka, shining star of the bolero-cha-cha, pope of the carnival *vidé*²⁷ in semitone, master of the *meringué*, connoisseur of calypso. He exercised his talents in the orchestra that supplied the ambience for the church fair each year at Eastertime. Whenever he had a moment to spare from his work as a chair mender, Alphonse Antoinette would slip off to the solitary savannas. There he would tease out a genius capable not only of making the clarinet wail but also – Oh maestro! – of reaching an end-of-the-world vibe that made hummingbirds home in on him and flowers fly to his side. And that is how Clarine first saw him, clarinet to his lips, in a fluttery cloud of rainbow-colored blossoms and hypnotized hummingbirds. She thought she'd spied a devil and ran to squeeze herself beneath the belly of a cow. Amused, Alphonse Antoinette cracked a smile – just a thin grin, but it broke the spell, freed the hummingbirds, and dropped the flowers dead, withered forever.

"Well now, why you get scared like that, girl?"

The adolescent looked up at the musician with those infinitely sweet eyes. Flap! He felt the hopeless giddiness that would crush his career, and fell flat into the pond. Clarine dredged him out, and from then on they were constantly together on that savanna, between those Bovidae and that stagnant pool. By the time the latter had dried up into a moist eye ringed by scorched soil, Alphonse Antoinette had already taught the girl how to speak, how to read, how to write, and of course, how to get pregnant. Emma was staggered when her daughter's belly formed a bubble so perfectly round you'd have thought it was about to float away. Like many of us, Alphonse Antoinette panicked at the news of his impending fatherhood. He lit out in a zigzag for Dominica, where he starved to death, cadging bread from the dogs in a dismal harbor where thousands of jellyfish washed up every day. A divine dizziness prevented him from living off his clarinet or even mending chairs. Exile, poverty, the loss of his gift, the chaos of his life, that child growing in Clarine's womb, and most of all, the vertigo forcing him to create ever-tightening circles inside himself – it all shriveled him down so much a fisherman out seining one day found his corpse in an abandoned conch shell, yes he did. At that same instant there escaped from the shell a cosmic vibration that mesmerized two thousand three hundred seventeen hummingbirds – I'm not joking – for life.

Emma took Clarine off to see Joubaré the healer, because Jesus-Mary, you don't have babies when you're seventeen. Joubaré ran out of attar of roses trying to chase away the unwanted child and exhausted his supplies of Jerusalem oil, Seven Blessings oil, and Holy Spirit oil. He wasted a foot from a black hen killed on a Friday, a bamboo flower petal, three horseradish leaves, three barren blossoms from a male papaya tree, a consecrated packet of vetiver roots, two mugs of milk, four serpent's heads, and a wicked bouquet of the most secret abortive plants. But the seed clung like a deaf devil to Clarine's insides. Then Joubaré, lapsing into a languor, lay down in his dispensary and spent four days there, meditating. Emma and her daughter waited out in front of his hut, through rain and through shine. At dawn on the fifth day, at the hour when Joubaré stood up with the intention of placing the matter in the hands of Beelzebub himself, Clarine detected at her heart's core the familiar vibration that, through its faintness, clearly conveyed the last sigh of Alphonse Antoinette. Grief-stricken, she crouched behind a tree and asked the unfinished child nicely to come out of there because papa's gone for good . . .

The egg obeyed in a trice. Then Clarine got to her feet and despite the wailing of her mother walked away without a backward look. Emma, doomed to be carried off with the roof of her hut by a future cyclone, never saw her again (adieu Emma my dear, your tomb – can you tell? – is in the sanctuary of the winds, what a way to go, my my).

Walking, walking, walking, Clarine soon came in sight of Fort-de-France. She passed the Dillon sugar mill with its braid of black smoke and crossed Morne-Pichevin, already dissolving into a night only pitifully starred by kerosene lamps. After Terres-Sainville, she sat back in exhaustion against the white-washed walls of the wealthy folks' cemetery. Behind her loomed the deluxe sepulchers: silver crosses, Boulogne marble, imperial wrought-iron railings. The whole lot looked like an incomprehensible palace, a bric-a-brac hodgepodge of elegantly chiseled laments and defiant challenges to death. When Clarine crossed La Croix-Mission, the night owls took her for a zombi and cussed her out to hound her back into her grave. Taking to her heels down Rue François-Arago, she veered right on an impulse and crossed the Gueydon Bridge to the right bank of the Canal Levassor. She had been resting for a few minutes in a fishing skiff when she was attacked by stray dogs. Encircled by some twenty of these feral creatures, Clarine thought she'd come to the dead-end of her life. That's when Gogo the Albino arrived. That night, he had emptied his chamber pot into the canal and was contemplating the usual free-for-all among the claw-waving "it's-my-fault" crabs around this godsend when he'd been alerted by the dogs' yapping. He put them to flight by looking at them upside-down with his head wedged between his legs, and then he took you back to his one-room hut where he let you stay, no strings attached, have I got that right? *That's the story.*)

On one of these walks during which Pipi would tell her the saga of her life, Clarine shivered like a blackbird taking flight, did a sudden about-face that stupefied all passersby, and began lumbering heavily toward reality. Her body – built for permanent struggle – had just shuffled off indecision. From that day onward, she displayed boundless energy in lugging charcoal before sunrise, cleaning stores, carting garbage. When October rolled around, she could be seen in the rich people's cemetery, washing the dusty petals of artificial flowers to prepare for the commemorations of All Saints' Day. In the evening, triumphant, carrying some black-market meat, she would come home to Gogo.

"Vié chabin, épi mwen Obê pé jan tué'w!" she would tell him. (Old *chabin*, Robert won't ever kill you 'long as you're with me!)

Once, Gogo kissed her in welcome. His red albino's eyes gleamed like the fruit on a mango tree in season. Clarine trembled at his tender touch, and when he crept over to her straw mattress, she silently enfolded his bamboo-thin body and warbled under the doctor's expert polishing, without realizing that this pleasure was setting in motion her future destiny as a forgetful mother. And just to show you how mean life is, that was the only time he ever crawled over to her . . .

Gogo the Albino was a prudent man: he'd had someone make him a two-sided picture frame, the first side showing one of the many photos of the Maréchal, the second a drawing of De Gaulle that everyone recognized because no one knew what he looked like. Thus, depending on the visitor of the moment, either the Maréchal or the Général was sitting in state next to a crucified Jesus on the chest of drawers. Gogo couldn't see the slightest difference between them and privately thought they were *vié blan fwans inm pwel* (two shriveled peas in the same Frenchy pod) . . . This stratagem had earned him a reputation as a Gaullist or a Pétainist among useful people and wherever it was profitable. His dissident customers were from all sectors of the city and came knocking on his door as furtively as rats on a midnight skulk. Gogo also recruited clients himself around the wireless sets of Rue Blénac, during the clandestine broadcasts to which his reputation as a Gaullist gave him access. There he would hook a hothead suddenly fired up by the flames of patriotism and dangle before him a glorious destiny under arms.

At first, Gogo and Pipi usually made two clandestine trips a week. Gogo steered the skiff with unerring instinct around the searchlights of the Pétainist ships. But a time came when their crossings grew rare. Patriots were deserting the ranks: the Germans, it was said, just plain killed people without asking questions. As for Admiral Robert, he became ferocious. From being fooled so often, his sailors had acquired a wisdom difficult to ensnare with any tricks. There were many arrests. Wireless sets, supposedly invisible to white eyes, were seized nevertheless. Some of the boatmen running the Passage were imprisoned with shaved heads, while some others must this very day be haunting the undersea plains in the flock of drowned souls. Gogo no longer found it so easy to slip among the battleships: the faintest splash triggered bursts of gunfire. So, since the albino wasn't one of those movie heroes from a four o'clock matinee, he made his funereal second-in-command a proposal.

"So you see, iffing it keeps up like this, those guys are going to kill us, and since we're not boneheads I don't see why we should keep risking our hides smuggling maniacs off to save De Gaulle!"

"You don't want to make the run anymore?"

Gogo had shaken his head and rolled his pink eyes.

"No, that's not it, Pipi . . . Listen . . . The dissidents pay us before they climb aboard, they've said goodbye to everyone, and anyways the Germans are going to kill them when they get where they're going, so why not toss them overboard with a knock on the head and just come on back home?"

And so, many an ardent patriot was of no use whatever to good old De Gaulle. A well-aimed slice with an oar sent them by the dozens to save a different France, the one in the bitter depths and gloomy abysses. The two confederates ran their little business without a hitch for quite some time. But then came the run where they found out they were ferrying some serious sort of monster. The fellow was so vig'rous (thanks to all that arrowroot pap and vitamin-rich breadfruit when he was a tad, oh yes) that the oar snapped on his noggin as though dashed against a hardwood locust tree and only made him gingerly poke his bloody pate with his little finger, in slow surprise. Flab-ber-gasted, Gogo the oar-wielder saw the colossus swell with unexpected strength, snatch the rest of the oar from him and snap it like a twig, grab him by the collar, and stave in his skull before tossing his corpse to the impatient waves.

Pipi survived only by jumping smartly into the current, which carried him away. Crazed by the brain-leaking hole in his head, the giant dissident went to work on the boat, ripping out nails, caulking, and planks in a hopeless battle against the invading sea.

Back from a day of djobbing, Clarine found the hut as empty as when she'd left it before dawn. Gogo, who had gone out the night before, should have been there, sleeping. Struck by the brutal certainty that her benefactor was dead, she sat down on the *paillasse*. Trying to start the tears flowing, she kept sighing, "Aie-aie-aie dear Lawd . . ." That's how Pipi found her the next day at sunrise. He was as wet as the opening of the rainy season and woozy from the effort of out-swimming drowning. He explained that a searchlight had locked onto the skiff and that despite all their zigs and zags, a bullet-burst had torn her into such shreds that she'd gone out from under them in little bits on the waters of the Passage. Gogo, Pipi, and another patriot had been left to the mercy of the currents.

"*Mêsi bondié* [t'ank Gawd], I was able to find a scrap of wood and clutch on it like that all night I'm telling you . . . When the sun came back I swam to shore . . ."

Gogo's disappearance, like all subsequent catastrophes, increased Clarine's energy tenfold. She scrubbed that hut top to bottom, scouring the cement, scraping the old boards, hustling down the steps several times to fetch water from the fountain, sinking herself into endless activity to escape painful memories of Gogo and Alphonse Antoinette. When the tiny hut could no longer channel her fearsome stamina, she plunged back into her djobs, renting her strength cheaply to the Syrians and the shopkeepers along the pier, who appreciated her talent for lifting heavy sacks. She immersed herself like this in a curious solitude, definitively indifferent to everything. In the evenings she did her cooking by the light of a coconut oil lamp. Bathed in a red glow, the shack took on an infernal atmosphere perfected by the sizzling of fish in a frypan, the spitting of charcoal and its flying sparks, or the

bubble-bubbling of meaty soups that steamed up the walls. During this culinary retreat she learned about spices, sauces, bouillons and daubes, and those peppery stir-ups that ravish   45
the taste buds.

As she was sitting down to a *blaff*[28] of red snapper, Clarine saw Pipi walk in. Her eyes were clouded by the mist that clings to the solitary bamboos of Le Morne-Rouge, and she did not immediately recognize the *dorlis*'s son, who burst out in sorrowful reproaches.

"But, but, but what's this, my dear? The wind blows so hard through your heart that your friends are swept away just like that, hey?"

Pipi, who had not seen her for ages, had brought her two packets of manioc flour and a piece of meat concealed in a banana leaf.

"I've brought some good things for you, but I see you've already got all you need to keep body with soul . . . Listen, my dear, listen to me . . . Gogo is dead, we know that now . . . If we haven't found him it's because the Passage never gives back what it has snatched away, right? . . . Okay . . . me, I haven't forgotten you. So tomorrow, 'stead of breaking your back for those Syrians, you'll go to the market . . ."

"Sa anké fè bô maché?" (What'll I do there?)

"You'll sell cane . . . Elmire the Voyager knows an old lady in Le Lamentin who's got some sugarcane behind her hut she's looking to sell . . ."

That's how Clarine wound up on the market esplanades, with bunches of sugarcane stalks, cotton-tender and sweet, oh my yes.

The market no longer had that intense hum, that sign of the city's good health. It sheltered an agglomeration of people peddling their personal famines. In exchange for her cane, Clarine harvested salt, oil, charcoal, butter, and sometimes even the occasional uneasy sou. Pipi brought the cane to her place every evening and left after the division of the day's take. It was during one of these divvying sessions that he noticed the unusual swelling of Clarine's belly, already naturally quite plump.

"Well Goodlawd, girl, could be Gogo might've left you a package in the mail?"

Clarine finally became aware of the child growing within her. She'd simply ignored her pregnancy, just the way she'd ignored a whole slice of life. Pipi's eye-opening remark did not awaken in her any ancestral and tremulous maternal instinct, even if her gaze did fill with a dizzying gentleness – the sight of which took Pipi aback.

"Don't move, don't move . . . I'll go get a lady who knows all about this sort of stuff . . ."

He returned with a *câpresse* as round as a doughnut, who examined Clarine with experienced hands and said, "Not long now . . ."

It was an easy birth. The midwife intervened only to cut the child's cord and bury it beneath a tree that, all things considered, must have been thoroughly unlucky. That very day Clarine clapped her son against her shoulder and left for the market, holding her bundle of canes balanced on a head wrap and carrying her sit-down stool with the other hand. She plunked herself in her usual spot at the moment when the first drop of sunlight scatters the nocturnal dogs. The child grew, nursed with the rich milk of a huge breast, soothed by the boundless sweetness of dark eyes, and the beguines Clarine murmured as she mused upon Saint-Pierre.[29] Pipi used to come and chat with her now and then. He hadn't had any work since the wreck of Gogo's skiff. The thought of having a *dorlis* for a father was racking him more than ever.

"It's nothing, you say, that's what everyone says. I agree. But then what is it that makes me scrawny and crazy like this, that beats on me like I was an old dog, dammit?"

Clarine gave him addresses for djobs. Pipi would go there, saying she'd sent him, but her former employers, used to the wonders of her Herculean strength, quickly dismissed this young clackabones (the wheelbarrow hadn't yet forged for you the iron arms of a master-djobber). Then Clarine would see him return, more wobbly and doleful than a coconut palm in the wind. The other vendors, won over by his limpid and good-natured loopiness, accepted his meandering among their baskets as just plain part of the market. Time passed like this. Clarine did a brisk business bartering or selling her sugarcane. She stayed seated, her eyes half-closed, her nameless baby in the crook of her arm, basking her strength in the genial sunshine, rising now and again to stretch her legs, calm the child's tears, or pass the time of day with the other market women, who were always astonished by the inexhaustible softness nestled in her eyes.

47

"My goodness, girl! They like forest pools in moonlight, well-well-well . . ."

While gossiping one day she heard that Admiral Robert would be leaving and that some fellow was coming in on the battleship Le Terrible to replace him. She learned that it was all over, people would finally be able to eat like God's children again, to forget that dog's life they'd been leading and get brand-new skiffs. Clarine was disappointed by the end of that arid existence she'd grown used to struggling against with all her might. Strangely detached from the feverish joy breaking out everywhere, she felt suddenly naked at the threshold of this rebirth, rather useless, and certainly too lonely.

"How much for a joint of sugarcane, mademoiselle?"

Beneath her droopy eyelids Clarine made out the silhouette of the handsomest mulatto in Creation. The gentleman in question, manmaye, was Ti-Joge [Lil'-Geo'ge], future mailman, about whom it would be useful here and now to say a few words.

(Here's the chat on Ti-Joge, mailman-to-be. He was born in Terres-Sainville, right behind the church. His father, so they say, was a Breton sailor just passing through who'd fetched up one blustery night under the window of a lovely mulattress. The Breton was charmed. The mulattress, entranced. This love was as brief as it was effective, because when Ti-Joge was born his mother Amédée had already forgotten the father's name and face. A seamstress, she worked at a treadle Singer that had given her the calves of a racing cyclist. She had acquired a reputation throughout at least half the city by specializing in mourning gaules, shapeless and lugubrious dresses. Making money off every funeral, she offered condolences several times a day, handing out here-there-and-everywhere a business card advertising:

AMÉDÉE BALTHAZAR

Couturière diplômée de Paris

DRESSES FOR WIDOWS AND OTHERS

3, rue Serviette—Terres-Sainville   Fort-de-France

She'd never seen Paris (but what use was a diploma from anywhere else?) and owed her profession as a seamstress to the chance arrival in her bed, one rainy evening (bad weather inevitably gave her an itch), of a customs officer supremely skilled in filching merchandise. He gave her the Singer sewing machine intended for some *béké* mother, with an eye to ensuring his welcome on other inclement nights. At first Amédée had puzzled over the device, wondering how it could ever be more efficient than a patiently plied needle. The appliance sat untouched, a home to dust and red roaches, until that other wet night that brought the Breton sailor, who knew – besides how to impregnate a mulattress – how to operate a two-speed treadle Singer sewing machine. Amédée found her vocation watching him mend a uniform somewhat the worse for its hasty removal. The perfection of the stitches so intrigued her that she stopped selling peanuts to devote herself to haute couture. She was quite content to copy the styles she found in photonovelas until one day at a funeral she had a profound inspiration and thought up those sinister *gaules* for grieving widows, thus providing a cozy future for herself. Ti-Joge's childhood was therefore a comfortable one. He became a man, after a short stint in school and an eternity in the city streets as a member of a teenage gang that fished in the drains for *sous* lost by the *bitakos*, the cloddish country folk who came to town on Saturdays. Since his mother's handiwork brought in enough to live royally, Ti-Joge never bothered with a job. His great beauty allowed him to keep living that life after his mother threw him out. Single women from Trénelle to Sainte-Thérèse provided him with food, lodging, love, and rum. The rest of the time, he played accordion in a small orchestra in

Redoute that never left the rehearsal space loaned to them by the priest. One day at the market, he met the woman who was to become his wife. *That was the chat, now you know.*)

Ti-Joge was immediately entranced by Clarine's strength, by the astonishing gentleness of her gaze; Clarine felt something quite ancient stirring inside her, the awakening of a vintage freshness that bedewed her skin, put a glint in her eyes – and enhanced their immeasurable marvelousness. She began to hear, to feel, became aware of the taste of her saliva, and with an imperceptible crackle, emerged from her drab massiveness with the elegance of a young girl.

"You have the most beautiful baby," murmured the mulatto.

"Sé . . . sépa ich mwen kilà non . . . Sé ich an adanm." (It's . . . it's not my chile . . . It's another lady's.)

She wanted, instinctively, to make herself new for this man.

"Ah, I thought so!" exclaimed Ti-Joge.

And he began hanging around every day, with a sudden interest in green sugarcane. He could talk a treat and had French at his complete command. Clarine listened in wonder as he recited the fables of La Fontaine, from which he'd drawn for himself one-two precepts for living. When he asked her for her address, a few days later, she could only babble it out, realizing at the same time that he would discover she had lied about the child. The day Ti-Joge announced he would drop by that evening, Clarine, already lost to love, lost her head. Her round and usually placid body fell prey to spasms and cold sweats. She could just imagine her lovely mulatto bolting at the sight of the baby, the way Alphonse Antoinette had done before. Clarine saw herself ditched once again at the gates of love, her heart thrown for a familiar loop. At the approach of twilight, she left the market like a madwoman, forgetting her unsold cane and even her stool.

As the first shadows appeared, Clarine arrived in front of the Cathédrale Saint-Louis, with its spire shooting into the sky like a stalk of sugarcane. She made the sign of the cross over the child, then knelt for a few seconds before lumbering across the marble floor and up the central aisle. The flickering candelabras, the death throes of the sun in the stained-glass windows, and the muffled echo rippling beneath the vault filled her with respectful fear. The cathedral was not empty. Shabby old ladies, devoutly on their knees, were planting a forest of tapers on the Virgin's toes. A few altar boys chased one another in the side aisles. *Quimboiseurs* were lined up to lap from the holy-water founts, and an organist was noodling around on an instrument somewhere beneath the crypt. This holy place was bestirring itself for the evening High Mass. Clarine wandered around between the altar and the confessional without finding the discreet darkness to which she intended to entrust the baby. Bells abruptly obliterated the silence. She thought she heard in them the voice of God in utter malediction, and she left the cathedral as one would flee the likely target of lightning bolts. Soon afterward she reached the square in front of the Église Saint-Antoine in Terres-Sainville. This other holy place was hardly taller than the trees, its walls were gray, and its windows bore no resemblance to pieces of the sky. Going inside, Clarine was welcomed by a moist warmth quite different from the cold majesty of the cathedral. The church was deserted. A few yards away, the tabernacle shone like a star. The surrounding shadows sported a rosette of burning candles. Clarine set the child down beneath a holy-water basin and left without a backward look, almost with a light step, her heart yearning for Ti-Joge . . . who abandoned his butterfly life for Clarine, became a mailman, gave up the accordion, and married her without pomp or circumstance, *gwoka* or *tibwa*,[30] so as not to alert his host of conquests.

Pipi had lost touch with Clarine. He had returned among us, in the market, where he lived by his wits, and barter, and dubious means, as the judge said reproachfully before sentencing him to seven months for who-knows-what theft. Pipi served his time in the main jail of Fort-de-France, in the ten-bed dormitory well known to us all: plaiting vetiver,[31] playing cards, taking endless showers, beating his head against the walls to counteract the anguish coursing through his veins. In the evenings, at lights-out, his cellmates would gather round his pallet, eager for his stories: he excelled in the dramatizing of events not worth mentioning. Pipi emerged from jail even more dilapidated than when he'd gone in, but with something lively stirring behind his eyes. Although Admiral Robert wasn't strangling the country anymore, meat was still rationed, and famine prowled the city. The markets remained as torpid as nap time in Lent. Rumors were rife: German revanchists were heading for our shores, and the slightest shadow in the harbor was a submarine. As the war wound down, Pipi just coasted with his mind elsewhere, lying belly-up on the crates, gulping down the afternoon heat, and he seemed to look at life in the way you watch a mangy cur go by off in the distance. But when he woke up, it was in fine style . . .

POST-WAR PLENTY: THE KING

After the war, our lives took on the color of good times and a breath of fresh air. The markets awakened like dogs doused with hot water. A breeze wafted along the aisles, for gasoline had brought the countryside and all its riches back to town. Under Admiral Robert, famine had spurred the return of vanished vegetables and forgotten fruits, and before boats arrived from France to reprovision the island, peasant women reigned like queens over the markets. There were so many vendors you had to hop over one basket after another just to move around. Neighboring streets within two hundred yards of the market happily absorbed the newcomers. Oh, those were the days! City Hall had laid things out with a compass: meat, fish, and vegetables were sold separately, beneath roofs, within partitions, and on counters. Every day was one long djob. The djobbers who had survived the war pumped up their arms, their muscular shoulders, their steely thighs. The wheelbarrowing skills we were developing discouraged amateurs: to be hailed as a master-djobber by the market women you really had to be cut out for it, as we were.

During this period of renewal, the vegetable market became the permanent home base of our group of djobbers. Other bands had sprung up in the fish and meat markets. Our clan was made up of five serious experts: Didon [Say-Hey], a lean couli with lustrous black hair; Sifilon, a former fisherman from

Les Anses-d'Arlets, as sinewy as an old rooster; Pin-Pon [Siren], a fellow from no one knew where with a mysterious talent for putting out fires; Lapochodé [Scaldy-Skin], a stand-up guy, speedy as a goat, disfigured with acid by a girlfriend; and Sirop [Syrup], a sort of angel, a powerful but thoroughly gentle man. Two apprentices hovered around us: Bidjoule [Beaut], the adopted son of an ancient market woman named Mam Goul, and of course, the one who was destined to astonish us all, Pierre Philomène Soleil, the *dorlis*'s son, whom we called Pipi. During the peak hours, our market swarmed with people. The vendors from Le Morne-Rouge came with their pineapples, their hands of bananas. The women of Saint-Pierre brought the juiciest Spanish limes, the choicest avocados. Batatas, dasheen, glorious yams from Le Lorrain, *pacotilleuses* from the island of Saint Lucia, *quimboiseuses* from Bezaudin with rare herbs, moon powder, and *bois-bandé*,[32] wickerwork from Morne-des-Esses to astonish the tourists, ice slabs from Pointe-Simon, buckets of lemons and peppers from Tivoli – this new life had simply everything. You could even find the yellow pumpkins of Croix-Rivail cut into thin slices, the last vendors of tanned leather and quicklime, small trades and crafts, seasonal fruits, and a vegetable cornucopia.

Coming in from miles around, the vendors arrived at La Croix-Mission, near the fish market. If the women didn't yet have a regular djobber, we'd squabble among ourselves to see who would carry their baskets. The brimming wheelbarrows would race to the vegetable market, with the vendors hustling along close behind, anxioused up about their produce: "Ho – don't you go bruisin' my tomatoes now!" After the deliveries came the arranging of the produce, at around eight-thirty. At that hour there weren't many customers, and the hubbub of activity was created by the market people themselves. Screeching unholy murder, the resale women besieged the vendors. We master-djobbers chased away the occasional docker trying to horn in on the unpacking and laying out of the produce. Children galloped up and down the aisles carrying a few fruits, crying their purloined wares to all and sundry. We would set out the displays: piling up tomatoes in blood-red pyramids, laying out the yams along the railings, brushing the carrots to the right color at the edge of the fountain, and dusting off the sweet potatoes. Flanked by his acolytes, the municipal guardian would check the location of the stalls, inspect the baskets, and braving curses aplenty, begin to collect the day's taxes.

"I haven't sold a t'ing yet and that damfool comes by to drain me dry!"

After paying up, the country women would get a receipt to tuck beneath their kerchiefs, and their early-morning anger would die down with the first customer.

After the stalls were set up, we'd sit together on the crates of potatoes, between the main entrance and the guardian's lodge. Bidjoule would remain with us, modeling his stillness on ours, keeping the same attentive eye on the market as we did to anticipate the vendors' wishes, but Pipi – he would stroll off among the baskets, prattling to himself as he checked out the spurs of the specially bred fighting cocks, hefted the cucumbers in his hand, applied his nose to the fragile curve of the arum lilies from La Médaille. He was gradually becoming popular among the peasant women. They'd call him over to taste their Spanish limes and mangoes, assess the flavor of a water lemon . . . I must admit we master-djobbers hardly gave him a glance: he seemed insignificant to us, floating in his dirty yellow jersey under a worn-out *bakoua*. We found Bidjoule more appealing: much younger, stockier, taller, with supple muscles under his smooth skin. Hearsay had it that during the reign of Admiral Robert, Mam Goul, the oldest of our vendors (she was probably eternal), had plucked him from beneath a holy-water fount in the Église Saint-Antoine. Ever since her son – a redoubtable giant who'd left to join De Gaulle – had died in the war, and her daughter had made a new life for herself in the wonderland of France, and her last companion (a girl named Anastase) had abandoned her for love of a Syrian bastard, the old lady had lived alone. And it was at the end of her rounds one day that she'd happened by the church where the priest had just discovered a baby sleeping as soundly as a rummy. The priest, who'd been about to lock up, was quite put out and completely at a loss. Then he'd marched hopefully over to Mam Goul as she prayed before the statue of the Virgin.

"'Scuse me, Mam Goul, is this child yours?"

Mam Goul wasn't expecting anything from life or the mailman. Her potato chips sold well enough but her heart was empty. She had only one friend left, Anastase, whom she would visit to sit listening to the radio and talking about life between mouthfuls of mashed arrowroot. So when the priest asked you that question, you answered yes-yes without really thinking about it. Clasping the warm little body, so alive, to your bony chest, you'd hurried furtively home. For the first time in a long while you'd double-locked the door, and fixed a baby's bottle. You bathed the infant lovingly before laying him down on your bed. You passed a wakeful night, without any rheumatic twinges: this new life disturbed your desolation, just as Anastase's stay in your home had done such a long time before. The child, named Daniel, became your adopted son, who always knew you weren't his real mother. For him, you stopped selling chips (and wearing your legs down to stumps) and went to sit in the market behind a basket of vegetables. Daniel grew up at your side until he was tall enough for us to find him handsome, and to baptize him Bidjoule, apprentice-djobber. Pin-Pon took him under his wing, teaching him our trade. Sirop was the one who looked after Pipi.

Somewhere in the middle of the morning there was always an indiscernible hour when customers grew scarce. Hopping off our perch on the crates, we would then carry out what had become a ritual: joining Pipi around the basket of Elmire, the *pacotilleuse* of countless voyages. All the dust in all the world was upon her shoes. To call up her memories, she'd shake her gray curl papers. We hung on her words like dogs on a bone.

> And Haïti, mama wounded by
> that nightmare Doc
> who paints her life naïvely
> outside of time and space.

> I saw Barbados [33] a limestone ham
> with a Hillaby frill on top

Eleven saints slice it up
and the English gulp it all down.

We would huddle around her talk. Her throat poured out the song of waves on the hulls of boats, the rush of wind in the shell of an ear. She'd seen the green gulfs and their little island eyes. Our other selves in English, Spanish, Portuguese, and often, in protean Creole. The starry center of our branching wheelbarrows, Elmire lost her wet-bird look to be reborn, as certain fruits grow glossy when washed by a storm. The municipal guardian would make his rounds. In the distance, Mam Elo, queen of *macadam*, would hail all lovers of *losis*, codfish fritters blooming with pimento. The peasant women hustled and bustled. Pipi stared fixedly into the eyes of the ancient voyager, astonished that those tiny stones could have hoarded up so much scenery.

Salute Grenada, my children.
They say she's sailing off to the other America
and that Carriacou, Ronde, and Petite-Martinique
are pointing us in that direction.

Grenada, she said,
amid Trinidad, Tobago, and Margarita,
you flourish toward the mainland
a calenda [34] of petticoats.

(A-ah! Here Elmire would shed a tear.)

The fever returned from noon until one o'clock. Customers would flood in from everywhere. Knives pierced the secrets at the hearts of yellow squashes. Coins jingled. Paper money, as soft as faded flowers, gave off its special scent. Sometimes a dog would manage to reach the cooks' stands and keep a hungry eye on the fish marinating in sour orange juice and red pepper. Mam Elo washed her rice as she sang a soundless song no mandolin had ever succeeded in courting. The market went full tilt, sending up lofty bamboos of noise. Serious heat began to come through the iron roofs. Fruits set impatient odors free, distant cousins of sweet liqueurs. Fresh sweats dampened our jerseys already yellowed by old ones.

Ééé Guadeloupe
Chalky and volcanic
tranquil and turbulent
from the waterfalls at Bouillante
you go suckle at the high winds of Soufrière
And from both breasts you descend to La Grande

There between high plateaus and ocean deeps
peeks out the eye of Grippon-Morne-à-l'Eau
(and Les Abymes dips a toe in the water).

Elmire always ended with Guadeloupe. She'd left a bit of her heart there, in the gray eyes of a black man. Her own eyes would close at the memory.

"Now leave me alone, will you, I've got to get selling!"

Elmire would shake herself, straighten up her vegetables, adjust her kerchief, and give a look-see for customers. On our own again, we'd go back to our crates.

During that hour between noon and one, something would snap in the market, like a step danced backwards in a quadrille. Without consulting one another, we'd all sprint to the sanctuary of a rum Mass. Our favorite spot was a nearby bistro, Chez Chinotte. Our regular table was always waiting for us. Chinotte, the proprietor, had stepped off a Colombian boat lugging a couple of suitcases so heavy they had to be stuffed with gold pieces. The very next day, the Adventuress bought the bar from Bonne-Mama [Grandma], a sixty-year-old widow so cruelly affected by the death of her husband that she was letting the place go to grit and grime. With Chinotte, the bistro came alive again. A young woman from Marigot worked there as a waitress, threading her way among the tables, weighed down by an impenetrable sorrow. Streaks of sunlight filtered into the shadowy interior through the crooked slats of the shutters. Glasses clinked. Tongues clacked. Rum splashed, mingling its fragrance with the heady aroma of plum wine. Silently, we partook of the sacrament of the first punch, and then came the rowdiness of the first intoxication, which Chinotte pretended to frown on from atop the stack of credit ledgers where she sat in state.

In spite of her embonpoint, Chinotte was elegant. And stout of heart: she could handle all by herself the bands of drunken sailors who swept through the city on Saturday nights. In addition, she controlled a tiny protective monster that helped her ward off the evils of mischance. She had hidden part of the treasure brought from Colombia in the apartment above the bar and wore the rest in the form of gold jewelry, from her Creole earrings to that *collier-choux*[35] with a bead containing dust off a black stone from Trinidad, an infallible counterpoison. One dazzling marvel, the spider pinned over her left breast, did not come from Colombia. We would all have sworn to the existence of this extraordinary brooch . . .

(*Here's the clatter on the wonder-spider.* Ever since Chinotte's arrival here without a husband, no man had been rash enough to proposition her or reach even one fingertip across the bar toward her breasts. The only one who tried to invite her to the Sages's Ball in Le Robert – so propitious for wild times – was a *quimboiseur*, a terrible sorcerer from Anse Gouraud. Chinotte's plump curves (and doubtless her fat purse) tormented the *quimboiseur*, who could be seen prowling around the bar even when it wasn't rum-punch time, all spiffed up and cologned. The Adventuress, protected by her monster, was not afraid of the *quimboiseur* and repelled his advances with a raised eyebrow. Luckily for the sorcerer, there was at that time a goldsmith on Rue Ernest-Renan who was leading precious metals a merry dance to the tune of his brilliant inspiration: Monsieur Nicéphore Adeldade. Appearing in Fort-de-France several days after a cyclone had passed through, the jeweler purchased the premises of a shoemaker undone by diabetes and rum (the man was no longer master of his craft, and we took our pointy-toed shoes elsewhere). Nicéphore Adeldade set up his jewelry shop and became instantly famous. The black women of Macouba or Grand' Rivière braved the dangers of a trip all the way down to Fort-de-France to order rings, pins, and necklaces from him. They came up from Sainte-Anne, too, and Le Diamant, rustling in their stiffly starched garments. The jeweler's fame soon spread across the water, and at the hour when the pippiree heralds the dawn, people from et-cetera would be waiting in front of his shop. The *békés* despised our artist at first, but as his success grew, they came around, too, and ordered their share of this sunlight fashioned by his fingers. Ladies and gentlemen, our comrade spun gold divinely into finest lace. The curve of his earrings was not of this world. His golden brooches *à clous*, *têtés-négresses*, wasps'-nests, dahlias, sweetsops, caterpillars, *gros-sirop*[36] chains, and cane pommels were simply incomparable. For the madras headscarf, he reinvented the barrette and the cabochon stickpin. For the torrid frenzy of the calenda he found a *tremblant* pin that secures the folds of the headdress, and at the ends of minute springs, jiggles tiny hollow balls enshrining love-locks. His fortune was made, and then misfortune annihilated him down to the very last hair.

So: one morning (Lord have mercy!) there was a knock on the jewelry shop's door. The sublime goldsmith opened up. As the *quimboiseur* from Anse-Gouraud stepped inside, a ring tarnished aborning on the black marble slab.

"I want your finest piece," said the sorcerer, "the one into which you pour so much of your soul that you'll never get it back!"

And he sprinkled Nicéphore Adeldade with sweat droplets from a *molocoye*-tortoise, then made things worse with eye-stickum from a he-mule on its last legs. Under this evil spell the jeweler's workshop rang with feverish activity in the moonlight. Quicksilver spurted from the window shutters. In the morning police experts cherishing no illusions searched for the goldsmith, poking through a workshop charred so black it seemed the sun had spent the night there, while the *quimboiseur*, on the stroke of noon, began poking Chinotte in her upstairs bedroom. He had presented her with the fabulous creation in which our greatest artist had burned himself out, and – *wouabap!* – the Adventuress had let down her guard.

After humping Chinotte for long hours without a hitch, the sorcerer made his entrance in the bar during a rum Mass with the relaxed manner of the master of the house. He poured a round for everyone with his own hand, and gave an entire bottle to Pipi, who had entertained him with an amusing story.

A taxi soon arrived with his suitcases, and Chinotte, back at the cash register, was treated all day long like a bitch brought to heel. The *quimboiseur*'s arrogance probably proved his down- fall. That evening, he was preparing to coil himself around his new slave like a conquering corset beneath her sheets when the monstrous Antichri'[37] that Chinotte kept tucked in her armpit at night showed its face. No one knows whether the Antichri' floored the sorcerer with a specific curse or simply looked him straight in the eye. Either way, our *quimboiseur* is now an unspeakable wreck, eating his own excrement behind the Adventist temple. After that fateful night, Chinotte appeared at her cash register, resplendent in the aura of her latest piece of jewelry. *There you have it.*)

The faithful always showed up for Mass: we djobbers, Ti-Joge the mailman (Pipi had no idea he'd married Clarine), a few fishermen from Rive-Droite, plus some country folk whose wives were busy at their market stalls and who'd come to pay their respects to Chinotte, sit down with a rum, and chat about soccer, *bois-bandé*, and putting themselves out of their misery by flitting off forever to France, the land of dreams. Chinotte had a welcoming smile, a good word for everyone, but she regularly reminded a few customers how big a tab they'd run up over the last six months. Because although rum punches were easy to get on credit, Chinotte wrote them all down in indelible ink in the fat ledgers that served as her throne.

Along about two o'clock, we'd head back to the market, famished, looking forward eagerly to Mam Elo's royal *macadam*. The market would be starting to wind down. A few customers lingered, haggling happily. Parked behind their mothers, children dug into their lunches, while the vendors were already calculating the day's profits with furrowed brows. Afternoons, in the deserted stalls, we'd all rest our fatigue on the peace of these sunbaked hours, after listening religiously to the funeral announcements broadcast every day on the radio. With the first coolness in the air, the market would gently return to life, as mixed bouquets and bundles of soup vegetables with herbs began to sell. And with the first shadows, the unsold wares had to be put away in boxes and bags and stashed out of sight beneath certain counters while the vendor murmured a raticidal prayer. Picking up baskets and racing them back where they'd come from would keep us hopping until almost seven o'clock. Then we'd clean up our wheelbarrows. Pipi and Bidjoule would help us, thrilled to be grooming these beauties. The clan would disperse for the night, everyone for himself in the solitude of a shanty or the warmth of a woman. Pipi and Bidjoule would go home with their mothers, to the ritual soup eaten by the light of a kerosene lamp. As for us, regarding this aspect of our lives, allow me to be discreet: I never heard tell that one must tell all.

Pipi, king of the djobbers, my my. Pipi and Bidjoule were in school on the djob, so to speak. Sirop and Pin-Pon were their mentors, and all day long – through little hand signals, winks, silences, and the odd word or two – they imparted to them the essence of the djob, the technique and knowledge of a master-djobber. Dealings with the vendors, the handling of delicate flowers and fragile fruits, how you stack up different clusters and bunches, assemble piles of firm or tender produce, and the subtle ways to hook a vendor, keeping her faithful to one djobber till the coffin lid's nailed down . . . All this is laughable today, but it's how we survived when others were going under for good. The time came for the two youngsters to make their wheelbarrows. This took them however long they needed; Sirop and Pin-Pon paid no attention to them meanwhile, and we paid even less: that's when the djobber is born, alone and his own man.

The construction of the wheelbarrow.

In germination

infinite desire for its completion all impatience
yielding to its vital assembly the back-breaking
problem of the axle the delicate determination of the
forward thrust and the anxiety over botching the arms
shafts essential to its equilibrium the chiseling of
their strength

You had to come into the world with it truly feel
quiet possession that increasing density of self
like a message revealed

To express lastly the love released to make everything
whole and begin something that never existed before

With djobs come
the modeling of the fingers
the patina of the handles
and
the development of the shoulder muscles
sole true tamers
of the Beast.

How to describe the pleasure of seeing young people following
in our footsteps, remaking us, inscribing us in time? Oh, the
vanity of those days: we thought ourselves immortal! Our clan
increased by two wheelbarrows, still stiff but giving promise
of a thousand supple moves. To us they seemed alike, handsome embodiments of the wisdom imparted by Pin-Pon and
Sirop, and it was impossible for us to see in Pipi's wheelbarrow
the one that, as it matured, would outshine all others. In the
streets, from djob to djob, Pin-Pon and Sirop showed the
youngsters the hip movements that assured a smooth advance,
the finger-tip control required for various swerves and detours.
When the apprentices were ready, when Sirop and Pin-Pon had
nothing more to teach them, when certain vendors began calling them master-this and master-that, and when they'd dem-
onstrated their full-throated expertise in the djobber's cries,[38]
Mam Elo offered us a thank-you macadam, and Mam Goul, the
vegetables-of-grateful-appreciation. That day – 'scuse me Lord
– the rum Mass was a genuine pagan feast.

Then came the revelation of Pipi, the event that without further
ado crowned him grand master of the wheelbarrow, king of us
djobbers. The rumor was flying that a vendor from the parish
of Ducos was coming to market with a yam so enormous she'd
had to hire an entire car. Sitting in a group on their crates, the
master-djobbers – Sifilon, Pin-Pon, Sirop, Lapochodé, Didon,
Bidjoule, and Pipi – all heard the news at the same time. The
advantages of this djob were obvious to everyone: the fame
(newspaper photo of the gargantuan vegetable and the djobber), the money (the vendor, surely in high flustration, would

be generous in relief), the balance of the wheelbarrow (transporting an undoubtedly magical yam could only mean good things for the lucky vehicle). Although she tended to favor Didon, the vendor from Ducos did not yet have a regular djobber, so the first to arrive at La Croix-Mission would snag the djob! Like a pack of rats fleeing fire in the cane fields, we took off with our wheelbarrows in a flurry of controlled skidding. There were shouts of *Ba mwen lê!* [Out of my way!] and *Pin-pon-pinpon!* – all our yapping cries rang out. It was a tricky business. On a Saturday, with cars and people everywhere, the markets were surrounded by dense crowds. It would take a genius to win this race, for it was essential that you calculate your speed and the length of your stride with the utmost precision while handling the heavy wheelbarrow like a feather so as not to hurt anyone or miss an opening. This demanded absolute familiarity with the local geography and the dimensions of each street, and above all, the ability to adjust to the unexpected. Now, since we were all doctors of wheelbarrowing, no one would have been surprised to see us arrive in one clump before the vendor from Ducos. And yet, Pipi beat us there by one minute and change.

Here's the story: Sirop, Pin-Pon, Sifilon, and Lapochodé galloped down Rue Antoine-Siger and came out together onto Boulevard Allègre, which runs alongside the Canal Levassor as far as the fish market. It was a good route (this market is right next to La Croix-Mission), but a conventional one. At ten o'clock, Rue Antoine-Siger is clear. The sidewalks of Boulevard Allègre are cluttered with vendors and a few parked cars, but the street is wide enough for a wheelbarrow to zip all the way to the fish market and over to La Croix-Mission. Which is what Sirop, Pin-Pon, Sifilon, and Lapochodé tried to do. Sirop took the lead because he tilted his wheelbarrow up onto one back wheel, which reduced his width and allowed him to charge ahead. At the end of Boulevard Allègre, Lapochodé, Pin-Pon, and Sifilon ran smack into a throng of people shopping for fish (they'd expected some traffic, but had forgotten about the late deliveries on Saturday: up until eleven o'clock, covered trucks block everything while they unload). They lost a minute and a half. Way too much. Sirop, having correctly gauged the cost of such an obstacle, left Boulevard Allègre via Rue Ernest-Renan, intending to run straight into La Croix-Mission on the last sec- tion of Rue François-Arago. It was a good plan, but he dropped seven seconds outside a Syrian store where a truck had pulled up sideways to deliver some bolts of the very latest nylon. He had to improvise a maneuver that ended up costing him first place.

As for Bidjoule and Didon, they immediately left Rue Antoine-Siger, swinging into Rue François-Arago. It was a dicey move. This street runs bang into La Croix-Mission but it's constantly jammed with cars and people outside the Syrian shops, where textiles are displayed. The djobbers thought they could sur-mount this difficulty by straddling the curb, rolling their wheelbarrows half in the street and half on the sidewalk. They'd forgotten the intersections at Rue Lamartine and Rue Ernest-Renan, where cars and pedestrians tie the traffic in knots. They lost almost a minute there. Besides, like Sirop, they still had to dodge around that truck delivering the nylon. Which cost them thirty seconds, and the djob.

Pipi proved his mad audacity, his lightning-quick imagination, and lastly, his flawless knowledge of the neighborhood. He ran along the edge of the vegetable market toward Rue Isam-bert. That took him four seconds he made up by charging down Rue Isambert, which was clear at that hour on Saturdays. Passing the playground at the École Perrinon, crossing Rue Victor-Sévère, he zipped down Abbé-Lecornu – a narrow alley, but completely deserted – and emerged onto Boulevard du Général-de-Gaulle, which was congested but broad as a black nose, thus posing no problem for a master of the wheelbarrow. Darting here-there like a yellow viper, up the boulevard went Pipi. He skidded triumphantly to a stop in front of the vendor from Ducos, who rewarded him with the yam. This route was thenceforward known as Pipi's Path, and we used it on great occasions.

The vendors had followed the action and welcomed Pipi back with delirious hoo-rah. The municipal guardian, who'd practically ignored us since his appointment, insisted on shaking his hand and asked him his name. People thronged around him, admiring his wheelbarrow. We couldn't even get close to him to show our love and respect. A crowd rolled in from all around, and a newspaper photographer had him stand on the yam next to the vendor from Ducos. On the municipal scale, the jumbo root weighed in at two hundred and eighty-one pounds one and a half ounces. That Saturday morning was awhirl around the whopper and Pipi's glory, as the market women and city folk clamored fit to bust. The vendor from Ducos – it was terrible – didn't know how to sell this gobstopper: By the slice? By the hunk? By the foot or by the pound? And anyway, no one had the heart to take a knife to it, so the monster simply sat there beside its bewildered owner.

On that auspicious day, Pipi met up again with Clarine, who was now Mam Joge. The mailman was with her, looking like a colonel in his post office uniform. The year of their marriage, they had had a daughter, Pauline, a *câpresse* with luxuriant hair, followed by a boy, Emile, whose tragic destiny was yet to be revealed. The market had not forgotten Mam Joge (Clarine as was), for she'd been a shrewd judge of vegetables with those marvelously gentle eyes, and she'd never haggled over prices. Chance had so ordained that she had never run into Pipi, until then. She saw him when he climbed on top of the yam at the photographer's request. In spite of those impressive royal shoulders and the knotty muscles of a master-djobber, she recognized the adolescent who'd eaten his heart out during the war over having a *dorlis* for a father. Now he was strong, lively, with a quick and clever tongue, and only a fleeting shadow sometimes revealed the lingering pain deep in his eyes. After their marriage, Ti-Joge hadn't wanted Clarine to keep working among us in the market, so she'd become a cook for a lady on Rue Lamartine. The mailman, a communicant like the rest of us at our rum Masses, had been happy to find his wife so well acquainted with the new grand master of wheelbarrows. He listened in delight as the two of them reminisced about the war, and to polish off the morning in style, he invited us all to Chez Chinotte to savor the rum of memory. Mam Joge (as becomes a lady) went along home. No one suspected that seeing Pipi again had reopened an old wound: her abandoned child . . . At Chinotte's bistro, the mailman put on quite a show, for he was dead set on pitting his knowledge of Fort-de-France against that of our new champion.

"Well then, Pipi," shouted Ti-Joge from his table, "how would you get to Le Calvaire in three minutes without taking Boulevard du Général?"

Often, Pipi answered in a drip-drop, filling the djobbers in the room with pride. At other times, he would finish his sip of rum, but his reply – albeit tardy – would prove correct. Solving Ti-Joge's stumpers that time put the crowning touch on Pipi's triumph. No one was supposed to know Fort-de-France better than the mailman, who tramped through it every day for six hours at a stretch with measured tread, up hills and down steep streets, on stairs and along hallways. That urban science was unique in this city, a city sprung from an unwholesome swamp found suitable by Governor Du Parquet, however, as a site for the king's next fort. A church was erected on the first land hauled out of that hell. They destroyed the mangroves to build houses they had to rebuild after every flood. Despite the thousand twinkling lights of Saint-Pierre, people came from all over to live in this new-born city. Rochambeau named it Fort-de-la-République. Later, it was called Fort-de-France. This city prevailed over epidemics of leprosy and smallpox, September floodwaters, and earthquakes so sudden the rats had no time to warn anyone. It even endured a calamitous forest of furious flames in the great fire of June 22, 1890. Houses flared up like dry canes, with bursts of red and a spectral yellow that coppered the whole horizon. All Fort-de-France became one blaze that licked a cloud before curling up on a bed of silent ashes. The city survived, but collapsed like a sorrowful negress into premature old age and stayed cringing in that bay facing the sea. That's how things were on March 30, 1894, when Béhanzin, the deposed king of Dahomey exiled by the imperialists for his rebelliousness, arrived in Martinique with a few of his wives, his ninety children, and his counselors – who no longer knew what counsel to give in this place so poorly risen from its ashes. To Béhanzin, the city was such a surprise that, keeping an eye on it from where he'd been tucked away in Fort Tartenson, he wore the eye out. He spent entire days observing the city, unable to fathom its secret. This enigma remained closed to him even after he was moved to a villa across from the seminary-college, where he studied the mystery most intently, surrounded by his counselors, who would tell him, "Highness, ask to leave this cursed city." His health irreparably damaged, Béhanzin left our country for Algeria, where he died soon after setting foot ashore . . . Unlike Pipi, who cared nothing for the past, Ti-Joge the mailman knew all this, and even more. He paid court to the city as he crisscrossed it daily, delivering an endless stream of joys and tragedies. He read letters to those who could not do it themselves (yes it's your daughter writing here, telling you everything's fine) and explained the administrative documents that flummoxed our brains with their impossible questions (they're asking you how old you are) . . .

Although he never missed midday Mass at Chinotte's place, Ti-Joge didn't touch a drop while he was working. He declined all offers until the last letter was gone, when he would finally sit down and take the time to talk about life, tippling a half-bottle in the company of Pipi, whom he quite liked. The master-djobber would recount his war stories, describe his distress at learning of his *dorlis* father. Ti-Joge would tell him about the widows and lovely young things who fell over backwards at the sight of his piratically dashing looks and snappy uniform.

Mam Joge came to the market every day. She would look for Pipi and ask him to buy vegetables for her, waiting for the right moment to confess her secret anguish to him. The tremendous yam from Ducos had the market topsy-turvy, and Pipi's extraordinary popularity left her little opportunity. One time, though, she was able to speak of her shame.

"So you abandoned Gogo's child?" exclaimed Pipi. "Where, 'zactly?"

"In the Église Saint-Antoine."

"A-ah!"

"Sa anté pé fè?" (What else could I do?) moaned Mam Joge.

No one paid them any attention, neither the vendors nor us, all busy jabbering about the gigantic yam.

"I don't see how I could help you . . ."

"Anlé sav là ti-manmay la pasé, Pipi . . ." (I want to find out
where the lil' one is . . .)

"You want to have him back?"

"Noooo, Ti-Joge doesn't know anything about him, and
wouldn't want him . . . I'd just like to help the child . . ."

Pipi, that day, made no reply . . .

Almost in spite of himself, Pipi went to the Église Saint-Antoine. Because he had never prayed, he entered the church
walking backwards, so as not to offend Jesus and his family.
After a useless inspection of the holy-water basins, he approached the priest, who revealed to him that the child in question had been taken home by a pious soul who lived only a few
steps away, a former potato-chip peddler. That didn't ring a
bell for Pipi, so it wasn't until he went to the address in question, knock-knock, Yes yes who's there? – and then Mam Goul
opened up . . . SWEET JESUS!

"Well, Pipi, so you've come to see me?" squeaked the immortal old lady.

The master-djobber stood there goggle-eyed like a fly before the syrup jug. In his head, it all fell into place: Daniel,
Mam Goul's adopted little boy, called Bidjoule because he was
cute, growing up around the wheelbarrows, smarter on the
djob than in school, "You fathead!" Mam Goul would scream,
but the boy loved hanging around the djobbers, clutching at
the wheelbarrow handles, trying out delicate maneuvers, he'd
been unusually promising material and he'd come along at the
same fast pace as Pipi despite being younger . . .

"Mam Joge, she's his mother . . ."

"Wha?"

"The wife of Ti-Joge the mailman . . ."

"What about Ti-Joge's wife?"

"She's the mama of Bidjoule . . ."

"Whoosat, Bidjoule? Whoosat Bidjoule . . ."

"Daniel . . ."

Bidjoule wasn't there. The old woman could blast out all her
rage at the revelation: "What, that fat bitch, it's her? Abandoning a child like that I ask you! Even if it's in the Good Lord's
house, you just don't do that after all I mean really! There's

people have no feelings . . ." But Mam Goul had lived too long to underestimate the ravages of love, and when Mam Joge – alerted by Pipi – appeared before her, the old lady clasped her to her bosom the way one does with someone who has suffered.

"We going to tell him?" whispered Mam Goul.

"I don't know," replied Mam Joge.

"It'll mess up his head . . . Let it go," advised Pipi.

"I always told him his mama was dead."

"Then let's leave it like that, Madame Goul," concluded Mam Joge.

The vendor from Ducos had remained by the yam's side, baffled, no longer comprehending the life parading before her eyes, the curiosity-seekers, the tourists taking photos of the phenomenon. Staying close to her vegetable treasure, she spent nights in a room across from the market, watching through the shutters for the slightest suspicious movement. More and more sightseers kept pouring in. So Pipi suggested that she charge money for the photographs. Shaking off her paralyzing indecision, the vendor from Ducos covered the marvel with a piece of oilcloth that she lifted up again only in exchange for francs, dollars, and lots of other kinds of currency that only Ti-Joge the mailman could recognize and evaluate. This business went on for several months until the yam melted into a wormy mush. The stench was such that we would have fled the market if the city sanitation department hadn't zapped that plague with a flame-thrower. The vendor from Ducos spent the rest of her life cussing out the clerks in the currency exchange offices she haunted in the company of Ti-Joge, whose calculations of thousands never exactly matched those of the bankers before whom the vendor would spread out her twenty packets of foreign bills. She battled on and on for her cosmopolitan treasure, surrounding herself with lawyers and experts whose bills kept mounting up, leading to the seizure of her land, her furniture, her baskets, and of course, the twenty packets of money, the judiciary valuation of which covered one tenth of a half-third of the debts of the miserable woman, who died of a sorrow beyond the powers of witchcraft.

So: The flood of people and money drawn in by the yam swept the pleasures and pains of first love into Pipi's life. In his spare time, the king of the djobbers helped the vendor from Ducos harvest the weird currency the tourists paid. The yam had become an object of pilgrimage, luring to the market people who otherwise would never – or only rarely – have come there. Thus it was that one day Mam Goul showed up with a creature named Anastase.

"Pleez Pipi, let my granddaughter see the yam . . ."

And the king set eyes on the *échappée-coulie*.[39] And he turned gray, staring at the wondrous girl with the look we usually save for lovely cars. She was tall, aeolian, with a quivering softness beneath her madras-cotton dress. Her eyes were sunlit nights, and her lips were as full of promise as hibiscus buds. Getting a grip on himself, grinning, and lifting up the oilcloth turned out to be so strangely difficult that Pipi spent a tad of time on this. Anastase gazed at the yam with a sad smile. She spoke a few words, but Pipi, in a daze, heard only the quintessence of music. When the apparition went off with Mam Goul after one or two thank-yous, the vendor from Ducos had to grab our man and lean him up against a railing: "Pipi, ho, feeling faint?" He did not answer, enslaved by the silhouette undulating beside the clomping Mam Goul.

"Who is that, huh, that girl there?"

Before the vendor could reply, he'd already caught up with the two women, going rigid with supplication like a dog desperate for a home.

"Ho, Mam Goul, what's the lady looking for?"

"Cucumbers and some forceripe fruit . . ."

And the king was masterful: hands in a flutter, mouth bubbling with words, he showed off his market expertise, pointing out to them the thirteen vendors of *massissi*-cucumbers bristling with soft spikes, delicious in vinaigrette, and haggling with seven other vendors over the price of those e-normous pale green cukes that are so refreshing to the heart. He unearthed for them the rarest of watermelons, yellow, with dark green stripes, and flesh like a pink elixir, plus a bunch of sapodilla plums for less than a pittance. The creature thanked him with gracious warmth, finishing him off with a smile that stuck him plonk in the middle of an aisle, as firmly planted as a fencepost. That afternoon, Pipi neglected his usual rounds and a few promised djobs. Sticking closer to Mam Goul than a noonday shadow, he fanned her, massaged her touch of rheumatism, killed seven vicious flies for her, and kept her company until he could ply her with impatient questions. We watched his little game with amusement from a distance; it was still impossible for us to imagine that love had suckerpunched him, and that, naturally reeling from the blow, he would be leaving us for the pernicious pleasures of a rum drunk all alone.

Mam Goul told him everything, without really comprehending our man's agitation. Yes she's this old, no she's not married, she sells sweets to children at the École Perrinon during recess, yes she lived with me a long time ago, now she lives alone, alone, yes alone, you don't understand alone? . . . From Morne-aux-Gueules, she comes from Morne-aux-Gueules . . . Seeing Pipi deep in conversation with the Immortal One, we drew closer.

"You have to hear the fabulous story of her father," Mam Goul was saying . . .

(A word or so about Anastase's father. Her father and grandfather came from India. Driven from Pondicherry by famine, they'd contracted to work here for a béké who supplied cane choppers to growers. Ever since the abolition of slavery, those damn niggers avoided all work in general and the fields in particular. The grandfather had traveled steerage on the boat and come ashore at the main square in Saint-Pierre, where he sat amid puddles left over from the last rain, waiting in front of the immigration officials to have his papers stamped so he could go off in the béké's cart. The béké had picked him out of the crowd along with five or six others and made them mark an X on their indentures into hell.

The man who was to become Anastase's grandfather had no one left but his son. The mother had been trampled to death in a Calcutta street during a distribution of food by the British. It took him two years to figure out what kind of a contract he'd signed: they'd confined him in a former slave-hut at the edge of a cane field where he toiled from one end of the sun to the other, jeered at by idle blacks, and the few sous he was to have earned had been replaced by thin strips of dried cod and lots of tafia. At the end of the contract, he tried to leave that very day for his native land, now a vision of loveliness. The *béké* chained him up with two or three other homesick would-be travelers in the infirmary (required by the immigration department) which became, in this situation as in others, a dungeon ghastly enough to inspire the signing of a new contract, the terms of which were then carried out by gendarmes-on-horseback. The future grandfather signed whatever they wanted when he realized, at the end of six days, that the irons were already eating into his ankle bones. He was sent back to the fields, where he found his son (who had been assigned to a small crew digging irrigation ditches) and most importantly, the *béké*, who, dressed all in white, was surveying his domain from up on his horse. Anastase's grandfather-to-be casually walked up and hacked open the *béké*'s thigh with six cutlass slashes, using the seventh to split open the head of the field boss who came running over. The gendarmes-on-horseback tracked down the murderer and, at dawn on the third day, cut him down without warning, as was customary at the time in dealing with unruly *coulis*.

Taking most seriously that wise proverb, *Ich tig paka fèt san zong* (Tiger's cubs aren't made without claws), the *béké*, crippled for life, handed the murderer's child over to the immigration department posthaste. Since no *béké* in the neighborhood was willing to hire that rebel's seed, a magistrate placed him in the care of the parish priest in La Trinité. The priest put him to work on a few acres of good soil (mysterious legacies from parishioners at death's door) on which he raised some tobacco that was not up to snuff. Although the child gave cause for great satisfaction to the priest, who taught him – among other things – a garbling of Latin plus how to read and write, the adolescent gave the saintly man cause for some distress. Kouli (that's what he was called, for no one knew his name) had seen a bout of *laghia*[40] one day, over in the Brin-d'Amour part of town, and he'd taken it into his head to become a famous fighter in these ritual combats. He spent most of his time toughening his muscles and packing more punch into his kicks. Soon, instead of passing the collection plate at Sunday Mass, he was following his *major*, the neighborhood tough guy, on challenge-walks through the territories of other majors in places like Anse-l'Etang, Vert-Pré, Lestrade, and Trou-Terre. The local hero was a certain Lassao. And he was one big fellow. A skillful dancer who, after choreography worthy of a dragon-fly, could crush his adversary's liver, or break his back across an upraised knee. Kouli idolized him and never missed one of his fights.

The world of *laghia* had been driven underground by the police, but there were ways of throwing them off the scent, and everyone knew who the great masters were. Lassao's reputation soon spread beyond the suburbs of La Trinité to the heart of the city. The majors of Pelletier, La Bélème, Balata, Long-Bois, and La Duchêne experienced that unforgiving kick of his. And out at the cape of Pointe Figuier, a certain Fidèle, whose name was mentioned in hushed tones, was killed outright: *jou malê pani pwan gad* (days of disaster don't give fair warning).

Going southward, Lassao's reputation bumped into that of Zouti, the major of Anse Carétan, whose renown was spreading north. Zouti was a *chabin* as gnarled as a stalk of twisty bamboo. His dance was less powerful than Lassao's, but his muscles were as hard as *baume*-wood. He was famous for the speed with which he would whip behind his opponent to snap his spine with a single kick. From Sainte-Anne to Grand' Rivière, people talked of nothing but their inevitable battle. Delayed time and again by police patrols, the fight finally took place at La Mancelle, near Le Marin, in the presence of a hundred lucky souls.

Lassao was the first to arrive, accompanied by two drummers on the big *gwoka*, those on the smaller *tibwa*, and the seven men in charge of his neighborhood's wagers. Lassao crawled around for a few minutes, speaking in a low voice to the earth, feeling it, sometimes tasting it, in order to determine the precise place for the match. He soon found it and struck the ground with his heel at a spot that instantly became the center of a circle of spectators, while a mighty shout and drum roll went up. When Zouti appeared with his entourage, Lassao began his challenge-round immediately, without even a glance at his adversary. This electrified the *major* of Anse Carétan. He 73 crossed himself, flung away his *bakoua*, stripped off his shirt and trousers, and to the *wop-wop-wop* of the crowd, entered the circle, where he danced his acceptance of the challenge. Then words began to zing.

"Zouti my friend, lifting me up is like lifting the factory in Le Robert, and if you lift up that factory, how the strain goin' affect your balls, tell me that?"

"Leave my balls alone and take care for your eyes, Lassao, 'cause I'm ready to go" – and Zouti launched his attack.

Unfolding his tales of an evening, a storyteller from Le Marin related that, in the sudden throbbing of the drums and voices, Zouti's first blow went wide, throwing him off balance. He was then grabbed by the waist, whirled around, and cracked like a stick over Lassao's knee. The audience swears to having heard his back crunch while Lassao's drummers struck up a victory barrage. Holy Mother of God, something incredible then happened: Zouti, whom everyone expected to see wriggling like a worm atop newly plowed earth, sprang right back to his feet. U N H U R T. Fresher and more lithe than at the beginning of the bout, he began circling his adversary in a new challenge-round. That was how we discovered he was *monté*: the earth, through an old compact, was infusing him with its power every time he touched the ground. Lassao was discombobulated. Zouti, fast as a fish, slipped behind him and oh mama, after *chassé*-ing to the left as handsomely as this world of *laghia* has ever seen, he popped off the definitive kick that was to extend his fleeting fame all the way to La Désirade and make of Lassao, caught in the spine, an invalid whom compassionate friends pitched off a cliff in Le Lorrain just to do him a favor, so there.

With Lassao routed, Kouli angrily demanded that throats and drums give voice to his defiance, and amid general disbelief, he began a challenge-round. Zouti, offended, tried to keep calm: "Anpaka goumen épi i-anmay" (I don't fight kiddies), he growled. But soon he simply could not ignore this outrage. Shaking his head with disdain and regret, he stepped into the circle. People were betting fast and furiously, but never on Kouli. Confident of victory, Zouti took no particular care with his passes and thought it unnecessary to use his unstoppable *volte*. As the more experienced fighter, he threw his opponent with five *levés-renversés* in a row, which left Kouli staggering. The high and mighty Zouti played to the crowd, smiling at the pretty girls. That was when Kouli put his hands behind his back and struck up this soon-to-be-celebrated song.

Kouli's Song

Hé Mérilo hé Mérilo
Saki vayan lévé lanmin
Saki vayan tonbé si mwen[41] . . .

In plain language, he was reissuing his challenge and urging Zouti to fight for real. Having delivered his warning, Kouli leaned to one side and worked out some completely unprecedented steps, destined to become classic *laghia* passes. Intrigued, Zouti straightened up slightly to get a better look. This uncovered his belly just enough for a *doublé-pieds*, a right-and-left kick that fried his liver. The police found his body the next morning, beneath the crossroads crucifix where to this day, the victims of clandestine *laghia* still wash up on a mysterious tide.

Kouli's fame fanned out like a passel of mongooses bolting from blazing sugarcane. Young punks came running, but Kouli was invincible. When spectators saw him clasp his hands behind his back, sing "Hé Mérilo," and trot out those steps that every self-respecting *major* today carries engraved on his heart, well they simply felt sorry for the other guy. The new master did not let success go to his head. His love for this dance was so profound that he performed it with the utmost concentration, becoming in each combat a carnal vibration as beautiful and deadly as an onrushing of bees. Along with the renown and the victories came the women. Every Sunday, Kouli carted one off into the bushes. And so the man who was to be Anastase's father came to Morne-aux-Gueules to challenge a *major* with a budding reputation. The *laghia* lasted one hour, after which that *major* was a rag-doll in dire need of a camphorated rum massage. As custom dictated, Kouli stayed overnight in the district, thus annexing Morne-aux-Gueules to his *laghia* territory. The neighborhood threw him a wingding. Kouli was cock of the walk, and a gaggle of women filled every inch of his shadow with tremulous desires. That was the evening, said Mam Goul, that an old black man, a former maroon,[42] gave his fate a twist.

This oldster's name was Hep-là [Hey-you]. He lived by himself in a tiny shanty in Morne-aux-Gueules, feeding on crawfish and wild yams. Hep-là called for silence and, addressing Kouli, the hero of the hour, he told the story of Ti-Boute [Lil' Bit] the hummingbird in an original style that enthralled his audience.

Ladies and gentlemen good evening, Kouli this word is for you, hummingbird was the biggest bird this side of a miracle, but, well, an evil spell shrank him so small that now sometimes his heartbeats blow him right up é kriii,[43] he had a papa, he had a mama, he had enough to eat and his fill of tender affection every day é kraaa, hummingbird lived fine thanks to his parents, but these lovebirds were shot on the very day of All Hallows' truce when the dead ask for peace, by a godless hunter é kriii, hummingbird swore taking blackbirds to witness he would avenge his father's blood, avenge his mother's blood é kraaa, but the godless hunter was a magician as well and so as not to have to live in anxious upset, he placed on hummingbird the cuss-cuss that made him as small and harmless as a tamarind leaf é kriii, what did hummingbird do I ask you, except to grow himself, with a thousand-year patience, the longest and pointiest of beaks, a beak capable of piercing the heart of the godless hunter and paying him back at last for his crime éékraaa, but what did hummingbird do? what did that ingrate and all his progeny do? this disrespectful son? he used his beak only to get drunk more easily on the tafia of hibiscus blooms: he'd spent so much time listening to his beak grow he'd forgotten the why of it éékriii, to punish him those blackbirds, seeing how frivolous his life was, frightened him just as he was flitting from a flower, his heart jumped boodoom-boom and made him explode, that's why ladies and gentlemen — and here's the end — you sometimes see today a startled hummingbird fly all to pieces among the flowers, Kouli this word was for you! . . .

While no one that evening understood the real meaning of the old man's tale, Kouli, on the other hand, was touched in a secret spot inside. Stumbling, he left the light of the torches to go collapse out in the bushes, where he was joined by a silent *câpresse* thunderstruck by love, whom he humped all night long in an unaccountable rage and abandoned without a backward glance when he left the district at dawn. The *câpresse* was called Féfée Célie. Nine months later, she gave birth to Anastase.

It's said that Kouli's head was never right after his match in Morne-aux-Gueules. He no longer smiled, would vex up over trifles, repeated over and over that his heart wasn't going to blow him up, because I'm no heedless hummingbird, and me I haven't forgotten the police shot my papa down like a mad dog . . . He was seen prowling around police stations, glaring at the officers with looks as poisonous as manchineel.

"But what's he want from us, this loony?" worried the gendarmes.

One day, an officer got down off his horse and grabbed Kouli by the collar – you're going to tell me what you're up to! – before receiving the magisterial *laghia*-blow that drove his belt buckle into his bellybutton. The evisceration of the lawman unleashed such a brouhaha that Kouli managed to escape. Hiding in the woods, fed and protected by everyone, for a long time he eluded capture by the police, who would only move around now in groups of five, ashen with anxiety atop their snorting horses. Their thin mouths set a little more grimly, they patrolled the margin between the shanties and the fields, gunning down the wind in clumps of canes or the flutterings of birds in fernbrakes. Kouli became a bit of a legend. When a gendarme sprained his ankle, it was Kouli. When another fell off his horse, it was Kouli. It was also Kouli's fault when those two sergeants, crazy in love with a mulattress, drew their weapons simultaneously for a mutual splattering with their own brains.

The man who was already Anastase's father soon turned blindly brazen, walking on roads in wide daylight and openly crossing fields. Waving breezily to the cane-cutters, he blew kisses to the women who tied the stalks into bundles. One day he even showed up at noon in the marketplace of Saint-Pierre, calmly drinking down two proffered coconuts without a single twitchy gulp. Another time, he popped up at the pit in Démarre to watch several cockfights without once checking his back. He was even spotted at the harbor festival in Le Robert, where he laughed his head off and slurped up some sherbets. And lastly, because fate always arranges a middle and an end, he grew accustomed to spending a few of his Sunday hours in his neighborhood in Morne-Poirier, where he enjoyed seeing his women again, rolling the dice for a game of *serbi* with his pals until the moon was watching too, and where, finally, a swarm of gendarmes swooped down on him, peppering with bullets the table, the dice, the torch, the demijohns of tafia, one of the women, three of the friends, and Kouli himself. *That was the word or so.*)

In spite of Pipi's protests, we begged Mam Goul to tell us Kouli's story again, and again. The old lady ran through it three times in a row, with slight variations occasioned by her weary memory. "And Anastase's mama?" protested Pipi, "what happened to Anastase's mama? . . ."

"Who, Féfée?" creaked Man Goul. "She had her baby . . ."

"And then?" implored the king.

Then then then then then that birth surprised the whole household, starting with Féfée's mother, Ti-Choute, a black woman whom poverty had run ragged before her time.

"Well now my girl, well-well-well so that's why your belly was that big well-well-well . . ."

But, tenderized by the newborn, Ti-Choute plastered the babe to her bosom and from then on carted it around with her everywhere, to the fields, the market, even the river on washing days, where she'd dandle it while waiting for the sheets to drink their fill of sunshine. Things went less smoothly with the father, Isidore Célie.

"You've set a bad example for your brothers and sisters," he'd shout with each spoonful of his meat soup, so automatically that the twelve younger children's spoons would pause, hung up in midair, whenever he kept silent between two swallows.

Even though he'd never asked Féfée or anyone else who the father was, one day Isidore Célie got out his blue cotton suit and his patent-leather shoes. He wrapped his carefully sharpened cutlass in a towel and, grabbing Féfée by one wing, commanded Ti-Choute to carry that child because we're going to ask Monsieur Kouli what his intentions are right this minute. The strange crew arrived at day's end in Morne-Poirier, a neighborhood outside of La Trinité, former stomping grounds of Kouli whom the gendarmes had just riddled with thirty bullets. Lost in the crowd surrounding the body, Isidore Célie, Féfée, and Ti-Choute were in deep dismay.

"Bound to happen," everyone was saying, "*laghia* is no match for the gendarmes' guns . . ."

The handcart from the local clinic carried away Kouli's corpse. Isidore Célie, Ti-Choute, and Féfée returned to their shanty, taking the same paths along which they'd come, but stepping along less jauntily, not because they were distraught over the tragedy (the exploits of murderous gendarmes were nothing new) but because Isidore Célie could feel the first stirrings of the fool idea that would drive him daft and to death-by-barbed-wire, lead to Anastase's departure for Fort-de-France, and, in the end, ravage our friend Pipi's heart with the torments of love. At first, Isidore Célie kept his idea firmly to himself. He was obviously cooking something up. His silences gave him a mongoosey look, and he displayed a quite sudden concern for his granddaughter: "Has Anastase had 'nuf to eat today? Why's Anastase blubbing? Uh-oh – that a cough I hear from Anastase?" Ti-Choute and Féfée were applying a poultice to a rooster's wounded foot when Isidore Célie came over to them. After wavering in hesitation like a palm frond on Holy Innocents' Day, he announced that he was now convinced Anastase had inherited all Kouli's genius: "And you can believe me because it's true, she'll be the first *laghia*-woman in the land, no one will ever have seen the like . . ." (Oh yes, ladies-an'-gemmen, that's how big sorrows get started from little tiny things.)

Isidore Célie paid possessive attention to Anastase's childhood. He went into ecstasies over her teeniest accomplishment, over the slightest foot-wiggle in which he always saw the beginnings of a *laghia*-kick. As soon as she could walk, he introduced her to the steps of this warlike dance, which plunged Ti-Choute into aggressive despair, for in order to pay the drummers he'd hired for Anastase's training, Isidore Célie was emptying out the small parcels of sous hidden in odd corners of the shanty in case of rainy days. These drummers were two local fellows, generally used by second-class *majors* for worthless matches. Their knowledge of drums had stopped just where it should have begun, and while the soulless mess they thumped up was all right for an evening with American tourists, no *laghia*-master would have risked his life to such accompaniment. But they were all Isidore Célie could find. Every Saturday they dumfounded the neighborhood with their stunning din. Holding Anastase's hands, Isidore Célie would demonstrate the movements of *laghia* to the bewildered child.

Forced to endure this intensive training, the little girl sweated her way through the basic steps of *laghia* but showed no inspiration at all in their execution. Still, her studious performance of the martial dance attracted so many people from neighboring districts that Isidore Célie (fate's plaything, yes) had to purchase on credit a roll of barbed wire and set up a bristling enclosure to protect Anastase's practice ground. After that, no one could get in without forking over a sou. This money went to pay the drummers, who'd always had to wheedle bread from dogs and tourists, but who were now fat and flourishing. Every Saturday noisy streams of curious people flowed toward the Célie shanty, where Ti-Choute and Féfée sold candies to the onlookers. It was beginning to seem as though Isidore Célie had had a bright idea.

Little Anastase began to enjoy this premature stardom. Her popularity followed her everywhere she went outside her own neighborhood, even to school, which she abandoned when she was sixteen at the urging of Isidore Célie. He had pointed out to her the uselessness of these French stories about fir trees and snow, and problems about trains leaving late that have to arrive on time, so forget all that flapdoodle and come practice what you didn't quite get last Saturday . . . But just when everyone was acquiring a taste for this syrup-sweet life, Isidore trotted out the next stage in his plans – which only goes to show,

you youngsters ignorant of life (Mam Goul told us most specifically), that the flowers of foolishness are the only ones you
can pick all year round in the minds of men.

One Friday, Isidore Célie left home without a word on where he was going. He arrived before noon in the neighborhood of Fond-Moustique, where lived a certain Siloce, a slightly simple giant singularly blessed with a gift for *laghia*. At Kouli's death he had become the uncontested master of this martial dance. His inordinate strength allowed him to squash his opponents. Siloce was a very gentle man, though. With the lentor of large leaves and the benevolence of imbeciles, he was always smiling at the antics of some amusing angels. His brain, too small to hold two thoughts at once, simply forgot all about malice. But in his matches, the first blows from his adversary would make that tiny brain heat up like a moped straining on a morne, releasing an irreversible violence that no one dared oppose. And the crowd would gape in horror at the savage dismemberment of the other dancer, until the monster, quivering and shivering, recovered his beaming beatitude.

Surrounded by the usual areopagus of men and women who sponge on the grand masters of *laghia*, Siloce was eating a *dongrès* of dumplings and red beans in the sunny front yard of his cabin. Isidore Célie pushed open the bamboo gate and planted himself before the now silent group. The giant went on gobbling his dumplings, as peaceful and massive as a toad in a misty drizzle. Isidore Célie took off his hat with the blue velvet ribbon to announce: "Ladies and gentlemen in present company *bonjour*, Siloce it's for you I'm here, myself Isidore Célie, son of Balthazar Célie and the unhappy Epiphanie, Kouli's last representative on earth . . ." Siloce wiped his mouth before guzzling half a demijohn of tafia and replying, in that castrato voice giants have, "*Bonjour*, Monsieur Célie, Kouli was what to you?"

"The papa of my granddaughter, Anastase, who dances the *laghia* better than you and could knock you down on the spot . . ."

This declaration provoked the mighty gales of unquenchable laughter that were to follow Isidore Célie right into his barbed-wire grave. Siloce, convulsed under the table, knocked over demijohns and cooking pots as he jiggled with mirth. His parasites all followed suit. Haughty and stoical, Isidore Célie waited for them to finish howling. It took him two hours to realize the inextinguishable nature of their delight, and he shouted his challenge with terrible wrath: "Siloce, my grand-daughter's going to kick your liver to pulp, she'll be waiting for you next Sunday in front of my place in Morne-aux-Gueules!"

"Hee hee hee I'll be there," gasped Siloce.

Word spread like the twenty thousand mongooses that take off whenever cane stubble is burned. Célie's house sat in a sea of merriment. Folks who'd come running to find out what was up were unable to leave: hilarity twisted them around like cork-screwed climbing vines. Ti-Choute and Féfée heard the news from the delirious crowd that suddenly came thronging around their shanty even before Isidore Célie returned. The two women just couldn't believe it, but then Isidore came home as gray and shut-up-tight as a clam in a market basket. Good Lord God it was true! Féfée, unable to make the smallest peep, clutched Anastase to her breast. Sitting heavily in a corner, Ti-Choute breathed through her mouth so as not to gag. Jolly pro-cessions streamed by the house. Isidore, parked at the front step, began to collect the bets . . . Of course, no one was giving much for Anastase's chances – that frail young girl, that tender liana – against the murderous enormity of Siloce. People were all the more eager to wager on the giant because Isidore Célie proclaimed the staking of his entire fortune on his grand-daughter's victory. The guffaws, the parades, the recording of bets lasted for the two days leading up to that fateful Sunday. As the time of reckoning drew nigh, Féfée lapsed into the tor-por of poorly watered flowers. Her eyes gleaming greedily at the bundles of sous gathered in, Ti-Choute wept all the same, which made her look really strange. Anastase felt childishly proud, for she knew she was the center of all this hoopla (and what she didn't know was one blessed thing about her adver-sary). On the evening before the inevitable day, they had an early supper and went quickly to bed, on Isidore's orders . . .

Isidore Célie awoke at dawn that famous Sunday. Dozens of spectators were already clustered outside the barbed wire. Be-

hind them, the countryside hummed with the advancing mul-
titudes. Isidore set his drummers going: "Start warming up –
are the criers here? . . . Good . . ." Soon the shanty was almost
swamped by a festive rabble. Isidore Célie ran around in all
directions, helped by his twelve younger children, feverishly
checking on everything, more and more irritated by the hee-
hawing and mockery. This vast laughter was abruptly choked
off as a galloping rumor announced the arrival of Siloce. More
colossal than ever, dressed in white, relaxed and debonair,
trailed at a respectful distance by his criers, *gwo-ka* and *tibwa*
men, and the usual batch of hangers-on, the giant hove into
view. The audience was transported with joy, which staggered
Isidore Célie. Siloce stepped up to Anastase's drummers, who
read the look in his eye, ceased their cacophony, and melted
away into the mob. Now it was the turn of Siloce's musicians,
true virtuosi on the *ka*-drums, who launched into one of the
loveliest salutes ever to open a match. The giant waited until
his criers had cleared their throats with some innocuous flat-
tery, and then, stripping off his shirt, rolling up his trouser
legs, gurgling with glee, he began a rousing marvel of a challenge-round: frankly it was one thing of beauty after another,
each the prettiest you ever saw. Enthralled, the crowd fell silent.
A few seconds later, it burst into a deafening haw haw haw at
the sight of Isidore Célie: dazed, his hair gone white, the
wretch lurched out of his shanty like a crab without claws. Am-
bling aimlessly, he finally collapsed into a tangle of barbed
wire. The mob thought he had just realized the folly of his
pretension after seeing Siloce's incomparable opening round.
They laughed themselves silly without ever suspecting he'd
simply discovered that Ti-Choute, Féfée, and Anastase had up
and disappeared: gone since midnight, the other children af-
firmed, and it was anybody's guess as to where.

They say that no one ever had such a belly laugh as that day
when Isidore Célie, caught in a wiry mouth of teeth, watched
the collapse of the one and only dream dredged up from the
depths of his misery. He died there like that, a Saint-Anthony's
candle slowly swallowing its flame. The hysterical hordes
never noticed a thing. That's why Siloce addressed a dead man

when, after no one had taken up his challenge, he gave the signal for departure and declared to the body in its prickly prison, "Isidore, you're one total ass." The gendarmes discov- ered the corpse and tried in vain to tear it from its spiky knot. They sent for wire cutters, hacksaws, experienced blacksmiths, and even an exorcist, but nothing could lift the curse, which is why Isidore Célie had to carry to his grave a barbed-wire garland snagged in his skin. At that disgraceful sight the cemetery shook with the cackling of the dead.

Ti-Choute and Féfée had awakened Anastase in the middle of the night: "C'mon open your eyes quick we're leaving . . ." Having finally learned her opponent's identity, the girl had obediently dressed, gathered her few belongings into a bundle, and set out into the land of night. They'd walked in hush to the highway, where they'd set about waiting for dawn and the first share-taxi to Fort-de-France.

They came to me, Mam Goul, Ti-Choute's old friend, around eleven that morning. Leaving Anastase with me, they headed back to Morne-aux-Gueules, where Isidore had already expired on his jaggy death-bed. A bad kind of despair latched onto them when they learned of that agony. Racked by remorse, Ti-Choute wore a crown of barbed wire. Féfée, who also felt guilty somehow, never appeared after that in the light of day except clothed in the white of mea culpa that blots out everything but the penitent's burning gaze. This behavior sent the neighborhood into crazed anxiety. A ring of silence soon surrounded the Célie shanty, confining the two women within an inviolable solitude. A social worker seized the twelve little ones, who vanished into the labyrinth of Child Welfare. Ti-Choute and Féfée still live in that shack, or else they've gone, it's possible, but you should know, you happy-go-lucky djobbers, that in Morne-aux-Gueules there is a shanty that's icy cold even in sunshine. As for Anastase, that hillside world forgot all about her . . .

The immortal Mam Goul had trapped us in the toils of a vague distress. Now, she savored her success, her head tilted back, eyes half-closed. What a patchwork of wrinkles! She still wore the garments of those far-off days when people slaved in the cane fields, and she put on shoes only to go to Sunday Mass. Around her everlastingness, the market had grown up and the

city had changed. Mam Goul had seen the horses disappear, and the carts, and the pigs folks used to raise until the new city sanitation department stepped in. She'd seen the sidewalks of beaten earth vanish, along with the ancient pine houses with their dusty shutters and flowery balconies. That city of old had been engulfed by asphalt.

"And now, beat it!" she commanded.

We obeyed, already forgetting Anastase, and Pipi's frantic face. Well, one Sunday afternoon, our man put on his white nylon shirt, his gray polyester trousers, his pointy shoes, and a small straw hat. He went to Mam Goul's, waited patiently with Bidjoule until the old lady came home from Mass, and simply said to her, "Take me to Anastase's place . . ." At her age, the Immortal One wasn't much surprised by anything anymore. She accompanied our master of the wheelbarrows to the tiny house in Terres-Sainville where the runaway lived. The paragon received them graciously, offered them Noilly-Prat and a few sweets, and made polite conversation about life the way one usually does. Sitting across from her, Pipi slipped into a daze and grinned like a mooncalf. Beginning to see the light, Mam Goul speeded things up a bit, because when you're as old as I am Pipi you've no more time to waste, so spit it out . . . Still all dizzy and smiley, Pipi gazed at the beauty's sad eyes, her gleaming brows, the various blue highlights in her long hair. Oh, for him, she had the freshness of cool fountains during scorching dry-season droughts. Her voice was a melody. Her gestures, every imaginable caress. He had but one desire, now: to melt into her and no longer exist. His confusion ruined the elegant speech he'd spent so much time preparing, and he could only whimper, " . . . marry . . ."

" 'Scuse me?" exclaimed Mam Goul, astonished. "That's how it's done these days?"

Amused, Anastase patted her sighing suitor's cheeks and told him she'd given her heart to another . . .

"Ki pi ésa? [What's this guff?] There's no man in your house," protested Pipi.

"I wait for him, he comes by, time to time . . ."

She had just confided to our man the great sorrow of her life, but it was Mam Goul who gave him all the details on their way back, so listen: between here and there love's going to snap up this young soul . . .

The arrival of Anastase, the fugitive from Morne-aux-Gueules, had brought the old lady back to life. She dumped out a big basket of wearinesss and brought laughter and smiles back from some lost corner of her mind. Every day, as tender as the heart of a coconut, she would kiss Anastase and murmur, "*Iche mwen* (my child), my home is yours . . ." Mam Goul earned her living at that time selling homemade potato chips fried in colza oil. The old lady spent her days watching over four greasy cauldrons while Anastase sliced up the potatoes. In the evenings, when they changed into fresh clothes, Mam Goul would slip on a dress with sleeves and a long, starched skirt, polished by the hot iron. Each carrying a basket of chips, they would follow an unchanging route through the center of the city, and Anastase soon learned the business. Mam Goul knew in advance where to stop to sell a packet of chips, and she never forgot a single one of the bars where she had to collect the money from the previous day's consignment before delivering a new supply. By the time they both reached La Savane,[44] the violet sky would be alive with fireflies. Couples strolled beneath the tamarind trees in the cool of the evening. Children rediscovered freedom playing breathless tag, weaving in and out among the trays of the peanut vendors. Mam Goul and Anastase would wander leisurely around the great esplanade, breathing salt air from the nearby sea, selling chips to girls in a dream of passion, their hearts petal-open around the park pavilion.

That's how life handed out its days to the two women, without too much excitement, without too many troubles, from the bleating voice of Chine, the Chinese who supplied their sacks of potatoes, to the smiles of their loyal customers. Anastase forgot Morne-aux-Gueules, Féfée, Ti-Choute, and all the others. She eagerly took up her new life as a chip-seller, with the diligence of a youngster off on her own. Soon she grew into a beautiful girl, with titties and just the right tingling beneath her skin for love (always on call) to strike her its usual bitter-sweet blow we all know so well.

Mam Goul had a bad back, so Anastase sometimes went off alone with her basket. She had adopted Mam Goul's pace, her short steps and heavy tread, her Barbados-tortoise bearing, and even just a little of her silhouette, curved like a coconut palm in the breeze. Baffled by this lovely flower with a witch's walk, young men neither noticed the swaying of her hips, nor spoke to her of love, dances, or walking arm in arm. The exception to this rule was committed one evening by a light-skinned mulatto with silken, curly hair and – this didn't hurt a bit – limpid eyes that could turn the dark glass-green of a fine demijohn on a rainy day: Zozor Alcide-Victor.

Ladies and gentlemen, Zozor Alcide-Victor was the offspring of the secret liaison between a Syrian and his servant girl. When the Syrian community learned that one of its own was living with a negress, it delivered a solemn warning to him during one of its gatherings around the huge radio receiving set that pulled in broadcasts in Arabic. The man who had just become the father of Zozor Alcide-Victor was threatened with a shunning so severe he would be forced to sell his stock and close up shop. Zozor Alcide-Victor's father, sick with horror, hurried to the house of the woman to whom he usually professed love-without-end, to play her that old familiar tune, the one that goes: No, he cannot bear my name, but you can be sure I won't forget him, I'm his father, and may Allah lay me low if ever I neglect him. After a year of loneliness, sustained by rancor and welfare, taking the full measure of Allah's indifference, the mother of Zozor Alcide-Victor had to call upon a bottle of acid and a pair of scissors to remind the unworthy father if not of his duties, at least of his promises. In response to the stab wounds and extensive burns suffered by its obedient member, the Syrian community gathered around the fabulous radio and set itself to thinking, coming up as always with a solution to a problem that risked shining a spotlight upon their discreet and prosperous existence. And so, from the cradle, Zozor Alcide-Victor, for lack of a father, was endowed with a fabric store located near the market, between Chez

Chinotte and Chine the Chinaman's place. This windfall enabled him to spend his years of compulsory schooling snoring by his inkwell, beyond the reach of the marvels of French culture, without thereby becoming a beggar of bread from dogs.
His store was run by a manager, and when Zozor Alcide-Victor was old enough to have direct access to its revenues, he began the rowdy, even licentious life that broke the hearts of one thousand eight hundred and seven black women, four hundred *chabines*, six hundred and fifty mulattresses, two Chinese, and a whole regiment of *câpresses*, quadroons, albinos, and *échappées-coulies*. He was already sadly famous when he left the area around the pavilion, where he was taking the air, to sashay over to Anastase.

Zozor Alcide-Victor bought her entire basket of chips, which he gave away to children with an imperial hand. He had a word with her, or three or four. He walked along beside her for about five hundred yards. Finally, with a graceful flourish, he regretted intensely having to take his leave so soon, but we will surely meet again. The whole thing had been carried off with such ease, such aplomb, with so many smiles, and inflections, and light touches with fingertips, and dewy moonstruck looks, and above all, with so many smoothly oiled French rs, that Anastase felt all funny in the days that followed. In the evenings, near the pavilion, when she saw he wasn't waiting for her, an unspeakable bitterness would wash over her (Oh budding young girls, flowers of innocent mornings, yes you, tender cane-shoots impatient to grow – the harvest is not soaring flight into the sky, but a slashing cutlass blow, oh-yes: beware of love!). Life had lost its flip for Anastase. The cauldrons no longer amused her. The gleaming chips nauseated her. Mam Goul's chatter bored and vexed her. She sank into a sleepy melancholy. The old lady, completely at a loss, thought she was the victim of some evil spell and worried herself to shreds. She was thinking about seeking out the appropriate countercharm when one evening, in La Savane, she saw Zozor Alcide-Victor approaching, holding out a triumphant hand to Anastase, who became so flustered she tripped over her own feet. Mam Goul figured it out flap! "Is she unwell?" asked Zozor Alcide-Victor of the old woman, who watched with a gimlet eye as he steadied the girl. The seducer seemed sure of his victory, but Mam Goul's hostility limited him to the simple purchase of two bags of chips, a few hasty compliments, and a speedy retreat into the shadow of the pavilion. This reappearance sank Anastase a little deeper into despondency. The old woman looked on helplessly as the girl lost her appetite, lost weight, and lost the bloom off her complexion, which lemon-verbena tea was powerless to restore. Mam Goul now avoided La Savane on her rounds, but her back acted up again, and she had to resign herself to letting Anastase go out on her own with her basket. Filled with the wisdom that flies in the face of fate, she kept telling Anastase, in a voice stripped of all illusions and strength, "Don't go to La Savane . . . ."

The first two evenings, the girl avoided the park. On the third, something inside her snapped, breaching her defenses and sending her straight to the forbidden spot. Just as in the most rubbishy Italian photonovelas, Zozor Alcide-Victor – gorgeous, smiling, and available – was there. Observing Anastase arrive alone and all aquiver, he put on his gala performance, the one for emergencies and high alerts, which enabled him in next to no time to lure the besotted girl beneath the tamarind tree where he usually applied the finishing touches to his impromptu seductions. There he revealed to her unsuspected joys and unfamiliar pangs, he laid her out in wondrous giddiness, paying pleasure its tribute of moans and hopeless tears. Mam Goul, seeing Anastase appear in the doorway with that look of a bird beaten up by the rain, her eyes misty and her feet dragging, knew that the inevitable had happened. She basted the girl with bitter abuse. She compared her to those women in Saint-Pierre, easy flesh for passing sailors. Anastase made no reply. She was hush-mouf on the days that followed, too. Shut clamshell-tight on her newly discovered bliss, she paid no attention to the old lady's despair. After selling her chips, she would set off openly again for La Savane, spending half her night there and coming home more lost-in-the-clouds than a street up in Morne-Rouge. One evening, Mam Goul followed her and rushed at Zozor Alcide-Victor, who was already opening his arms to his new conquest.

"You unmannersable stink-pig two-faced dog, *ich Man banse et ich kône* [facety hellspawn an' whoreson], are you gwine to let my granddaughter be?"

As one used to this type of attack, the seducer faced Mam Goul calmly and riffed off a tirade of incomprehensible French that purely struck her dumb. Then he strolled away with Anastase on his arm, toward the undoubtedly aphrodisiacal shade of his time-honored tamarind tree.

This deplorable episode widened the gulf between the two women. They no longer even looked at each other. Anastase didn't lift a finger to help prepare the chips. Mam Goul lost her smile all over again and grew reacquainted with her old wrinkles and solitary rounds. The little shack now had the atmosphere of a hole housing two he-crabs. This spoiled Anastase's new happiness so much that Zozor Alcide-Victor noticed the problem and solved it, because it's not a problem after all, just change houses, I'll find you one . . . That's how Anastase left Mam Goul. She paid the rent on her little place by selling rainbow-colored sweets at the end of the street. During recess at the École Perrinon, she would set up her tray in front of the gates, and the kidlets would come frolic around her. In time, Mam Goul's rankling resentment faded away. She often visited the girl who had been the light of her life. At first she took her some pots, knives, sheets. Then she went simply to talk, for pure friendship, and lingered there as if loathe to return to the dreariness that had moved back in with her. She avoided Zozor Alcide-Victor, however, who – for the moment – stopped by regularly to attend to his latest conquest . . .

Pipi was not in the least discouraged by the details of Anastase's amours. He went through an initial period of dotty hopefulness. Dabbed with scent, he visited Anastase frequently, on Sundays or weekdays, at noon or in the evening. Bearing litchi nuts, mangoes, custard-apples, and other treats, he did his best to shine, and managed to wring one-two smiles from her. At the market, during this period, Pipi became as vaporous as a mountain peak, never resting his gaze anywhere at all. Often he would remain so-still, daydreaming away. Mam Elo would tease him: "Well now, my son, what's her name, huh?" Then his visits annoyed Anastase. No longer smiling, she refused his fruits, and finally suggested to him gently that he shouldn't come around like that anymore, what will the neighbors think, and if Zozor . . . ? So the next phase began, the one of lost illusions. He began to drink alone, at any old time, without even an honest thirst and good company, and to go reeling down alleys bawling bawdy songs that offended the Christian decency of certain market vendors and deeply distressed Mam Elo. Forgetting his duties as a master-djobber, he flew his flag on a wind of hot air and fetched up every day in the gutter. We thought he'd had it when he wore his polyester trousers forever, stained with vomited liquor and street grime. In his worst moments of delirium, he would plant himself beneath Anastase's window and belt out love songs. The poor girl was quite upset by his suffering. One day, she came outside, took him by the hand, and with a helping arm around his waist, led him inside. Taking a towel moistened with warm water and eau de cologne, she washed his face, smoothed his hair (now twice as nappy as normal), sponged off his body. She wrapped him in a clean sheet while she washed his clothes – something Mam Elo had attempted in vain, but Pipi, in ecstacy, let Anastase do whatever she wanted, watching her with glazed eyes as she moved about the room. She spoke gently to him as she dried his shirt and trousers with a hot iron. Pipi listened, hypnotized. She drove away his alcoholic fog with salty coffee, that old-timey remedy, and he dropped right off, slumped in his chair. She had to wait for Mam Goul to arrive to get him moved to the bed. The two women sat down on either side of Sleeping Rummy, gabbing aimlessly as they always did on their evenings together. They woke Pipi up for some meat soup and two smoked sardines. After Mam Goul had gone, Pipi and Anastase were tête-à-tête, watching each other through the steam from their soup bowls. Our friend might have been able to reach an understanding there with the woman who had set his soul on fire. She was treating him so sweetly, and looking at him so tenderly, but since fate has no feelings, the old hallway floor began to creak under the dancing step of Zozor Alcide-Victor. When the seducer opened the door, Anastase was already shooing Pipi out with both hands. Our colleague now sort of went to hell in a handcart, wreathed in a permanent cloud of rum, explaining incomprehensible things to the angels, which grieved us sorely when we sat watching him on our crates during slack time at the market.

He was fetched back from the abyss of passion by the unexpected death of the immortal Mam Goul. The old woman's lifeless body, found sitting bolt upright behind her basket, had brought everyone together in the seine of sadness. Her skin had gone the ashy gray of volcanic disasters. Pipi became himself again: he picked her up and carried her across the city to her home. With Anastase, Bidjoule, and Mam Elo, he helped with the paperwork at City Hall, and with finding a coffin. During the wake, he never once slid a look at Anastase, who prayed in silence. Two days after the funeral, when he'd returned to his wheelbarrow and his djobs, Pipi climbed up onto the fountain, imposing quiet on the market as he shouted, "Mam Goul, ho, poverty never robbed you of that green-plant twinkle in your eye . . ."

Listening to that tribute, did we ever water the ground with tears . . . The only dry eyes around were Bidjoule's.

Today, in the grueling conjuration of these memories, when we look back on that postwar prosperity, a wave of nostalgia washes over us: Oh season of market plenty! Despite our graying hair, we master-djobbers – Didon, Sirop, Pin-Pon, Lapochodé, Sifilon – felt indestructible: there was such vim in Bidjoule, and vigor in Pipi, that great master with whom we so identified! Watching him survive, overcome the misfortune of his *dorlis* father and that impossible love for Anastase, proved to us that he was solidly rooted in life, tough and hardy like logwood. Ho, there was a glint of bitterness in his glance, and one or two furrows on his brow, but in the market at midday, amid the peasant women and the crazy pace of our djobs, he unleashed his astonishing energy – and he was royal. We did not yet know that for him, as for us, suffocation would soon follow.

2 Expiration

ê-ê-ê! . . .

(Bonne-Mama's sole philosophical commentary on the shenanigans of fate.)

more boats and planes kept coming from France. They brought crates of inexpensive merchandise, exotic apples and grapes that capsized our hearts, unfamiliar produce in cans, in vacuum pouches, or wrapped in cellophane. The *békés* sold their agricultural land to low-income housing developers, or to civil servants eager to live in the suburbs, and erected import-export warehouses on the harbor. Soon they were covering the country with self-service grocery stores, supermarkets, and megamarkets that made ours look pretty sad. Overjoyed at having been officially welcomed into the Republic (made French by a stroke of the pen[45]), the market folk were proud of these sparkling shop windows, these endless shelves groaning with goodies. Stores covered their old wooden façades with plastic, and blinking neon signs made the streets look like Christmas every night. The world had finally reached them: television sets were cram-full of more pictures than Elmire's memory. We celebrated that law with torchlight carousing, with the frenzy displayed by most orphans when a mother opens her arms to them.

DÉPARTEMENT, DÉPARTEMENT! . . .

The extinction was imperceptible, at first. When the evidence finally jumped out at us, it was too late. The elderly peasant women gave up, the middle-aged ones abandoned their baskets for housekeeping jobs in office buildings or huge villas, and the young vendors went off to France with the help of the Division of Departments Overseas, a state company created in 1963 that organized a mass migration from the island. Around the deserted market stalls, we transported baskets that were much too light, and the wheelbarrows lost their balance. Only Saturdays had kept some of their old spark, for Sunday stewpans still featured a few local products. A djobber's life became harsher than in the time of Admiral Robert. Pipi, Sifilon, Sirop, Lapochodé, Didon, Pin-Pon, and Bidjoule – we were all like scarecrows in our jerseys, raising Chinotte's throne of notebooks even higher with our requests for credit. The market women weren't nice to anyone anymore. Elmire hardly said a

word, and Pipi would cut short his rounds among the stalls. Baskets of unsold wares spoiled in the heat. At the end of the day, we'd fight over the wrinkled tomatoes, the shriveled carrots, the oranges going rusty with age, which returned to the share-taxis in our wheelbarrows under a damp cloth and a protective rosary.

At around this time appeared a student revolutionary who flogged us with an idea she wielded like a whipping vine. Her voice blotted out the cries of worried vendors seeking customers for their ripening breadfruits, their star apples opening at the first touch of heat.

"We must stop the importation of French products, tax them when they enter the country," shouted our beauty, "or you'll stay mired in this endless poverty! Your yams will be beaten by potatoes, and your Spanish limes can never compete with their grapes! You have to get organized," she would yell, "apply modern methods of efficiency to your crops, gather your energies into the strength of a cooperative that could purchase refrigerators, allowing you to store your produce and sell things all year round! You're still tied to the seasons, that's not real production, it's just picking stuff! You've got to wake up, poke your heads up out of your graves! . . ."

This echoed through the market without any more effect than the jabber of an *haute-taille*[46] for tourists. We simply enjoyed contemplating her youthful enthusiasm. Pipi, who was always shrewder than we were, would answer her in riddles.

"Don't turn up the heat, my girl, or bring us green wood for a thrashing: we're tearing out bitter hairs . . ."

The student didn't get it, not a jot, just as she didn't understand who we were, either, or what we were doing there: But you're completely unproductive, you don't even pick anything! . . . She was only interested in the peasant women. Ignoring Pipi, she preached her faith from the four corners of the market. We quickly forgot her, for we had more urgent needs to see to, and you had to look sharp if you wanted to eat, setting out early to "pick" the first scattered vendors, completing the trips in less than no time so as to accommodate more customers. Hard-luck cases would call themselves fully qualified porters, driving down prices and making things dicier for us. We threatened them with knives and nasty acid. Their blood and ours splattered in the same hell on earth. If the last vendors from the good old days had not stayed loyal to us, we'd certainly have been up to our eyeballs in mud, like crabs at low tide. Oh, we envied those young market women who'd flown off to Paris on one-way wings, we envied them that continental life, and it was dreaming of voyages that we'd doze off on our crates, during our long – and often fruitless – waits for djobs. Gently, harmlessly (for the moment), we were going off our heads. Our only science, our wheelbarrowing, was losing its edge. The vehicle was slipping through our fingers with subtle cracking sounds. The tools we used to handle so deftly now seemed strange, as though we were becoming the useless foam on a changing life.

Bidjoule on the skids. Those who clung to the market often succumbed to a kind of madness that became commonplace. For us aging master-djobbers, there was no escape: the market was all we knew. And it was as though trapped in the bottom of a demijohn flung overboard that we watched the shipwreck of the two youngest among us. The first to waver without warning was Bidjoule. The alarm went up when his barrow lost a wheel and snapped its axle. A trifling repair. But our colleague spent a whole Sunday in perplexity before the unfathomable enigma of his open toolbox. He could only slap together a shameful makeshift that cast a pall over his gaze. On the days that followed, we saw him stop every ten yards, whipping suddenly around in an effort to surprise the abyss he claimed was following him. Then he began rubbing the same ten words together in a furious discussion with himself. He seemed to be carrying an impossible sorrow around in his head, and darted looks of terror at our world. Tears sometimes drowned corrosive flames in his eyes. Helplessly, we saw him go slowly under, saw him botch his djobs more and more badly, saw the scrapes his wheelbarrow inflicted on cars. At times he would fly into mad rages and attack passersby, drawing police truncheons

down on himself. Baffled, Pipi hung about him with the woeful
face of a dog stuck on a boat. Pipi had alerted Mam Joge, who
had always been extremely kind to Bidjoule, especially after the
death of Mam Goul. She came to the market every other day,
asked after him when he wasn't there, entrusted the transport
of her purchases only to him, and in payment for these minor
djobs, would offer him – inexplicably – more sous than they
were really worth. We thought for a while that the mountainous Mam Joge was feeling frisky and looking for a way to pay
Ti-Joge back for his infidelities. But that didn't make sense:
the looks she gave Bidjoule never stemmed from that ancestral
frisson. And seeing him in trouble distressed her more than
anyone else. Neither Pipi, nor Mam Joge, nor Pin-Pon his former mentor could bring rain to that fellow's parched soul. His
downfall, it was clear, had begun the very moment when his
eyes had found no tears to shed for Mam Goul. When he vanished, Pipi went looking for him, but without much hope.
"What's the use, what's the use," he kept saying, yet for five
days-and-nights without faltering, while our legs were giving
out beneath us, he searched the blind alleys of Terres-Sainville,
the bushes around the seminary-college, the labyrinth of the
Rive-Droite neighborhood. He hunted for him in the rocky de-
serts of Pointe-Simon and beneath the walls of Fort Saint-Louis,
where those in despair go to talk to the sea. Le Calvaire, La
Folie, Morne-Pichevin were combed in vain. Mam Joge, who
came regularly for news, even wept over him one time . . . On
the sixth day, the police found him in the brushwood of Bois-
de-Boulogne, just behind La Savane, buried up to the waist and
claiming to be a yam. He was packed off without delay to Colson, a psychiatric hospital we found so appalling that even Pipi
never-never dared visit him there. Mam Joge made a request to
see him, which was denied, since she was unable to admit her
precise relationship to the patient.

OH, THE GRIEF! A devastated Mam Joge came to tell us of
Bidjoule's death. The doctors had found him curled up in the
fetal position, a smile on his lips. The ultimate mystery of our
mountain: she cried like a cyclone. Mystified, we watched her
stagger away. The news went through the market, leaving si-

lence in its wake. What? Mam Joge, wife of Ti-Joge the mail-man? Why would she weep for a djobber? This conundrum accompanied the funeral procession, where we were surprised not to see Ti-Joge. His wife, leaning on Pipi, walked in the first row, djobbing a sorrow even heavier than ours.

"Pipi must know," Elmire whispered to us.

Leaving the cemetery, Mam Joge went home to Ti-Joge, who was said to be tied to his bed, a victim of delirium tremens. Our mailman no longer looked like a dashing colonel: asthma had slowed him down, so his bosses had pulled him off delivery and assigned him to sorting letters. He'd taken to drinking in a destroyful way. Pipi, lovesick at the time, had matched him drink for drink. Then Ti-Joge had vanished from our hori-zons: he no longer attended the daily rum Mass, and nothing brought him to the market. We would have forgotten him if he hadn't popped up at his window now and then, white-haired, haggard and pale, with the papery skin of men old before their time. He would send us little waves and trot out one of his jaunty smiles, and we'd salute him by tipping our wheelbar-rows. Not seeing him at Bidjoule's burial, we had the painful presentiment that for him as well, this life was wandering off its course.

At Chez Chinotte, where we gathered for a funebrial rum, Pipi threw himself weeping into our arms.

"She was his mother, *manmaye* . . . Mam Joge was Bidjoule's *mama* . . ."

TALK ABOUT SURPRISED! That threw us into some serious rum punches. As far as the market was concerned, Bidjoule's mother was a holy-water fount, and Mam Goul had never told us otherwise. Then Pipi unpacked his memory for us. Perhaps he revealed to us at the same time that unspeakable torture: Bidjoule was the son of a forgetful mother, and no one had ever suspected it! In this life where each man is the scab on a wound, how hard it is to recognize the secret sources of sorrow . . .

Raising his last punch, Pipi sobbed, "Bidjoule ho! Remem-ber only this, that our sole mother is misfortune, our father is courage, and that at the end of your day, it was the Forgetful One who paid for your coffin . . ."

No one knows exactly when the idea of gold entered Pipi's mind. Bidjoule's death had so upset Chinotte that she'd begun bemoaning the miserable figure we cut here below. She was practically delirious up on her ledgers, babbling about snatches of her adventurous life in Colombia. That reminded us of those old stories about her hoard of gold and jewelry. Pipi started studying Chinotte, staring harder and harder at her every day. Finally he went over while she was counting up her takings one noon, and stood right in front of her. It was going on one-thirty; the fishermen were heading back to their boats. The other rumhounds were getting ready to transport a touchy load of booze fumes. We djobbers had gone back to the market for a picture-taking session with some Canadian scholars.

"Whacha want?" the Adventuress asked Pipi without glancing up from her work.

"I'm going to go look for gold . . ."

(Ho! How destiny does sprout sometimes from an innocent little seed . . .)

Chinotte continued her calculations with single-minded concentration.

"Listen, Chinotte," insisted Pipi, "you're an expert and I'm telling you, this country's full of treasures, pirate chests, the moneybags of mean rich *békés* . . . There's legends about them, after all . . ."

The Adventuress put down her pen in irritation.

"Well that does it! No wonder this country's going to pot! Children in school learn stuff about France no one understands, young people are carted off to Paris by the thousands, the sugarcane is sick, even blighted, the bananas have gone into a tailspin, the pineapples are already cemetery dead, every year the police kill two or three farm workers who've gone stony broke, the market women are pragging bread from dogs outside the fancy grocery stores, poverty's raising a ruckus everywhere, and you, you come to me blabbering about pirate treasure!"

Surprised by the violence of her tone, the barmaid had stopped collecting dirty glasses. She looked at Pipi, who'd taken on the cringe of a castrated mutt before a bitch in heat.

"What else can I do?" he moaned.

Chinotte's anger died down. She knew that Pipi, like all of us, couldn't pay for his rum punches anymore. The market was growing shabby. There were more and more rats and ants among the stalls, and there was more and more silence. The djobbers were falling back on the Syrians. Pipi carted off empty boxes for Ahmed, and cleared the animal waste away from the doors to his shops, because the smell tarnished the beauty of the silk fabrics. Ahmed didn't really need Pipi (just as the others didn't need us), but these djobs made his payment look less like simple charity. In the evenings, so as not to be a burden on Mam Elo, Pipi would beg some withered vegetable from the market vendors. Chinotte knew all this. She tried to be sympathetic: "Sure, I'd like to see you find a nice treasure chest . . ."

"Can you help me?"

"Helping is bad for the back . . ."

"Everyone says you found a treasure in Colombia!"

"Saki disa?" (Who says that?)

"Elmire the Voyager . . . According to her, that's the only place your gold could have come from . . ."

"Poppycock."

"Why?"

"Because I've never seen a single piece of gold in my life, and in Colombia I worked, just worked, you understand, WORKED! That's all I've got to look back on . . . I sweated blood digging in the Panama Canal, and I pissed blood working on rubber plantations! And do you know what I can look forward to every day?"

" . . ."

"Work! More sweat and more toil and nothing but!"

"And your monster?"

"What monster?"

"The Antichri' . . ."

"Barfly bullshit! If I had it, you think I'd spend my youth in this haze of lemon-and-rum? Or even in this *ababa*-idiot town baking dry in the sun?"

These revelations made Pipi so dizzy he had to grab hold of the bar, where he clung for a few seconds, as shaky as a poisoned rat. Unconcerned, Chinotte went back to her figures.

Pipi walked stiffly away; the rum that had just seemed so exhilarating was seeping into his legs with a vengeance. He spent the next three hours in one of Ahmed's stores, flattening cardboard boxes from the latest deliveries, more pensive than an *anoli*-lizard stalking a fly. Impossible to imagine Chinotte without gold pieces or Antichri'. What else could ever have put the *quimboiseur* into such a pickle? Not possible, just not possible to picture her sweating in the marketplaces of Colombia or the rubber-tree plantations of Amazonia. Tearing up the last carton, Pipi concluded that she'd lied to him. She didn't want to share the wonderful secret that had helped her find a treasure somewhere in the world and alight here, royal and mysterious. By attempting to dissuade him, the Adventuress proved the existence of chests hidden here-there-and-everywhere, in layers of ancient earth. Pipi could clearly see strongboxes with gilt hinges, coffers with drawers, a mass of gold so vivid in his mind's eye it made him walk tilted to one side, which Ahmed pretended not to notice, convinced this was an aftereffect of the midday rum coming late into bloom.

As this gold fever – well known to all – took hold of Pipi, he lost his sense of wheelbarrowing and any interest in his djobs. He often broke one of his wheels (unthinkable!) and no longer knew how to avoid traffic jams. With the eyes of a candidate for Colson, he worked on his idée fixe. He sought out old treasure hunters in the Citron neighborhood, who confided to him their suspicions as to the presumed locations of a jar filled with écus and sealed with red wax. The existence of this jar was vouched for by a fantastic rumor that the old men related to him in detail over the course of several visits . . .

(What hearsay says about Afoukal, the zombi-slave. A béké master of days gone by, learning of the compulsory abolition of slavery, emptied his woolen stockings, his coffers, his waistcoat and trouser pockets, his money pouches, his wife's caskets and jewelry boxes, tore the silver buttons from his old army uniforms, scraped the gold plating off his watch, unscrewed the carved ivory door handles, the bejeweled pommel of his cane, pried the silver filigree from his saddles, and stuffed the lot into the Provençal jar in which the plantation's oil was usually kept. In the secrecy of a moonless night, he awakened the slave Afoukal, the faithful coachman who had managed to escape the agony of field work and who devoted his life to the elaboration of a slightly piratical English lord's mustache. This master had him load the jar onto a handcart and set off with him to a certain place then frequented by embittered mongooses and friendless manicou-possums. The béké, it seems, was strangely cheerful and kept humming old Breton folk songs under his breath. This threw Afoukal into vague distress. The master did not normally wander around as a singing somnambulant.

"Afoukal my son, tomorrow you'll be free . . . So this is the last slave service you will ever perform . . ."

"Oh, you know, master, freedom . . ."

"What about freedom?"

They were passing the dusky fields where the Long-beasts slither. In the ravines, stands of bamboo told their creaking tales, spread far and wide by the night. The sky teemed with bats, with lampflies lighting up their own souls.

"Freedom doesn't change service . . . I'll be staying with you, yes . . ."

They plunged into the undergrowth. Leaving the handcart by the side of the road, Afoukal carried the jar on his back. In front of him, the master parted the long eyelashes of tree ferns and towering bushes. The crowns of acacias erased themselves into the sky. The blackness rustled with herds of leaves.

"Well now, as far as staying goes, you'll be staying all right," chuckled the béké.

Uneasy though he was, Afoukal dug the hole his master ordered and settled the jar nicely inside it with a few round stones. He was about to climb out when the béké, leaning over the edge of the pit, spoke to him like this.

"Afoukal my son, you see this jar?"

Afoukal felt an ancient hissing begin to sound in his ears, but he replied, flashing his largest smile, "Ah well, I see it, and how! But why, Master?"

"I'm counting on you to protect it well, not let anyone take it . . ."

"You can depend on me, Master," replied the fellow, feeling

ever so icy cold, "but give me a little hand to help me out of here, please sah . . ."

The *béké* held out his hand, hauled him up, and – flap! – sliced open his skull with a clever cutlass blow. Afoukal fell back on the jar, to begin defending it with a rancorous ferocity that discouraged the *béké* himself, who didn't even try to recover his treasure after his first fears of abolition had passed (aside from the chains, nothing was really different). It was easier, he admitted, to recoup his fortune on the backs of free niggers (which he did, I swear, within less than a generation of nigglerlings). He told his close friends about that excellent joke played on Afoukal. These friends then told theirs. Since words have no brakes, this planted a grapevine that can grow forever, one big mama of a rumor . . .)

Of course, the old men weren't the only ones to know about the location of the jar. A whole lifetime of foolhardy schemers had beaten themselves bloody against the fierce vigilance of the zombi Afoukal, who kept his word as stubbornly as a deaf devil. Sitting on the jar, Afoukal had first dragged it a thousand yards deeper. He wanted to warm himself at the earth's fire, to stave off the permanent chill left over from the sudden surprise of his death. Homesick, he rose again each midnight with his charge, stagnating just beneath the surface, listening to the night, accessible to a stout shovel and even stouter heart. Alas, before it could reach the jar, the shovel would run into Afoukal's bones and crumble at the touch of his vertebrae, bursting into flames when struck against his ribs. Horrified, the imprudent digger bewitched by beckoning gold would find himself the epicenter of a whirling round of crossed clavicles, of blooming humeri and tibiae. This bone dance had the unfortunate characteristic of inviting the skeleton of the intrepid prospector to the ball. He would feel his bones begin to shiver. They'd find him in the morning, tattered like an empty sack. That's why the jar was bothered only once every fifty years, by some poor fellow too young to have heard what had happened to his predecessor and too dazzled by what looked like easy pickings.

Armed with a shovel and a kerosene lamp, Pipi visited the suspected locations. As they were all on private property, he did so at night, dragging himself back at dawn behind his wheelbarrow with the puffy eyes of a *dorlis*. At the first spot, the garden of a luxurious villa, he'd barely started digging at the foot of a tree with yellow leaves when barking broke out, and a strikingly prolonged stinging sensation in his buttocks warned him that he'd been the victim of a shotgun blast of coarse salt. Scared shitless, he put on a burst of speed that spared him receipt of the second barrel. At the next site, somewhere around the Château-Boeuf neighborhood, he climbed over a fence, walked along the wall of a handsome house toward the waste ground where the jar was supposedly enshrined, and entered a maze of cages fitted with swinging doors and set atop piles, where he sowed indescribable panic among a hundred grouchy roosters and excitable laying hens. At each step he took, his lamp shone upon a pandemonium of combs, of furious spurs, of wings flapping in fright. The house lit up, and a man's voice rang out in threats. A panicky Pipi crawled through a forest of piles and hid stone-still in a far corner beneath the demented poultry, where he suddenly became aware of the infernal stench all around him: he had crept onto a deposit of chicken crap so fabulously thick it was probably prehistoric. He was forced to spend the night there, for the master of the house, armed with a cutlass, walked up and down this daedalian structure until the pippiree peeped at dawn, when a freezing rain allowed Pipi to slip away, for the poultryman, obliged to take shelter, had stomped off muttering about chicken thieves and other sombitch niggers.

The third place was the right one: in other words, fate had left a commission for him there. Following the old men's directions, he'd wound up between the neighborhood of Tivoli and the De Briand property, in a clearing where even at Easter (prime crab-eating time), no one went to lay traps near the holes. Burned by his earlier experiences, Pipi went to scout out that clearing first, with his lamp and familiar cutlass, but no shovel. The night was so bright he could extinguish his lamp and easily find the precise spot where, on the dot of midnight, with his ear pressed to the ground, he heard the scraping of the jar and the clicking of Afoukal's bones: the earth was quaking as it gave way before this uncanny ascent. Pipi was spellbound by the muffled rumbling that seeped from the ground, heightened by the dry, chalky soil, spreading along the layers of fine sand, slowed and muted by the surface crusts of red clay and the thick pelt of guinea grass that covered the area. About fifteen minutes past midnight, the noise ceased, in a murmuring of foliage abandoned by the wind and the last shufflings of the disturbed earth. Cheek to grass, in tremendous turmoil, Pipi sensed the close presence of the jar, its attentive stillness. He felt as though he could touch it by sticking his finger into the dirt, or that by pushing aside a web of surface roots, he could easily grab the jar and carry it off. But he had also detected, haunting the silence, the tikitak tikitak tak tak of a loose-jointed skeleton. He decided to put off any digging until later, and went away filled with a pensive joy he carted around with his head in the clouds on our djobs, among the market stalls, at noon in Chez Chinotte, and amid the boxes, bolts of fabric, and animal turds at Ahmed's.

And he carried it with him when he began revisiting the old treasure hunters. Familiar with this symptom in candidates for the bone dance, they laughed silently through their rum-seared gums.

"Aaah Pipi, Afoukal's no pushover. He was already hard-headed when alive; dead with his nut cracked open, it's two hard heads he's got! What to do (I ask you!) against two hard heads at once? Plus listen here: sometimes in that clearing roams a *jablesse*, a she-devil who charms and carries you off: the terrible Mam Zabyme. Watch out for her 'cause she complicates things . . ."

"I'm not scared of she-devils, but of Afoukal! There has to be some way to bung him up," groaned Pipi.

The oldsters kept laughing softly and scratching their pates. Sometimes they glanced keenly at the four points of the compass before returning to their gummy chortling.

"But Pipi, if there was a way, just one, wouldn't the jar already belong to us, hmm? Don't be fool-fool . . . In this business," they continued, "you have to have patience, Pipi, and you have to have luck. Enough patience to wait for Afoukal, and enough luck for him to come . . ."

"But come where?"

"Into your sleep."

"Wha?!"

"If you know how to wait, and if you're lucky, he'll come one night into your sleep. And then you'll learn how to go about getting the jar with nary a problem . . ."

Hope blazed up in Pipi like parched brushwood in the dry season.

"He'll come?"

The old men scratched their heads again, still crazed with their super-secret glee.

"If you're lucky, he'll come."

"He'll come when?"

"Quickly, if you're patient."

"Quickly means what? And not-quickly – that's how long?"

A bitter flame flickered through those arid eyes. They all answered with the same intonation, and the same words.

"But Pipi, come on now, it can take a lifetime and more. Look at us: we've spent ours waiting for him. And listen closely: we're waiting for him still . . ."

All this had shaken our hero, but he'd laughed in the old men's faces: "Wrong, you're wrong! There must be another way . . ." Perhaps this was what he was looking for during his sessions in Chinotte's, brooding over four fingers of rum he no longer even touched – or when around noon, at the market, he would fly off into silence without a net, stranger than a mango out of season. He had lost all heart for his djobs. The masterly wheel-barrowing that had crowned him king one Saturday was obviously beyond him. He was content to lounge beneath Elmire's rare pronouncements, enjoying the breeze, or to find amusement in the ranting of our student revolutionary. Now and then, he returned to Afoukal's domain. Lying on his stomach, he would get drunk on the eerie music of the jar's ascent. Sometimes he'd murmur to the guardian, "Yes it's me Pipi, a hardship djobber like you Afoukal, I dig holes without knowing if they're my grave and every day something splits open my head . . ." The zombi seemed to listen to him, to appreciate his presence. Pipi often heard sighing, but he could not determine whether it was coming from the growing roots of guinea grass or drifting up through the earth from Afoukal's throat. The

place became familiar to him. He watched the white cows that passed over it, browsing on the transparent pastures of an aerial plain. He grew accustomed to the bands of maroons, as flimsy as faraway haze, who came to cackle on Afoukal's tomb, sneering at his docility, reproaching him for not having run away like they had. There Pipi learned that at night candleflies draw the outlines of their souls, and that they illumine, for crawling insects, the constellations of a dream world. A passing slumber would carry him off, with his head facing the warmth of his lamp, its flame turned down low. Awakened by the cold rain that sweeps clean for dawn, he would sound his dreams for Afoukal, in search of words the guardian might have said to him. He would find only a nameless woe, the clanking of chains, foul odors from dark holes, the splashing of cruel waves. Afoukal would leave his own memories in Pipi's head without telling him one jot about the jar. Pipi tried this experiment many times. Afoukal enjoyed visiting his dreams and began speaking to him more and more clearly about plantation life during slavery, that most searing day-after-day distress.

(The eighteen Dream-Words that Afoukal gave him. It is through them that Pipi went back into his own memory cleft open like a calabash by oblivion and buried in the farthest corner of himself.

1. The Kongos, captured in more profusion than fish fry. Each wave out at Pointe-des-Nègres is one of their souls. In your tree, they branch out in the densest foliage. But there were also: the Nagos, the Bamanas, the Aradas, the Ibos, and the Minas. And those frequent maroons, the Riambas, the Sosos, the Taguas, the Mondongos, the Kotokolis. They were all so different that they created the beginnings of your language to bind us together. In those days, the evil tides beached these thousands of jellyfish who had to re-invent life brutally, without any water save that of memory.

2. There were three names. The one from the Great-Country (lost through futility or force), the one on the boat (given

by sailors during sea-water showers and the exercises that loosened up our muscles), and the one in the fields. That last name bespoke your certain death: you died with it and left it to children who had already forgotten you. So for us names no longer mattered. When the master named you Jupiter, we called you Crickneck or Big-Butt. When the master said Telemachus, Remus, or Mercury, we said Syrup, Afoukal, Pipi, or Tikilik. Has that died out?

3. Before the piping of the pippiree, the overseer whistled. His whip often cracked. In the distance pealed the bells of the big plantations. Still stiff with sleep, lines shuffled to the rhythm of the steward's roll call. Then we moved on to morning prayer and the break-fast. The foredawn and the lingering chill of the wind kept our voices low. Imagine not misery or anguish, but well-trained reflexes for which there was no reason at all to Exist. We would set out for the fields without even raising our heads. The Long-beasts knew how to bring us down when, bent over the soil, we combed out the long, burning hair of suffering. Imagine not grief (that was too absolute to be constant), but the slow vertigo of absence. At noon, old-granny would bring us salt meat, boiled plantains, manioc, and harsh *guildive* rum. We'd eat hot food and talk would well up (new words forged there in the fields). That was when the body sank into pain: hands were raw, singing with scratches from saw grasses. The overseer, with whip or whistle, would cry us back-to-work. And the field swallowed us up until the anus of nightfall. Think of that, repeated times without number, with those incomprehensible cutlass blows among ourselves, the poisoned deaths dealt by the Long-beasts, and the death suffered each hour in the almost fatal acceptance of this slow drowning.

4. Imagine this: you disembark, not into a new world but into ANOTHER LIFE. What you thought was essential breaks apart, dangling uselessly. A long ravine cuts its way through you. Now you are no more than gaping nothing-ness. In truth you had to be *reborn* to survive. What unholy gestation, what uterine hell, aie-aie-aie!

5. At the mill, it was best to be the one who slipped the fresh-cut sugarcane between the grinding wheels, the stiff cane that you shoved from a distance into the mechanical maw. But think of the second man, the one who for endless days gathers up the already crushed cane, flat, shredded, too limp to catch well in the wheels, so that it must be pushed by hand as close as possible to the rollers. A moment of fatigue, or a daydream, or the wrenching cry of a loved one in the far-off-country, or else a touch of sunstroke, a trickle of sweat into the eyes, a slight dizziness . . . Oh a finger's caught! The beast awakens in an inexorable slushing of ground-up bones and flesh. The hand is tugged in before your helpless eyes. Then the arm. The shoulder. You can barely cry out. The cane juice turns rusty with blood and marrow. The water of your soul is squeezed out and gushes down into the tubs. What greater horror than a sugar press jammed with the stubborn, grimacing head of a nigger? (So, there it is: the second man started carrying a cutlass. If his finger got caught and he had enough courage, he had to hack off his arm. That was better, after all, the master said. Surely. Besides, at the mill, there were double rations of salt meat and all the *guildive* you wanted. It was better, after all, the master said. Surely.)

6. We moved backward for the holes and the planting. Forward for the weeding. Our row stretched across the field. Behind, the work-crier raised the Kongo in song. Backs endured blows, and heads lolled. The sun beat down during those hours. The earth was beautiful and touched us on the shoulder. Some of us knew how to talk to her. She was, it seems, quite surprised to see us there. Heavy rains stuffed us under our bags in groups of three. Heads down between our knees, we'd watch the ground spit the water back between our toes. Snails and worms came out. Impossible to count them, because the raindrops put us in a trance. The overseer's footsteps slopped through mud, back and forth, as he counted our huddles: troops of hunched-in tortoises, shivery-chilled by sorrow. Does that still happen, that spell cast by the rain?

7. On Sunday, we rose early. Without whistle or whip. While the steward checked the cleanliness of the huts, we lined up in front of the store for the weekly rations. The stew- ard's assistant kept watch, discouraged pushing. We would move forward, not as solemn as ants, but fairly patient and orderly. The salt meat or fish was put in the small calabash-*coui* in the left hand. The larger one in the right hand received the manioc, plantains, millet, dried beans, the slices of yam, calabaza, sweet potatoes. Not all that all at once all the time, but a bit of one of them sometimes. We'd go stash everything away in the huts before catechism. The rest of the day, while sunlight lasted, we'd speak to the earth of our own gardens, or depending on the season, go off to hover around crossroads, selling our produce. That brought in enough to buy *guildive*. The militia would check our passes, but they rarely shot at us. *Guildive* was our passion. Dice, cards, dancing as well, dancing, dancing, dancing . . . 'Zat changed?

8. The most faithful of our yawings was starvation. The cane, that grass of calamity, lent us its roots. Can you imagine such a mooring? We sucked on it constantly. Sugar turned our lips rosy. And when times were hard, we'd chew even the tender bagasse of the violet stalks down to that fibrous paste we swallowed in one gulp. It made a nice weight in the stomach and kept us properly cleaned out. Can you see us, cane-suckers, drugged on sugar, dreaming all day long of the crusty salt on a dried codfish?

9. God. The Trinity. Redemption. Eternity. All that was spoken of in a mystery language when we disembarked. An old catechist drilled us in those words morning and night. The white priest lobbed them at us in sermons every Sunday before the long story of Mass. They were the first things to slip from our lips outside our own language. The black catechist was our godfather at baptism. He accompanied us, one hand resting on our shoulders as on the horns of a sacrificial goat. Glowing himself with a grace that fed upon the baptism of each one of us. In the evening,

shunning the dancing and storytelling as the priest demanded, we would stay in our huts, listening silently to ourselves, watching for the awakening of the whites' magical power we were now certain of possessing. We gave ourselves wholly to this new God, hoping to partake of his white strength to understand, if not vanquish, this life, this country, this bewildering mess. The old catechist, flush with the souls brought that morning to the god of this country, would get dead drunk, dance the wrong way round from his skeleton, and leap unscathed onto ten cutlass blades. But we, trembling from this baptism, would seek a slumber wherein we might dream of this newly tamed god, now ever so slightly in our power, who would help us to defeat the master. We didn't know, you see, that this god could not be swayed. That the master did not fear this god: ticks from the same *chien-fer*.[47] Has this mirage faded away?

10. From the boat we brought with us scabies, scurvy, dysentery, smallpox. They doused us with mustard, vinegar, lemon, and sorrel-tea. What they truly feared from us were scaly leprosy, madness, and the epilepsies that rendered even the oldest sales void and devalued all relatives of the afflicted slave. But more than elephantiasis, lockjaw, fevers, ticks or fleas, the irresistible craving for red clay, more than crabs or sores, more than the Siamese Sickness,[48] venereal diseases, headaches, merciless diarrheas, it was *sorrow* that beat us from the branches of life with the most efficient of misfortune's switches. Neither live-forever syrup, nor palma Christi oil, nor *sagon*-herb, nor the rarest emollients from whales' brains, nor althaea ointment, nor cochlearia water, nor calaba balsam, nor Kaiser's pills in their sacred boxes, nor cinnabar, nor mercurial honey, nor litharge, nor tartar emetic, nor *aillaud* powder and sarsaparilla for endless decoctions, nor even Venice treacle could rival our elders' knowledge of ancient herbs. We would have given a salt-cod tail for some wild purslane or American sage, both eyes for some fine peppergrass, blue vervain, or stink beans. And nothing could keep us from dreaming about wild pimpernel, verbena, and cresses. Is it still like that?

11. The women had learned how to expel all life from their wombs. They had command over tetanus, which carried so many children of the light off into the sky. Distraught, stripped of life like those palm trees bent so low over desolate waves they refuse to dream about clusters of coconuts, the women were trapped. Can you imagine how much love and despair it takes to kill your flesh and blood? We men were wrestling with our own misery and cared little for their suffering, which was twice as ferocious as ours. We'd tumble one of them every night. We were trying to break their backs, to make them heave the most strident sighs. Each humping reinforced our own existence, straightened our backs a bit, and like true dogs, we'd leave them in the infinite anguish of a fruitful womb. In the torture of loving for nine months a life that must be rejected. In the lonely tragedy that left them more bruised than fallen mangoes: giving birth and having to kill in the darkness of the hut and the suddenly yawning chasm of the soul. As for us, you know, always far from them at that moment, we'd be wallowing in thoughtless rum and joyful dancing. Do you think they have forgiven us?

12. Telling stories at night, we'd speak of the Caribs' great leap from the cliff.[49] There the sea opened up the most beautiful of graves for them. A splendid trail that confounds the mastiffs of slavery! But we kept silent to recall more truly our own dashes toward death: on the boat or after coming ashore, at the first hut or in the middle of harvesting. Do you know that some, at the moment of suicide, had white hair? Do you understand the strength and patience needed to swallow your own tongue? We would count up the dead: the army of their spirits marked down each *béké* for the most savage vengeance, as a viaticum for their return to the homeland. Meanwhile, the *papas-feuilles*, the bush-medicine healers who knew all about plants, would poison the plowing and carting oxen, the horses, the mules at the mill, so the whole plantation staggered along like a crab without a shell. They would also poison the master's favorite obedient slaves when they began giving us the looks one darts at

dogs. Soon the master was regarding us askance, sometimes with the stunned eyes of a storm-soaked bird. In daylight, our submission in the fields; at night, the clandestine power that could do so much. It took us several generations to send the poison directly to the master, tainting his jars of rainwater, infecting the bamboo gutters. The chambermaids would sprinkle the strength of our plants inside his boots, his underwear, along the edge of his chamber pots and the mauve enamel basins for his morning ablutions, on the sweatband of his hat where it stuck to his forehead, and in each end of his pipes. The kitchen women put it in every dish, on the tines of the silver forks, in the sparkling bowls of the spoons. It was amusing to see him afflicted afterward with relentless diarrheas, spasms, hiccups, reddened eyes, and a puffy face. His skin became transparent and we could see his veins. Our first heart-in-the-mouth came when we surprised him consulting one of our *papas-feuilles*, he was so sick. Can you imagine, him, a petitioner before our bush doctor? The second surprise was to find him dead one morning in the stable, swollen and unrecognizable. Can you understand? So, they could die like us!? But we didn't have time to dance our fill. Two months later a letter of appointment from the owner in France restored the master to life. That was when we learned they were eternal.

13. Think first of all about marooning to the edge-of-the-woods. That's what we turned to most often. You just took off, spurred on by some heartache or a flash in the brainpan, to run fullpelt into the free *raziés*. You got drunk cutting endless capers, daydreaming on beds of warm grass. But soon night was all around you. You drifted irresistibly toward your plantation and lurked nearby for several days. Living by stealing. Drinking from a freedom powerless to cut that umbilical cord tying you to the womb of your sufferings. This usually lasted six months. Then you went back. The master, who had always known you were around somewhere, whipped you on principle. As for the steward, he hadn't even struck you off the list. Anyone still go off on little maroonings these days?

14. Real marooning took more heart than I had in me. All those years of setting your dreams root-high – they rob you of your understanding and love of lofty foliage and even the wind. Ah, freedom isn't a broody hen! First she leaves you misery and the cold rains of sinister woods. Your heart hurls cusses at the silence. You must hold tight to a beeline, hitched firmly to the Star, or else you soon start to swerve round, and at dawn you stumble into the dogs. You must fast find those who are already there. They will not call to you. You will have to ferret them out to prove worthy of their band. You live like a *manicou*. Moving little by day. Distrust. Vigilance. Escorting the women into the most distant ravines to gather roots and healing plants. Retreating before roving militias, packs of wild dogs, solitary bounty hunters who haunt the shadowy undergrowth with those white lizards the Caribs called *mabouyas*. But, you know, a few of those men have told me of the intoxication of night attacks. The savage rush at the plantation! Not some petty plunder, quiet and quick, to fetch away chickens, a few tools, manioc, salt, oil, sweets, black girls. No. The true shrieking charge on the master's house when the militia is far away. The cascade of torches. The wicked cry of the flames. The windows you can shatter at last. That world of gleaming furniture, of rugs, paintings, napkins, carafes, mirrors, that you can finally invade, touch, destroy. And those white women you absolutely must rape to really live . . . But you know, face to face with the master, there is also the sudden numbing of your body. The old fear raising its head. A supreme moment to learn if you are a black-maroon or not. Either your cutlass strikes or the master calmly kills you. Do you know he often did just that?

15. You have to experience genuine marooning off alone, far from the bands of runaways. Those who had been hamstrung spoke of this during the long evenings by the fire. Ah, those black-maroons of silence! Planted like trees at the back of beyond, they stayed so still that spiders encircled their domain with long, creamy curtains. When you met them in the woods, their smiles were sad, their movements slow, their eyes wild from not seeing any sense in

what was happening to us. The silence enabled them to
listen to the earth. To understand the leaves. They tended
the wounds of the maroon bands and warded off the yaws.
They seemed as solid as *baume*-wood, as rugged as a rocky
shore, sturdy, but adrift. Theirs was the most noble of sorrows. Disquieted and stirred, maroon girls loitered outside
their huts or sat nearby waiting to be called, to be made
pregnant. The bands of maroons took in their children,
whose dark and stricken eyes harbored a gaze keener and
more distant than a memory of the Great-Country.

16. I left the fields behind because I knew how to talk to horses.
How many maddened stallions, after escaping into the
woods, came willingly to my furrow to dry my sweat with
their muzzles? How many times did they come clustering
around my hut when the steward emptied the stable to
clean and air it out? When old Prêl-Coco [Coco-Fuzz] the
coachman died, hoary with age and scurf, they naturally
offered me his place. I thus put a little distance between
misery and me. I was responsible for the horses, mules,
oxen. The only animals I didn't take care of were the dogs.
What's more, as the master's coachman, I traveled around
through all the parishes. I knew the ferrymen, innkeepers,
coast sailors. Once even, oh la la how wonderful, I spent
a day in the port of Saint-Pierre. My only misery in those
times was having to keep quiet when the animals died, sac-
rificed in our name by the *papas-feuilles*. Then the master
would see me so sad that he never suspected I saw anything
amiss.

17. I hated the whites and our misfortunes, but I had learned
to love the master. I watched him live every day. I knew his
friends, the freed black women he frequented. I saw his
distress when the harvest was late, his quivering excitement when the steward's report was good, the way he sat
up respectfully when letters from the owner in France were
opened, which he had read by the accountant. His fate
seemed linked to those papers from France. They deter-
mined the life of the entire plantation for months, come to
that. After they arrived, he would decide to step up the pace,

have us spend nights out in the fields. Or else slow everything down and put half the field slaves to repairing buildings, tools, and thousands of padlocks. It's true, I'd find
myself liking him. I was attentive to his wishes. He often
spoke to me about his Brittany of mists, green plains, dark
little farms (his coarse, common voice still rumbling with
peasant accents almost unchanged by exile). Each time he
died (poisoned by the *papas-feuilles*), I would grieve as if for
my best horse. Then I would sink into torpor like a crab
until a letter from France brought him back to life. It would
all begin again. First our silent company, side by side,
lulled by the horses. Then the subtle complicity of routine,
and the meshing of our habits. I would begin to speak up,
to advise him on decisions regarding the fields and stubborn slaves. He would listen to me, touch me on the shoulder. Some evenings, in fact, despite his wife's disapproval,
he invited me to have a drink on the veranda. The aromatic
liquor sent me into raptures. Can you understand these
little sips of pleasure in that vast calamity?

18. I was so bound to the master that I could no longer envis-
age life without him. When abolition came, I was more
dismayed than a column of ants in a downpour. The master
loved me the way he loved his mules, his fields, his boots.
I understood this when he split my skull open on that jar.
But even today, I remember him almost with affection.
With that shudder one still feels when recalling a friend
who has proved treacherous. Or who was never a friend at
all. Can you understand that dead image I had of my life
if it had to go on without the master? Does that still happen today? *Those were the eighteen Dream-Words that Afoukal
gave him.*)

These words rang in Pipi's head as clearly as church bells. He
heard them without understanding them. At first, whenever
the phantom fell silent, Pipi would beg, "And the jar? Afoukal,
what you say is true, but tell me about the jar! Can you let me
touch it? . . ." But he forgot the gold at the eighth Word and
let himself be carried away by that bitter muttering, that sinister whispering rising up from Afoukal's night.

During this period, Pipi had the tiny eyes of insomniacs yet the healthy gaze of those who, for the first time, possess a memory. He studied us the way tourists do, examining the shape of our noses, the texture of our skins. He took an interest in our profiles, in the way we swayed as we walked. A few market regulars asked him if he hadn't gone and turned into a *macoumê-tantieman*. Without laughing at the joke, Pipi took refuge in a starchy gravity and murmured as he walked away, "Kongos, Bamanas, Mandingos, all sons of Africa . . ." He often prowled around over by Boulevard Alfassa, in front of the import-export businesses to which the *békés* had turned, and looked at the owners' names painted over the doorways. When he thought he'd recognized the name of Afoukal's master, he felt queasy. In a trance, he doubled his noon rum punch, tripled his quarter-past-twelve, and multiplied his one o'clock before climbing up on his table, as sozzled as a Mexican, to proclaim with comic solemnity, "*Gentlemen, they're still here! . . .*"

That day, we had to haul Pipi back to the market. He spent the afternoon in his wheelbarrow, as motionless as the smooth-browed caymen of Guiana. The *macadam* tickled his nostrils in vain. The theme song of the funeral announcements radio program did not produce one twitch. Toward five o'clock, at our request, Elmire sat down on the edge of his wheelbarrow and told him a story about Kouli, Anastase's father. After listening quietly, Pipi launched into his own nightmarish tale. He spoke of chains. Of sunless prisons where the slightest wound could turn into the yaws. Of whips. Of the iron bar. Of spiked collars attached to necks by padlocks. He described the "dwarf" that would forever after haunt our dreams, an iron clamp sealed around an ankle that quickly went numb, then to pieces. He told us of Tripe, a captured maroon who destroyed himself with such determination that not one of his bones was found intact. Bordebois [Edge-of-the-woods] and his forty-eight black rebels. Séchou, who brought together Negroes and Caribs, and who was first hanged, then quartered. Pipi spoke of them all, and beat his forehead as he cursed our forgetting.

Curiously, instead of leaving us indifferent, these names revived old feelings, and we felt steeped in gall. Sirop doddled around in circles like a bedraggled hummingbird. Sifilon gaped like a blind man. Didon scratched his head with both hands and squeezed his eyes tight shut. Lapochodé and Pin- Pon tracked the chiggers between their toes . . .

"Manmay, it's an ancient memory of the flesh that's doing this to us," sobbed Elmire.

These revelations gathered up our dreams and poisoned them. Mam Elo felt impelled to prepare us some lemon-balm tea, which we took in small doses at around five o'clock, collapsed on our crates. The queen of macadam now had white hair and wrinkles, and her cooking, once so sought-after, hardly attracted anyone anymore besides us djobbers, always looking for credit. The new market vendors preferred chicken'n'fries from the fast-food places or hamburgers from movie-theater snack bars. Sometimes Anastase would appear and buy a few fritters from Mam Elo. Oh how that lovely one had changed! She now had the drab look of dried-up coconuts. Mam Elo offered a discreet diagnosis when she left: "Now that, my children, is the heartbreak of love . . ." Whenever Anastase came by, Pipi forgot his obsessions and straightened right up with a sparkling eye, but once she'd gone he collapsed back into his gloomy ways. On Saturdays, the only time when the market shook itself awake, Mam Joge would hustle by, say a few words to Elmire, embrace Mam Elo, and buy a cornet of pepper from a new vendor, once known as Mam Paville, whom we now called Odibert. Mam Joge, she was still the same, always getting rounder, her gaze a flickering of sweetness. There again, Pipi would come to life: "How's Ti-Joge, huh?" Her Hugeness would make a face and waggle one hand, a way of indicating serious sadness. The former mailman was bedridden and still out of his head.

Well, weird things now began to happen, omens of the great shipwreck to come. Odibert, the new pepper-seller, announced she was a nun. Pipi emerged from his far-off reverie to worry along with us about the white dress she'd put on, her thirteen rosaries, and the psalms she recited every ten minutes. This sudden and divine purity of Odibert's prevented her from selling her pepper to men, or from allowing men to use her section of the sidewalk in front of the market gates. Only girls, ladies, and certain pederasts could come near her from then on . . .

Mam Elo was well aware that Odibert had not always been a pepper-seller. Pipi, who heard it from his mother, told us about that period in Odibert's life when her name was Mam Paville. She lived in one of Ahmed's apartments with her two boys and her mother, Mama-Doudou. Widowed at an early age, she had opened a spruce shop selling funeral goods and nothing, no nothing had suggested she would wind up on a stool at the market. Once we were officially declared French, however, made-in-France funeral parlors began offering complete service packages: hearse, interment, and all the trimmings. People no longer had to buy what they could now rent. Mam Paville started to feel that end-of-the-month pinch, to receive bills she could not pay. Her stock of funeral wreaths ran low. The ribbons and artificial flowers as well. She tried to specialize in candles, but that didn't fill the till enough to dissuade the bailiff from seizing her goods. Evicted from her shop, she found herself left with only the same small cookie tin she'd had on starting out. Trying to help, her mother, Mama-Doudou, announced that she was ready to take up her basket again and go back to selling fish.

"If you do that, I'll become a vendor, too," said Mam Paville.

"And whatever would you sell?"

"Pepper."

"Huh?! Why pepper?"

"Because you can buy big bags of it on the cheap . . ."

They began a new life. When the afternoon drew to a close, Mama-Doudou would sell buckets of *titiris*, fry she obtained from a fisherman in Case-Pilote. Mam Paville took her place at the vegetable market, selling ground pepper in small cornets of kraft paper. The sound of her mill roiled up the lethargic atmosphere, and then we grew used to it. When her first son, Pierre, announced to her (as he was leaving a meeting of the Young Christian Students' Association, where he had found love) that he was abandoning the path to the priesthood to enter the field of marriage, she took out her rosary and threaded it through her hair. When the second son, Bernard, declared to her a couple of months later that he'd been smitten by a Jehovah's Witness girl and was going to be married in the temple, she spent several days babbling "Oh dis Bernard, oh dis Bernard." [Oh say it's not so, Bernard.] So we called her Odibert, a true Sister of Misfortune. Four months later, to the day, she showed up dressed in white, with those thirteen rosaries draped on her pepper tray, and without further ado ordained herself a nun.

Pipi paid keen attention to this Odibert business for a few weeks. He'd park his wheelbarrow nearby and watch her freak show. Now and again Odibert would lather him with a *ouélélé* of maledictions, a ruckus of cusses to make him look away, then she'd return to picking at her rosaries and feverishly murmuring her prayers. Soon the nun faded into the background and Pipi, like the rest of us, lost interest. He went back to meandering through the market like a mongoose and collapsing cataleptically into his wheelbarrow. A little later, his squinty-eyed look in the mornings was the sign he'd also begun hanging out again in the accursed spot where Afoukal stood guard on a jar of gold, but not no one not nobody could make him talk about what went on there. Some afternoons he washed his wheelbarrow with great splashing of water, then rubbed it with beef tallow until djobbing time, when the vendors went home. He emerged from his sullen silence only on the afternoon when Odibert learned of her own death from the funeral announcements program. We were all in a circle around the transistor, goose-bumping as we listened to the list of deaths, when My-oh-my-oh-my-oh-my!

"The obsequies of Madame Paville Elyette, called Odibert, active in all the organizations of her church . . ."

Upon hearing her name on the radio, Odibert quietly closed up shop, placing her pepper cornets in a Prisunic supermarket bag, wrapping her cookie tin in rags, and put everything in her basket. She folded her tray stand, straightened up, smoothed out her nun's robe, whispered an unrecognizable prayer, and with her rosaries around her neck, walked over to the fountain with all this stuff, watched by our sorrowful eyes. What happened next was prodigious . . .

At the fountain, Odibert bent over to intercept the tranquil stream with her lips. Around her, the market held its breath, petrified. At the first swallow, the nun took on the cloudy quality of cold rain in December, then the blur of the horizon when it gathers up its last things. At the second swallow, she rippled like a damaged film, and reaching into a corner of the fountain, grabbed a handful of dirt and stared at it, desperately seeking something. Finally, as when parched sand drinks its fill, her body was veiled in a sound of frying sizzling from a thousand tiny holes. We saw her as luminous dust and a myriad gaseous bubbles. When she disappeared completely, the throat-gurgling of the water tap welled up again in the incredulous silence. The market ran a fever for a day and a half. Pipi joined us in the general foofaraw. Fists on hips, the market women leaned over their baskets to explain what had really happened. Curiosity called its children home as customers poured in. Fifteen hundred *quimboiseurs* from the countryside brought strange bottles to collect water from the faucet, which was later disconnected by the mayor when this excessive usage began to throw the municipal budget out of whack.

Taking root in the cursed clearing. Pipi resumed his nocturnal visits to Afoukal's domain. Lying flat on the ground, he told the zombi about our life and times. The doings at the market. The death of Odibert, Chinotte's spider, and Adeldade Nicéphore the miraculous goldsmith. He spoke of his *dorlis* father's appearance in the marketplace in full sunsplash, Kouli the master of *laghia*, the student revolutionary we found so interesting, the impossible two-hundred-and-eighty-one pound yam, the travels of Elmire. He told him about the great fire in the city that we used as a reference point in time, and Béhanzin, a black man who was nonetheless supposed to have been a king. He spoke to him of anything and everything, and even taught him, they say, about the handling of the wheelbarrow and the anguish of its construction. This intrigued the zombi Afoukal, and the bony clickety-clack signaling his laughter or contentment clambered up roots like marmosets on a spree. A peculiar complicity was thus established between the living and the dead. In many ways it resembled that of black Phosphore and his son with the denizens of their cemetery. Perhaps our life of natural death was the real reason behind it. The warmth Pipi brought to the clearing heated up Afoukal's icy bones. Lying on that spot, Pipi forgot about the world and would always be startled at dawn to find himself half-eaten by red ants, drenched from a midnight downpour, or caught in the first clutches of a parasitic vine. Pipi and Afoukal grew so close that soon Pipi didn't even bother to come back to the city, neglecting his djobs and his magnificent wheelbarrow. Sunrise no longer chased the jar back into the belly of the earth, and Pipi stayed put in the hollow where he lay. His disappearance from the market threw us into consternation. Nothing is more awful for a djobber than an abandoned wheelbarrow, a fragile flower that begins to fade on the spot, loses its luster, shrinks into itself, and becomes a target for dust and stains. For those who know how to listen, the wheelbarrow whimpers. That tells you how we felt about Pipi's, forsaken at the entrance to the market. We knew without searching for him that he was held fast by the realm of the zombi with the jar of gold. We lavished on the wheelbarrow all the care necessary to retard its ruination.

Word was that Pipi talked to the earth in his cursed clearing, drank rainwater, and fed on blackbirds grilled without salt or spicy pepper. By now his hat had sunk down to his eyes. The hairs on his chin stood at attention. He had grown thin as a day without bread, and his gaze displayed a lunatic fixity. He stayed in that clearing for the longest time, which Elmire counted up for us on several calendars. When the rains and blistering sunshine dissolved his clothes, he covered himself with woven coconut fronds. Soon there was nothing left of the Pipi we knew but his *bakoua*, blackish and indestructible, warped by tufts of happily growing hair. His days were devoted to talking and listening to the zombi. Refusing to stand up, Pipi crawled around to trap his blackbirds with breadfruit glue or slip knots, and he never crouched except to relieve himself behind a wall of cabuyas. To drink rain or dew, he lay flat on his back, arms and legs outstretched. The rest of the time, face down, his body conversed with the zombi. A tribe of Rastas[50] who were reinventing our life not far from there would bring him breadfruit patties, batata slices, and pieces of fish. The Rastafarians never spoke to him, but often sat in a circle around him to smoke their divine weed in an attempt at respectful communion. This flesh that surpassed theirs in its return to the earth, the universal mother, impressed them no end. Hunted by the police because of their cannabis plantations, the tribe moved on, deeper into the forest, passing trackless through the leaves, but they took care to leave behind in the clearing several calabashes of fruit, a few sweet potatoes, and three wild yam plants.

Accompanied by Mam Elo, we would sometimes visit Pipi. His welcome was one of cold unconcern. Without a glance at our food, he would stare in our faces with unbearable intensity before bursting out with his: "Aaah here's a Kongo . . . Say, he's a Bamana . . . My my but this one's a Mandingo, what do you say to that?" His raving remarks, his sad indifference, his way of swallowing our eatables without a thank-you or the play of teeth, and above all his inexplicable disdain for our gift bottles of rum that piled up in the sun until they burst – all this snared us in sorrow like a school of alevins driven by the moon and trapped by the current.

When the blackbirds deserted the spot and we lost our taste for visiting, they say that Pipi fed on commelina grass chomped with a ruminant's resignation. This unlikely nourishment afflicted him with the quakings of hunger, and he had to fall back on bees, anolis, bugs, dragonflies, swarms of insects and vermin he lightly grilled at first but wound up gulping down glook! in a gluttonous greed unheard-of in animals, and that includes dogs. Mosquitoes chatted with him. His skin became covered with pimples. Followed by crusts. Finally, it changed into an indescribable hide, repulsive in the light but gleaming glossily in the dark. This phenomenon, of course, set tongues to flapping. Word had it he was a *papa-quimboiseur*, and right away furtive throngs began leaving shacks and villages to consult him after nightfall on the vicissitudes of life. These almost religious audiences seemed to entertain Pipi. People would stop a hundred yards from the clearing and sort themselves out, approaching the papa-firefly one after the other to beg him for advice.

"The heartless woman went off, left me with three lil' ones, yes! Can you make her come back, huh?"

"Papa ho, you know the lucky number for the veterans' benefit lottery?"

"I got some mis'ry that's taken hold of me and I don't feel so strong as I used to, can you take this hoodoo off me, papa?"

In spite of Pipi's addled answers, the crowds kept coming. The petitioners, moved by a generosity that was anything but selfless, arrived lugging witch-doctor offerings: black roosters and white hens, Saint Anthony's candles, hams from albino *cochons-planches,*[51] big pots of stink peas, holy water, medals of the Virgin Mary, the left tibia from a fathead burned to a crisp in Saint-Pierre, locks of hair from virgins, drops of sweat from a black girl's nightmare. All this was mixed in with the gifts of food heaped up around Pipi's glistening body. Soon the clearing looked like the stockroom of a Chinese grocery, and the wind stirred up sewer smells from the rotting, uneaten piles. For Pipi kept chewing his grass cud, busy with the osmosis between his luminous body and the beaten earth that faithfully reproduced the topography of his reptations. When the procession of his supplicants so disturbed his peace that he ceased to find them amusing, Pipi welcomed all intrusions into the clearing with a barrage of maledictions, of Your mamas here, Your mamas there. The place was quickly forsaken by normal folks. Only a few nitwits – sons of Colson on the loose, *engagés* derailed by their compacts with the devil – still braved his bitter invective to seek his help with one of life's low blows. The rest halted a few dozen yards away, behind a curtain of ferns, and tried (by dint of special prayers expensively purchased from a second-class spiritualist) to obtain a long-distance cure. These nightly gatherings drew the attention of the authorities when the daily *France-Antilles* ran a front-page headline: "Quimbois in Tivoli Forest." A deputy public prosecutor with an interest in witchcraft went to eyeball the situation in person by the light of a full moon. Also astonishing was the fact that the public television channel, France 3, broadcast the image of the sorcerer in his incredible clearing for seven seconds during a program on snow in the Alps and the unseasonable weather in the Paris basin. Three times Pipi was whisked off to the police station only to be promptly returned to his woods, since his arrests stirred up all kinds of autonomist and pro-independence politicians and other sorts of black hotheads who claimed they had made him into a *symbol of the degradation of West Indian man under the colonial regime.* They had moreover paraded into the clearing in great pomp, with a flag and *gwoka* drums, to rally the symbol publicly to their cause. But the symbol had greeted them with a hail of unspeakable debris and so many This-that-and-the-other your mamas that they felt it preferable to let him do his symbolizing unawares, unrestrainedly, but on his own. After that, Pipi experienced in his clearing the most absolute of solitudes.

Moths were drawn to the glimmering of his skin. They fluttered around him before settling on his *boubou* of woven leaves, where they continued to cling even when day cleaned with the morning dew. Covered in the geometric designs of these lusterless scales that trembled at night with the strange awakening of his shining skin, Pipi's form grew monstrous. He expended less and less energy, and to eat, simply swallowed handfuls of moths. This diet afflicted him with stomach cramps, fevers, and a nervous disorder that shook him like epilepsy. An ugly weakness seized him and laid him out there as flat as a spot. His skin lost its light, and the moths drifted away. Sun. Cold rains. His breathing became wheezing. A vise closed around his chest. Aches straggled through his body. He exhausted every kind of cough before being shaken by fits of painfully silent hacking. Only in the depths of delirium did he sometimes croak out the hoarse barking of a done-to-death dog. His life was flickering like a cemetery candle in the last hours of All Hallows when Marguerite Jupiter burst upon the scene. This stout *chabine* owned a hut in the vicinity and was rooting through the underbrush for the wild yam called Sasa (with an eye to perking up her stewpot) when to her great despair she strayed into the accursed clearing. The discovery of the dilapidated body released her entire supply of pity. Hoisting Pipi onto her shoulders, she took him straight back to her hut, where she sent two of her sixteen boys hurrying off to find a *papa-feuilles.* In the meantime, she dribbled down his throat some verbena tea made from plants gathered behind her house, and despite his agonized screams, she rubbed his swollen skin with camphorated rum. Frightened by the ensuing rash, she massaged him for a long time with the avocado oil that usually served to make her thick braids more supple. This ointment calmed the flayed patient, who plunged abruptly into the abyss of dreams, his breath whistling in his congested chest.

Guided by the boys, the *papa-feuilles* arrived when night was trotting out its first shadows. He was an ageless black man, as lean and tough as a liana, who lived way off by himself, ceaselessly elucidating the inexhaustible secrets of his plant world. The repository of a wisdom whose origin he no longer remembered, the *papa-feuilles* always abandoned his herbal arcana in a trice to answer the distress calls of those who still distrusted the new wizards of the Faculty of Medicine in Paris. When he found on Marguerite Jupiter's bed the broken-down body of the great sorcerer of the cursed clearing (the moth-tamer who shone like a Coleman lantern), the *papa-feuilles* felt faint. To pluck up his courage, he had to suck on some mysterious bark that he poked tremblingly beneath his suddenly dry tongue. With pastes of purple leaves, decoctions of red grasses, bouillons of succulent plants, savanna-scented soups, stems of green wood to chew on, sachets stuffed with unknown petals slipped between his teeth, root-slices as melting-in-the-mouth as communion wafers, endless baths in jungle infusions, and spaghettis of vines, he had the former king of the djobbers back on his feet within a month. Declining Marguerite Jupiter's repeated invitations, he had set up camp out in the open, in a nearby ravine, and slept on a mattress of cool banana leaves. Nocturnal rain showers were deflected above his slumbers by a clever arrangement of tree ferns that did not, however, block out the splendors of our starry sky. Fascinated, the sixteen Jupiter boys followed the *papa-feuilles* wherever he went. The children's eyes could make out things invisible to those who had reached the age of quibbling reason: the leafy rustle that haloed his every move, for example; the rhythm of his limbs, the same that sways the branches of a silk-cotton tree; his inevitable immobilizations, when he would instantly take on the

majesty of a cliff at Grand' Rivière; or his immediate disappearance whenever he came near a thicket of underbrush; and
finally, his timidly remorseful reappearances, when he would reveal himself to the tearful children who'd been vainly seeking him for hours.

When the sun's height pocketed all shadows, the *papa-feuilles* would come scratching on the door of the hut with apologetic smiles, asking to see his patient, whom he was treating as if Pipi were a plant: a bit of sun on his chest, a sprinkling of lukewarm water on his head and ankles, a touch of fresh air to build up his sap. He forced Pipi – along with all the Jupiter children, I might add – to breathe in a curious manner, using their bellies like pumps. Sitting in a circle a few yards from the hut, in a place where the breeze flowed freely, Pipi and the Jupiter boys had to oxygenate themselves daily like that for an hour, after which they'd flop down in the grass, drunk on who knows what, happy as giddy hummingbirds.

"It's rum!" Pipi would yell, "I tell you it's rum!"

"'Zactly," the *papa-feuilles* would giggle. "Air punch, that's just what it is . . ."

"How do you manage to breathe like that all the time without getting dizzy?" wondered Pipi.

The ageless one looked shyly away, hung his head, and (moved by a quiet joy that seemed to drive him to scalp-scratching) answered Pipi as though he were revealing a secret.

"Does rum make a rummy drunk? And what can air do to me, a rummy of every wind that blows?"

Pipi was not his only patient. He treated the Jupiter children's dry skin with carrot juice downed first thing in the morning, plus weekly applications of home-grown lemons, mashed savanna cresses, a paste of pigeon peas thinned with alcohol, and a lotion brewed from the bark and leaves of the *bois-canon*.[52] He alleviated their chronic bronchitis with infusions of parrot weed, crushed garlic boiled in milk, and a syrup of carpenter's herb. He brewed warm, strengthening baths with elder flowers, mango leaves, thorny *marie-dèyè-lopital*, and Caribbean vervain, in which the boys splashed noisily every Sunday, emerging glowing with the best of health. Their mother wept with gladness.

"*Papa-feuilles*, ho Papa, you're some kind of Good Lord," she kept repeating.

"But Madame Jupiter, please," protested this child of nature, "an old fellow like me can't be a Good Lord . . ."

"Well so what are you then, Papa?"

"Oh nothing, a lil' brother to the leaves, a friend of the trees . . ."

Marguerite Jupiter herself had her hypertension treated with scurvy-grass teas and male breadfruit blossoms. Her bad breath was banished with the juice of carrots and garden spinach, and with the eucalyptus leaves she was told to chew all day long. Her stubborn hemorrhoids left her in peace thanks to enemas of logwood water and sitz baths concocted from the bark of ox-heart soursop trees. And she saw a night angor that had long plagued her disappear after the tenth infusion of basil leaves. Weeks slipped by like this. Pipi was slowly improving, and the reinvigorated Jupiter family discovered the wonders of a sound body. The *papa-feuilles* was still convinced Pipi was a redoubtable sorcerer. He would appear before his patient very humbly, his manner expressing the most extreme devotion, and he always asked permission before taking Pipi's pulse or listening to the music of his lungs. Pipi had tried many a time to remove that idea from his skull: "But Papa, stop treating me like this, I'm a simple market djobber, a wheelbarrow-pusher, it's me should be showing you loads of respect . . ." The old man said nothing, however, or laughed softly like a simpleton before declaring in a tone of sincere reproach, "Lordy-Mary, Monsieur Pipi, heavens you do say silly things . . ."

Once during the last days of the old man's stay, when he was examining every inch of Pipi's skin, his patient asked him, "Papa, where does what you know come from?"

"Oh la la, Monsieur Pipi, who can say? I know what my late father knew, and he always said he knew nothing more than what his own father knew . . ."

The *papa-feuilles* seemed truly disconcerted by the question. Desperately seeking a good answer, he wrinkled up his little forehead, got a far-away look in his glistening eyes.

"How, Monsieur Pipi, how can we know where things come from? Grass grows up from the roots, but where do the roots come from? The roots come from seeds? But the question is, where does the seed come from, and the seed of the seed?"

"Me, I know where your learning comes from, I know, Papa . . ."

"Really," the old man said admiringly, "then tell me, Monsieur Pipi . . ."

"From the country where the black folks here came from . . ."

"I know this land is a stranger to us, she tells me this all the time, but do you know where we came from?"

"Africa . . ."

The answer sparked no gleam in the old woodman's gaze. He relapsed into the silence that swept him far from this world, and continued his thorough examination of his patient's skin.

"You're ready," he said at last.

A few days later, when Pipi precisely matched the freshly-turned-earth color of a healthy black man, the *papa-feuilles* collected his things and left, refusing the chicken Marguerite Jupiter had offered him. Pipi tried to catch up with him, but he vanished into the first *raziés*.

"Thank you Papa!" shouted Pipi anyway into the underbrush. "You can count on me from now on . . ."

Pipi didn't know that the old man had heard him. This simple debt of gratitude acknowledged by such a great sorcerer lofted the *papa-feuilles* into bliss. Pipi saw him one more time, a few days afterward, when he popped up unannounced from a bushy hairdo of ferns to ask humbly, "'Scuse me, Monsieur Pipi, but where, where is Africa?"

His eye was faintly troubled, the trace of a tranquility forevermore perturbed. He beamed devotedly at Pipi, and seemed to think the heavens would open at his reply. Of course, like all of us at that time, Pipi couldn't answer squat to that question.

A migan[53] *of love with Marguerite Jupiter*. When Pipi rose from his sickbed, Marguerite Jupiter grabbed a pair of scissors and applied a haircut. With a jackknife, and then a bottle shard, she scraped his cheeks clean. With her cutlass, she trimmed his nails. With a toothbrush, she picked off the tiny scabs that flecked his face. Finally, she set out to stuff him with breadfruit, bonitos in lemony *court-bouillon*,[54] rice-and-red-beans with salt meat, and all the treasures from our cooking pots hereabouts when famine isn't paying us a visit. The unfortunate woman (Pipi learned this only later) ran up eight notebooks of credit with such bounty. This colossal debt led her to forget the address of the state-managed store where she did her shopping, and even to avoid all paths that came within a thousand yards of the place. Armed with a bottle of acid, the grocer attacked the shack one Sunday evening, screaming "Lajan-mwen lajan-mwen lajan-mwen!" (My money!) Pipi's appearance on the threshold stopped this charge dead but in no way prevented the man from flinging acid at the hut or from threatening Marguerite Jupiter, who was tongue-lashing him from one of the windows. After this incident the menu became skimpy once again: ti-nains in the morning, ti-nains at noon, ti-nains at night. Variations on this theme ranged from wild yams to breadfruits swiped a few leagues away by the eighth of the chabine's sixteen sons in an orchard belonging to some official. Still, it was enough to fatten Pipi up a tad, stop his bones from poking out so fiercely, and – ye gods! – revive his interest in screwing. For Marguerite Jupiter found him handsome: his smell and presence sent shivers right through her. She had nursed him when he was peeking through death's door, and the blind urge to bind him to her household sprang from deep in her flesh. The children were forbidden to say the words "clearing" and "jar of gold." The chabine did her best to befuddle him with twaddle, to make sure he was never alone, for fear gold fever would take hold of him again. Needless efforts, because the jar and the clearing were gone from Pipi's thoughts, leaving behind nothing of his former obsession. He was behaving like a new skiff on the endlessly shifting tides of life: with the clear eye, strong voice, and precise movements of those who know exactly where they stand, or don't get all lathered up about it. Life in the Jupiter hut, the cheerful squealing of the children, the attentions of the stout chabine and her fond looks filled Pipi with an inner peace that provided no compost for the flower of departure. When he had begun to mend, Marguerite Jupiter had taken back her bed and made up a pallet for him in a corner of the one-room shack, where it remained at all times, while those of the children were rolled up and hidden beneath the bed at sunrise. The walls were covered with newspapers in which magnificent white folks paraded their faces. One light bulb dangled from the fiberboard ceiling, which was supposed to keep out the heat from the corrugated-tin roof. Each wall had a window, so there was a nice breeze. The rest: a table, three stools for the oldest children, a chair for Marguerite, her bed, two kerosene lamps, a gas ring for cooking, four aluminum pots, a few tin plates. Clothing and household linen were hung on nails behind an oilcloth curtain in one corner of the room. Bathing was done outside at the spring. A hole sheltered from the wind served as a privy. At night, with the chair and stools piled on the table, the pallets of the sixteen boys covered the floor. Five little bodies separated Pipi from Marguerite's bed. From where he lay he could make out the young woman's appetizing contours. Her endless tossing and turning revealed a flusteration comparable to his own. One night, unable to stand it any longer, he picked his way across the five small obstacles to restful slumber, and leaned over the bed of the woman he desired. Strong arms clamped him to the impatient curves of volcanic flesh: "Well Pipi what took you so long I mean really . . ."

From then on, when the rustling-foliage respiration of sleep rose from the sixteen pickneys, Pipi and Marguerite hurled themselves into the sole happiness here below of those who spend their days down on their luck. Our beauty had had a tumultuous love life. Among her twenty or so transitory lovers, the five most frequent paramours might be considered the fathers of her sixteen boys. There'd been no sign of life from them ever since Pipi's arrival on the scene. Firm believers in the essential brevity of the commerce of love, they were waiting for Pipi to leave of his own accord. So Marguerite Jupiter's hut was removed from the circuit of those where they stayed sporadically to relieve their glands. But this thing was dragging on, disrupting their sexual routine. Which is why, without discussing it among themselves, the five paramours each began to prowl around the hut, watching from behind bushes to find out who was breaking the rules of the game of women this way, perverting the nature of love by taking root in a single hut like white people do. Unaware they were being watched, Pipi and Marguerite spent sportive nights making exuberant love. Thanks to a decoction of *bois-bandé*, Pipi labored away, almost engulfed in his lover's generous plumpness. When the old Creole bed, weakening under these tender *laghia* matches, creaked loudly enough to awaken the children, the couple went outdoors to experiment – leaning against the walls of the hut, the posts of the chicken coop, or the sheet metal of the pig pen – with the gymnastics of vertical love. Soon they collapsed onto the grass, rolled into ravines, and one night when red ants had mysteriously carpeted the ground, they had to clamber up into a mango tree. There, on the strongest limb, they indulged until dawn in carnal acrobatics so perilous that the five spying paramours forgot their resentment for a few hours to become admiring and even supportive onlookers. Out under the stars, far from the children, Marguerite shrieked hysterically, agonizing and dying each night beneath her burden of pleasure. When Pipi would fall back limp and half-fainting, betrayed by exhaustion or inferior *bois-bandé*, his enormous lover would shake him up right away, and run to fetch one of the bottles of aphrodisiacs her suitors knew so well. There was the carafe containing a few avocado pits macerating in white wine, the one containing celery roots, the one of tomato juice with ginseng, the one of peppercorns and aged rum, the one of smoke-dried green plantains preserved in honey, the one containing hearts of pineapple, the one of sour oranges and carpenter's herb. There was that magical bottle holding a liquor brewed from the leaves, flowers, seeds, and stems of yellow loosestrife, kept up on the roof, exposed to the sun and rain. Finally there were the carafes of hollow float-wood, *paproka* roots, and vanilla scrapings in *samos*. Pipi had to try them all, with varying results. While Marguerite was off at work, he spent the day sleeping and recuperating. She would return at the end of the afternoon, prepare a meager supper, and pack the boys off to bed after waiting impatiently for the oldest ones to finish their homework. Life might have gone on as pleasantly and tranquilly as this if the five spies, united in their cause after sizing up the opposition, hadn't resolved to sabotage these immoral amours.

Not daring to attack head-on the man they took for a wicked *quimboiseur*, the fellows sent two of their number to parley at first, in hopes of a compromise. After Marguerite had left for work, they asked the ever-present children to wake up Pipi.

"Leave her for us on Saturdays and Sundays, keep her during the week . . ."

Pipi proved obstinate, even nasty.

"Pack of dogs, unbaptized bastards – we're not living in slave shacks anymore after all, oh la la!"

His attitude and those uncalled-for insults ticked off the paramours. They began bombarding the corrugated-iron roof of the hut with stones every night while shouting, "Pa koké la, pa koké la, pa koké la!" (No more jooking in there!) That frightened the children and dampened the ardor of Marguerite Jupiter. Constrained to abstinence, the *chabine* became frazzled, and cried if you looked at her cross-eyed. When one of the stones broke the carafe of loosestrife stashed up on the roof, she shrieked like a madwoman, grabbed her cutlass, and barreled out into the night. Finding no one, she turned her impotent rage upon the mango tree, which suffered a grievous gash. Another time, a poorly thrown rock crashed through a window shutter and grazed one of the boys on the head. Finally, the paramours set fire to the henhouse and let loose the *cochon-planche*. While Pipi was off chasing it through the *raziés*, the firebugs played hide-and-seek with a tearful Marguerite Jupiter, who tried in vain to slice one up. On another night, Pipi lay in wait for them. When their shadows glided down the path, he stepped out of the hut wearing a white sheet, with a lighted candle stuck on his *bakoua*.

"A curse on you, scoundrels: your balls will dry up, your *lolos* will shrivel, your balls will dry up, your *lolos* will shrivel, your balls will dry up, your *lolos* will shrivel . . ."

In a twink, this appalling perspective of their privates in such distress plus Pipi's reputation as a *papa-quimboiseur* struck the paramours with true horror. The night was filled with the trampling of leaves, pratfalls, imploring prayers, dull thuds against tree trunks, moans melting into the distance. The five men lived from that moment on in fear that the curse would come to pass. They wore underpants sprinkled with holy water and (Jesus-Mary-Joseph what a sacrilege) a rosary wrapped around the target member. All caught up in their terror, they forgot about Marguerite and Pipi forever.

The miracle-gardener. Marguerite Jupiter had a job in a secondary school in Terres-Sainville. During the day, she worked there in the cafeteria; after classes, she cleaned the school. She caught the seven-thirty bus every morning and returned at around seven at night. Six of her sixteen boys attended school and were gone all day. Pipi hung around the hut with the ten others, who were more or less famished and always quite querulous. Their daily diet of ti-nains did not much agree with them. The rare steaks or boxes of powdered milk their mother brought home fed no one when divided into eighteen shares. Green plantains sat heavily in swollen tummies, and young bodies lost their bounce. Pipi himself, whose nightly exertions required prodigious energy, felt the vigor restored to him by the *papa-feuilles* slipping away again. To improve their usual bill of fare he began working in the kitchen garden that provided Marguerite with hot peppers, lemons for her punches, and the various flowers-herbs-seeds for her aphrodisiac concoctions. It also haphazardly coughed up a few scraggly sprigs of cress, one or two limp lettuces, and twice a year, by some miracle, a rather wretched yam. Revolted by the family's poverty, Pipi labored in the little dirt patch with a sullen fury. He weeded, slaughtered root-loving insects, expanded the area of the garden by burning out bushes. The kids helped him with an enthusiasm both joyous and disorganized, yet effective enough to clear a cultivable space behind the hut in almost no time. From a tribe of Rastas discovered by chance deep in the woods, Pipi obtained batata plants, island onions, three banana trees, two pineapple crowns, a few slips of beans, and – God bless them – a breadfruit plant (fated to be incinerated, alas, just when it was bearing its first fruit). Once the garden had been put in order and copiously planted, Pipi turned his attention elsewhere. He repaired the *cochon-planche*'s pen and fixed him up a waste channel. The hutches for the Guinea pigs, the two hens, and the old rabbit were renovated and even significantly enlarged. He installed a latch on the door to the shack. He built another table, thirteen stools, a small cupboard in which to store the dishes. He separated the *chabine*'s bed from the rest of the room with a panel of woven coconut fronds. These amenities allowed the Jupiter family to live more decently but still did not pluck them from the basket of penury. Time went by, went by, went by, it went by so much it often went by again. Thus Pipi reached a period of relative inactivity. Seedlings were already poking their tiny heads up in the garden. The breadfruit was sturdily beginning a tree's long climb into the sky. The spruced-up hut and its weeded, sanded, tidy surroundings announced the presence of a family fighting the good fight against misfortune.

Pipi told his stories of slavery, complete with names and places, to the children who kept him company during the day. He described for them the way life once was on the now ramshackle plantations, the unsung heroism of black men, women, and children shut up in the most terrible of life's drawers. Wide-eyed, the boys drank in his words, and when he gave them the signal, they swamped him with questions. Was it ox-chains or goat-chains they had on their feet? But Mama she said those nigger-maroons were bad men? . . . At the supper table, over the beef-shin soup, Pipi resumed his stories of the great darkness. Marguerite Jupiter, too tender-hearted, would cry her eyes out. Like cruel beasts, the children would eagerly lap up tales of torture or deepest despair, and they capered with wild abandon when Pipi, carefully calculating his effects, would murder the wicked master and lay waste to the plantation . . .

One day, a day too much like all the rest not to turn out different, Pipi's destiny took a new turn. As usual, kitty-cat-quiet, he'd stretched out behind the hut to rest his back after his nightly frenzy. Marguerite Jupiter was long gone, and the ten children, sitting in a circle around him, were clamoring for more of the exploits of the brave maroon Séchou. After exhausting what he'd learned from Afoukal, Pipi had begun making up tales of fanciful prowess featuring Séchou, a real person in his imaginary barracoon. Every day Pipi invented for him some episode with various heroic deeds that were a big hit with the children. That's how he came up with Séchou versus the magic chain, Séchou versus the thirteen hunting dogs, Séchou versus the slave-catchers, Séchou attacks the big plantation, Séchou in prison, Séchou castrates the governor, and so forth. Pipi was pleased. This way of telling about the past was proving more effective than the grim historical facts he'd previously related. Enriching reality with myths had a lasting effect on the children, who could identify more readily with the rebellious slaves in their games of war and derring-do. On that particular morning, he was telling how Séchou and a few Carib Indians had snuck onto a plantation in outright daylight to rescue a slave woman who was being tortured, when the youngest child burst out miserably, "Pipi, I'm hungry!"

Ladies and gentlemen, one should never underestimate the power of words. The boy's cry tore at Pipi's body and soul and anything else he had. He leaped up as if lashed by a whip. Haggard, holding tight to the child, he searched the hut in vain for something to eat. Guilt-stricken over feeding stories to famine-pinched bellies, Pipi wept like the rainy season, kissing them all in turn, noticing their sickly color, their too-big eyes. He cooked them up the few eggs Marguerite had hidden away for a festive Sunday surprise, and while they gobbled them down, he attacked the garden with a vengeance. From then on he spent all his days there and even, to the huge despair of his banana-yellow lover, part of his nights. Sometimes he vanished into the forest with the tribe of Rastas, greedy for the secrets mother earth confided to them. While we had forsaken her, the Rastas – held in the utmost despisement – had renewed that ancestral complicity between mankind and the earth. Rich in humility, with the simplicity of humus, they had entered into the harmony of the forest interior, the thickets and insects, the sun and the soil, harvesting a natural science. They accepted Pipi with their usual benevolence toward those who sought them out. Pipi gave them a hand with their farming, and they provided him with a wealth of information about the life of the soil, the workings of plants, roots, green things thrusting up toward the sun with a telluric energy. Thanks to those visits and the experience acquired during his long hours in Marguerite's garden, Pipi became a plant expert and agricultural artist just like some of the Rastas. This knowledge was not the same

as the learning of the *papa-feuilles*, the pope of union between human and vegetable flesh, but a mastery of the arcana linking
plants, water, sunlight, and soil. When Pipi pressed the Rastas for ways of speeding up the maturation of yams, for cultivation techniques suited to the steep inclines of ravines or the rocky feet of cliffs, for grafts that might change the growth rate of certain vegetables and even their size, he met fierce hostility. The Rastas' humility before the forces of nature was so profound that they scorned these sacrilegious ideas.

"You must go along with the energy of the world, brother, not conquer it."

Engrossed in the application of his new powers, Pipi ceased visiting the Rastas and devoted himself to the Jupiter family's garden. He practically lived in it – Marguerite even had to bring him his meals when she got home from work. The *chabine* wasn't too happy about this, especially since their riotous sexual romping was now seriously curtailed. Touched by her lover's horticultural successes, however, she made no complaint.

On the slope of a ravine, Pipi managed to grow twenty-five tomato plants that quickly bore medium-sized but sublimely fragrant fruit. He forced the germination of some nameless yam that the children were able to harvest three times a year. He made rice sprout on the river banks. He managed to raise a stand of wheat that mysteriously refused ever to ripen. This was his only failure, because he planted manioc and harvested it five months later, feeding the blissful admiration of Marguerite Jupiter, who had expected a wait of from seven to eighteen months.

"We don't have time to wait, we won't have time to wait," Pipi would say. "We have to move these plants along smartly in an *haute-taille*, the children are hungry-tummy every day . . ."

Sometimes, lying with Marguerite in the garden, he would confide in her, revealing his new obsession.

"Why does the bamboche yam grow the year round and not the bastard yam, which only appears in October? Why the bamboche all year long and only December for the Guinea yam, the wild yam, or the cush-cush yam?"

"The Good Lord knows what he's doing," the *chabine* would

moan. "No one would do a lick of work on this earth if all kinds of yams grew every which way all the time . . . The bamboche is so plentiful because it's bitter . . ."

"Yes," Pipi would reply, "but it tells us what the others can do, and that's the work cut out for us, we black folks of today . . ."

And he never bothered to count the hours he spent fiddling with yam tubers, calculating in school composition notebooks the duration of their dormancy, that vital period during which they remained sound without germinating. He was constantly planting them on dates chosen to throw the plants completely off their natural cycles. He studied their diseases. Tracked penicillium molds and anthracnose. Marguerite Jupiter often had to drag him in from the thickets or the now impressively labyrinthine garden when the night would turn rainy. The neighbors goggled at the rollicking junkheap encircling the Jupiters's hut. Big domes of plastic. Margarine tins hanging up in the air, periodically releasing a mysterious yellow liquid. Trellises of bamboo and string overrun by a thousand and one climbing plants. Live charcoal buried and kept glowing to warm specific sections of the soil. Bizarre constructions of corrugated tin that deflected or channeled the wind. Mirrors that redirected sunlight to specific spots. An aerial network of bamboo stalks split lengthwise, distributing water from a cistern perched on the roof of the hut. And above all, a madhouse of plants that seemed free to run jungle-crazy. There was talk of witchcraft; a priest had come secretly from Tivoli to sanctify the site. Pipi might have run into trouble if he hadn't let it be known that he harvested his yams five times a year, and malangas every three months. That he could pick white, black, and even yellow dasheen throughout the twelvemonth. That eggplants were a snap for him. That okra now stood crisply at attention and even came without being called. That chayote squashes, cucumbers, melons, calabashes, pumpkins were driving him out of his gourd, because he could harvest them every day, from the tip of January to the tag-end of December. He also allowed as how he'd found the secret of *boussoucou* beans and pigeon peas. That he'd figured out the ways of red beans and black-eyed peas. That it was useless to go into detail regarding his mastery of hot peppers, Creole saffron, Seaside grapes, of cinnamon, nutmeg, litchi, passion fruit, soursop, sweetsop, red mango, apricot, avocado, orange, mandarin, papaya, Indian tamarind, or – Jesus Christ – star apple trees.

In front of the hut he constructed an open shed where he displayed to one and all the results of his endless harvests. An impressive stream of hard-workers and hard-luck cases came to stock up on native fruits and vegetables. Marguerite Jupiter left her job to preside over the cash box. When the news got around that Pipi's prices never went above four francs a pound for any of his produce, the market in Fort-de-France emptied out so fast the weeping vendors and we idled djobbers were left in flabbergastation, as though to illustrate that old proverb: the more dogs tear at you, the quicker they hit bone. Convinced Pipi had completely forgotten us, we didn't even dare go reproach him for this misfortune. When he heard about it, he surprised everyone by closing his stand to the public and selling only to the small-fry retail vendors. During this brief period, the vegetable market reached a flurry of activity comparable to the hectic success it had enjoyed for a much longer stretch after the war. The vendors' prices were so reasonable that the supermarkets with their made-in-France fruits and vegetables found themselves facing stiff competition. Since no good deed goes unpunished, the small farmers way out in the countryside were forced to adjust their prices and wound up wearing their pockets inside-out. Standing on the hoods of their trucks, they wailed in protest every Saturday, and fired off telegrams of distress to the prefecture plus the presidents of both city councils. But the agricultural exploits of the former djobber stole their thunder. Independence-minded political parties and other groups of modestly marooning black activists awarded Pipi medals, inviting him to meetings where he sat up on the speaker's platform patiently listening to reams of nonsense. He had proved, people trumpeted, that independence was a viable option. *France-Antilles* published his photo in that choice slot usually reserved for rapists and murderers. He was invited to the Communists' neighborhood youth centers and to the municipal theater of Fort-de-France, where he was personally clapped on the shoulder by Mayor Aimé Césaire's assistant, old Aliker himself. Pipi was filmed in his garden so that seventeen thousand video cassettes could be distributed throughout the island by the cultural services department of the capital. And flap-flap! To Pipi's befuddlement, he'd once again become the chief symbol of the country's anticolonialist organizations.

He was thrown into a dither when the municipal council of Fort-de-France, led by the mayor, marched up to him in great pomp. Seeing Aimé Césaire[55] in person come forward to hug him and call him a *fundamental Martinican*, Pipi went *ababa*. Sweating, stammering, he no longer understood a thing they said to him and proved incapable of explaining his methods. The workings of the garden were suddenly a complete jumble to him. Patiently, gently, Césaire questioned him.

"How do you manage to keep the yam tubers so long without them sprouting?"

"Hah? Wha? Kesse ti di misié limè?" (Whadjou say Mussieu Mayor?)

Pipi muttered. Stuttered. Tried to reel off a nice piece of French. Straightened his clothes. Combed his hair with his fingers. From behind, Marguerite Jupiter finished him off in a loud voice.

"Hey Pipi, damn but you're dumb today, Papa Césaire's not going to eat you I mean really come on after all, shit . . ."

This visit from the municipal council was a fiasco. The councilors wandered off into the miraculous garden, bumping into the stakes, putting their feet into the live charcoal pits, drifting under the bamboo sprinklers at just the wrong moment, miring themselves in dirt up to their knees, and having to crawl around in horror, looking for a way out of this maze. Césaire, who had stayed well away from all that, hustled back to his official car after assuring Pipi, "Dear friend, I will personally support any large-scale enterprise employing your methods . . ."

Ensconced behind his chauffeur, he lowered the rear window and beckoned to Pipi, who was gazing at him like an *agoulou*-glutton ogling a casserole.

"Please, tell me," asked Césaire, "what motivated you? Where did you find the energy to come up with all this?"

Vaguely grasping the meaning of the question, this time Pipi forgot about his hair, his French, his appearance, and blurted out, "Ebyen misié limè, séti manmay la té fin, danne!"

Which the announcer on the news that evening, after a report on the *département* of Loir-et-Cher, translated as, "Monsieur Mayor, the children were so hungry!" That's why everyone at the market, for ever so long, thought Pipi had become a Doctor of Proper French.

A quick trip down a slippery slope. The period that followed was agony for the miracle-garden. Aimé Césaire had pried millions of fat francs out of the regional council for the industrialization of Pipi's garden techniques. A slew of black botanists and agricultural engineers arrived to help Pipi. Their fantastic equipment was piled in front of the hut. A small laboratory was set up at the door. The learned gentlemen asked him for his formulae, for his statistics *regarding the physiological stages of maturity of the primary tubers*, for his opinion on rinditis as an activating agent of germination. In formidable French, they spoke to him of Convolvulaceae, of Dioscorea, of *Xanthosoma saggitaefolium*. When they realized he was unable to put his practice into theory, they deluged him with documents.

"Read this, monsieur: mastering this vocabulary and these basic principles of agronomy will help you to impart your knowledge to us . . ."

Pipi read and reread these esoteric texts in vain. By the light of a kerosene lamp, Marguerite Jupiter would help him in the evening, advising him on how to untangle it all.

"First look for the verb's subject, an' then the direct object . . ."

"Then what?"

"Then? Well I don't know, check see if the subject agrees with the verb . . ."

"And after that?"

"After after after, don't try hauling in all your nets at once, in school the teacher'd already've given you an A for that," the *chabine* would harrumph in exasperation.

When the learned gentlemen worried about his progress,

Pipi would reply, "Gettin' there, gettin' there, but all the stuff behind the verb's back ain't always the object doodad." These announcements tipped the experts into ravines of anxiety, and they abandoned Pipi to go figure out the fabulous garden on their own. The master of the house began to lose faith in himself, in his bamboos, his glowing embers, his mirrors, his watering mixtures. He performed his usual maintenance procedures without any confidence and let himself be influenced by the scientists, who clearly understood the garden's alchemy better than anyone else.

"Why do you do that, Monsieur Pipi?"

"*Anpa save* [I dunno] . . . I've always done it . . ."

"Tut tut, be logical! You waste time that way, don't you think that if you do it like this . . ."

"Oh yes! That's better . . ."

Something gradually went awry in the garden. Caterpillars flourished there. Mysterious mushrooms appeared. One day, a breeze toppled the aerial network of bamboo. The mirrors no longer sent the sun's energy to the right places. The stakes rusted, poisoning the irrigation water. Mockingly observed by the men of science, Pipi ran around in circles like a rat in a demijohn. He corrected, straightened, rummaged, weeded, tried fruitlessly to liberate his creative instinct. He changed the composition of the sprinkler-water, the placement of the bamboo channels, upped the dosage of his protective mixtures, and finally, losing his head, began to dance the calenda in his dying jungle while Marguerite Jupiter pelted him with caustic curses.

The learned men took the situation in hand. Fertilizers. Pesticides. Additives. Electronically controlled scientific watering. Sprayings. Thermometers. Plastic greenhouses. Grafts. Removal of specimens judged to be without interest. Soon the garden looked different. The plants had turned black. The trees were as sterile as male papayas. The wondrous fruits were shriveling up like rabbit turds. Riddled with pests, greenish roots were prematurely heaving out of the earth all by themselves. A foul odor of vegetable desolation hung over the area. The neighbors began some serious mud-slinging. Sneering, the experts packed up their equipment, certain they'd been dealing all along, as they explained in their reports, with a huge humbug.

The Jupiter family lived for a few more weeks on their savings from luckier days. Traumatized, Pipi wandered in the fetid ruins of his garden. Water kept trickling in through the remains of the bamboo aqueduct. The sodden earth began to look in places like a backwater marsh. Soon a population of toads set up house there. A myriad mosquitoes from Rivière-Salée moved right in. So the Jupiter hut became a little hell. Miasmas and mildews affected the children. The *papa-feuilles* was sought to no avail, and it was a witch-doctor from the Faculty of Medicine in Paris who looked after their sores, their asthma, their chronic bronchitis. Until then Marguerite Jupiter had been content simply to mean-mouth Pipi, especially since she still hadn't been able to get her job back. When real hunger reappeared, she became ferocious, smacking the children for the slightest little thing, screeching like a loose screw every three and a quarter seconds. She'd lost all interest in lovemaking and spent her nights sorting out soul-destroying nightmares. Her head had begun itching up a storm. She would plunge her hands into her hair and scratch out tornados of dandruff. Sometimes, beside herself, she would shove apart her thick braids and rub her scalp with camphorated rum, blissfully savoring the salutary sting. The itchiness would soon return, intensifying her hysteria and aggravating the mad glint in her eye. Trying to mollify her, Pipi spent his afternoons, habitually somnolent, raking her skull with a comb of bone. At first this treatment soothed the suffering *chabine*, who now limited her invective to the scabs flying all around her, but soon Pipi had to comb harder and harder, spurred on by Marguerite's swelling rage, which subsided only when her scalp had been scraped raw. Sometimes this itching would vanish for a few days, giving the wretched woman time to poison everyone's life or go create her monthly scandal at the clerk's window in the Aid to Families with Dependent Children office.

Pipi was once again as idle as a disenchanted cat. Despite round-the-clock mosquito attacks or parades of toads, he snoozed the day away in his usual spot behind the cabin, stirring only to fetch a doctor for a sick child or lacerate the scalp of the embittered chabine. The welfare authorities got wind of the Jupiter family's decline. A social worker began to march around the hut as stiffly as a general, darting official looks through the windows or the half-open door, at which latter she finally presented herself. Marguerite Jupiter, who associated such people with the distribution of subsidies or food coupons, welcomed her with the smile of a Syrian shopkeeper before a fresh-from-the-country customer. The social-worker police-woman, after wads of questions, pronounced her verdict.

"Alas, Madame, you are no longer able to take care of your children . . ."

"Whazzat?"

"The youngest are in real danger here – this air is most un-healthy. Look at the condition of their skin, listen to their wheezing . . . Your financial situation . . ."

"Give it to me straight," said Marguerite impatiently. "Just what is it you're trying to say here?"

"Your four youngest children are in such a state of malnutri-tion and precarious health that I'm forced to petition the judge for their placement in . . ."

Ladies and gentlemen, Marguerite Jupiter super-slapped her with what oldtimers around here call a palaviré. Retrieving her from under the table, the chabine administered, in spite of some moaning, some zinging ziguinottes. Grabbing her by the breasts, she hoisted the lady up and treated her to a thump in the thigh. Nose-biffs, ear-boxes, pinch-tweaks, claw-scratches, and head-bonks completed the treatment. The social worker found herself flat on her back out in the garden muck. Roused from his drowsing, Pipi misread the situation when he spied her sprawling there and shot his mouth off without delay.

"Well excuse me Madame but just what-all do you think you're doing? This is no place for you to come and take a crap . . ."

When the police car tore up in a blast of sirens and whirling lights, a terror-stricken Marguerite watched, slack-jawed, as her four youngest were carted away. The social worker, cleaned up and bandaged, insisted with great compassion that she would not be bringing charges against her for assault and battery because I understand perfectly your maternal feelings at being informed of such a measure but you understand we have no choice in the matter, I'll take steps to see that your situation improves so that the children can be returned to you . . . As soon as the police had gone, the *chabine* fell on Pipi like the summer sun pummels the huts of Le Prêcheur.

"It's all your fault you goddam devil!"

She tenderized him like a chunk of chewy horsemeat before flinging him out the window with an invitation to hit the highway. A bewildered Pipi went straight to his old clearing, where he resumed his interminable conversation with the zombi Afoukal. After that we heard nothing much about Marguerite Jupiter. It seems the social worker kept her promise. The city sanitation department cleaned out the garden. The *chabine* was treated for her scalp disease and recovered both her job and her children. Her new lover – jealous of who knows what – set fire to the breadfruit tree. And so, the last trace of the most wondrous concubinage this side of love went up, ladies and gentlemen, in smoke.

Rats, ants, and zombi-vendors. News of the miracle-gardener's downfall reached our devastated market. It gave us something to chew over for a few days. Then there was no further word of Pipi. People said he'd gone back to his clearing, but time slip-slipped by and no one would have chanced a dice-roll anymore that it was true. His wheelbarrow had become a blackish smudge on the cement floor in spite of all the municipal guardian's stubborn scrubbing. Life was planting only hot peppers and creeping bitter-melon around us. Rats and ants appeared in our derelict market. First two or three rats took to strolling around during the day. They bumped into ankles and baskets, trotted along the stalls, and fled at the first hint of a threat. The time came when, in packs of from five to eight, they simply attacked the basket of their choice, scaring the vendors, chomping on all the produce, and vanishing presto! when everyone had recovered from their fright. The municipal guardian, alerted by the victims of these fierce hordes, sent a report off to the health department. A team of exterminators, specialists in delayed-action poison for vicious rats, was dispatched to the scene. A curious thing happened just when the team was unpacking its equipment before our grateful eyes: thirty-two groups of ten rats each began to race along our aisles. The panic beggared words. People lit out for the doors. Hampers were stomped flat. Fruits, vegetables, little kids, and four of the six exterminators sailed through the air. It was crab-basket chaos, and the market suspended operations for three full hours. The guardian closed up exceptionally early to allow the specialists to apply their raticidal science. Free to deploy their talents, the sanitation experts worked for a long time setting out foolproof traps. The next day, when the market opened, the guardian collected here and there thirteen cats in endlessly agonizing convulsions, twenty-two dogs in rigor mortis, fourteen hundred anolis, one hundred and fifty spiders, three hundred thousand red cockroaches, fifteen moths, two birds that had ceased fluttering, and one very dead rat. Everyone gathered around that last item. Opinion on the success of the operation was quite divided and a tongue-storm was raging when a new florescence of rats produced a panic similar to the flap of the previous day. This time, people were just plain squashing up against the railings. They climbed the posts. They swung from the electric wires. They somersaulted over the stalls. There were tramplings. Overturnings. One oldster, reliving one of the worst moments of the city of Saint-Pierre, howled in the grip of a *nuée ardente* as searing as it was imaginary. The rats seemed to fly. They were big, dutty gray, nasty. This unusual behavior, their apparent madness, and their pale color unfamiliar in these parts all contributed heavily to the terror that overtook us. There were two fatalities that day: the elderly survivor of the fire of Saint-Pierre, who drowned in the fountain basin, and a vendor whose heart had surely upped and quit. The country was all agog. The television preempted two reports on the sex life of Breton oysters to show the devastated aisles, our wheelbarrows, the bodies, and the dead rat.

This time, after a futile search for holes and nests, the extermination team spent the entire night deploying its arsenal of anticoagulant poisons and tricky traps. Unable to determine where the rats usually congregated, the team scattered its materiel according to the laws of chance, reinforced by a few theoretical principles of ratology. The following day, only a hardy few dared venture into the market. Vendors, *quimboiseuses*, cooks, street-singers, children, the guardian, hangers-on, and we djobbers all thronged outside the gates, blocking streets and sidewalks, aggravating the normal downtown traffic jams. Surrounding us in a jiffy, the police herded everyone into the market after the doctor who ran the city health department had briskly explained how it was scientifically impossible that a single rat could have survived. Inside we found the usual litter of dogs, cats, various insects, and a bumper harvest of twenty-five poisoned rats, around which we danced uttering the savage cries of fishwives. Well, ladies and gentlemen, that was the last time we cavorted around any dead rats.

The day passed without incident, but the next morning, at the pippiree point, they erupted from ev-er-y-where, with fresh bursts every five minutes. They knocked over the scales. Zipped around the stalls leaving messes of bouncing produce in their wake. Streaked the air with piercing squeaks. This time, not everyone joined the stampede. While about thirty chicken-hearts were palpitating at the doors, Madame Carmélite (a placid vendor who was about to leave for France, the land of no bad luck) climbed up onto her counter to 'buse the rats – An landièt manman zot! [Your mama's ass!] – and trumpet her exasperation. Lapochodé hauled a cutlass out from under his wheelbarrow and sped off after the vermin. Zozinette, arms akimbo, straddling her baskets, glared at them contemptuously while growling "Here ratty ratty ratty" in a wee-bit menacing manner. Mam Elo, cracking open her shell of patient silence, brandished a furious fist overhead as she delivered a definitive curse on all sizes shapes and styles of rat. Elmire the *pacotilleuse* rose from her stool to shout, "Better watch out for me, dammit!" before sitting back down with studied nonchalance. These new attitudes had no effect on the rodents' madness, but they stemmed the human panic. Day after day, fewer and fewer people were terrified by the infestation of rats, which soon became a symbol of our decline as they skibbled along the aisles and between the stalls, escorted by a massive tide of ants impervious to Fly-Tox, amid our almost unanimous indifference.

Many weird happenings plagued the market like that while Pipi was out of circulation. One episode upset us so profoundly it made getting used to the ants and rats seem a snap. I'm talking, now, about ghosts. Three *chabine* peddlers, in a haze of dust motes, wreathed in an aura of eternity, for they were dressed in garments more ancient than our dreams. They appeared the first time in pink and violet petticoats, short-sleeved white blouses covered with embroidery as lush as leaves, sumptuous laces, scarves of yellow, rose, and green, with delicate *tremblant* stickpins quivering on turbans of cheerful madras. Wearing silk ribbons, necklaces with four rows of golden beads, gleaming brooches like Chinotte's, with roller and *chenille* earrings grazing their cheeks, the women advanced in the colors of the sunset, floating a few inches above the ground. Moving from one end of the market to the other in a deepening silence, they vanished at the entrance gate like reflections in a shop window, leaving us as dead-still as bamboos on a windless day. Scalding tears sprang from the eyes of the oldest vendors when they beheld this mirage from years long gone. The youngest market women, wearing fish-mouths of astonishment, were shaking their heads. Sitting on the crates or behind our wheelbarrows, we djobbers were as distraught as those caterpillars that must hand their lives over to butterflies.

At their second appearance, the specters wore Creole princesse gowns adorned with flounces and laces, and towering, pointed head scarves secured with golden brooches.

At the third, they were clothed in chemises of embroidered batiste trimmed with wide bands of lace and pleated around golden buttons. Their *matadora's* hips swayed in skirts with a bold floral pattern, full in the back, short in front, with batiste pockets that fluttered like eyelashes. Their *colliers-choux*, brooches, stickpins, and buttons bespangled the outfits with glints of light. The women hovered in their auras and offered large, empty baskets to all and sundry, as though crying invisible wares. Their faces were blurry and they had no eyes, oo mama we cried ours out over that . . .

The fourth time, they had put on quilted *douillettes*. The bodices, close-fitting at the back and loose in front, were gathered in at a yoke and joined by a belt to full skirts that were also gathered in the back, and piqué on either side to reveal taffeta petticoats with layers of flounces trimmed with satin-backed Chantilly lace. Their yellow hair was tucked under *madras calendés*, saucily tied turbans of stiff, bright cloth, and their braids, coiled over their ears *en macaron*, peeked out at the temples to show off clips or barrettes. Their jewelry this time included golden *gros-sirop* necklaces, chains with fobs, rings and pendeloques, cat-erpillar brooches, and drop earrings of black stone worthy of the wizardly Adeldade Nicéphore. These ladies appeared time and again, steeping the market in such anxious bewilderment that the municipal guardian had to call in the police and then the archbishop, since they were zombies, I'm telling you . . .

An arrest warrant was issued by a district attorney, and a police car parked itself at the entrance to the market to await the peddlers from dreamland. When they materialized the officers rushed at them angrily, as though to roust out a tribe of Rastas. In the name of the French people and the clacking of handcuffs, they enlivened the stroll of the Eternal Ones with a furious struggle that didn't jar the ladies' serenity one jot. The police-men clutched right through the apparitions as though grasp-ing the air itself. While all this was going on, news of Pipi was brought to us by Rastas who'd come to hawk bamboo sculp-tures at the market. They claimed he was almost completely covered by a blanket of earth sprouting white mushrooms. Doctors from Colson came to visit him now and then, taking photos and noting down his ravings about a slave guarding a jar of gold. There were periods, it was said, when he changed himself into grass, for he was nowhere to be seen. At other moments he must have found a way to move about under-ground along with the jar. He had to have died more than once and rotted away to dust, because the clearing was often in-vaded by yellowish fogs and unbearable pestilential odors that gradually drifted away. Otherwise, he was right in plain sight, a kind of quivering root curled up in the grass beneath a panoply of toadstools, chatting with the earth. Afoukal no longer spoke to him of slavery. He had begun asking questions, curious about our life, and especially about our future.

"What you going to do with all these races living in you, these two tongues tearing you apart, this mix of blood working inside you?"

Pipi had never wondered about these things, no more than we had. His jabbering dismayed the guardian of the jar.

"No fear, master-whoosis . . . We'll go back to Africa . . ."

"What? What Africa?" the zombi would exclaim. "Ain't no more Africa dammit! First place, where is this Africa? Where are the paths, the tracks to follow back? Got any memories of this way across the waves?"

"We'll find it, don' worry . . ."

"Find what? What can you do? Like pottery still to be fired, you people are. A strange land you never set foot in, blood and races all jangled up together . . . So whatever could you do with Africa?"

"Enough! I made this earth sing," Pipi would shout, "I conquered cabbages, yams, sweet potatoes, and so on and so forth and so don't you come moufing silly at me . . ."

"Well then, what," the zombi would whisper, "just what you doing here, glued to the ground like a cowpat? You think that's what life is?"

Pipi didn't answer that question. Pressing his cheek into the bare dirt, he would desperately seek a reason for his miserable presence in that clearing. The ancient dew of misfortune sometimes pearled on his eyelashes. Afoukal had become second nature to him. A few recollections – of us, the market, Anastase, djobs, his wheelbarrow, Elmire, our sleepless nights, Mam Elo, and the dorlis – lived on, perhaps, in a ravine of his mind. But he'd clean forgotten, and no mistake, having left all that to hunt for gold, sinking part of his life into the search only to wind up on his belly out in the back of beyond without why or wherefore. Trying to escape Afoukal's inquisition, he would lose himself in the fragrances of pink guavas or hog plums that laced the wind. His feral dog's nostrils caught the discreet scent of the last cacao trees or their dehiscent pods.

It was a game to him, in the depths of this distress, to identify in the swirl of emanations the bitter aroma of the cashew
trees with their red hearts, their cluster of woody flowers above
crinkled leaves, or the pungent breath of the roots of guaiac
trees, whose resin is treasured by *papa-feuilles*. On rainy days,
these smells were lost within a wild awakening, a unique and
variable odor that eddied through the undergrowth. This hu-
mid, fetid vegetal essence seeped out from everywhere. Its raw-
ness overpowered Pipi, who burrowed deeper into the warm
earth and lay motionless in the soaking rain. On sunny days,
he covered himself with Guinea grass, which spoiled and dried
out, keeping him as cool as the inside of a watermelon. Pains
would drive him from his hollow to search for the scurvy-grass
that soothed his teeth. Compresses of thistle relieved his headaches. Hunting for these plants, he encountered ailing cats and
dogs on the same errand, following their instincts. This bush
medicine learned from the *papa-feuilles* saved him from the
physical deterioration of his previous stay in that fateful clearing and even, most certainly, from death.

After the arrest warrant was canceled, the police car abandoned the zombi-peddlers to their exhibitions of a vanished
life. A sybaritic indigence kept us draped on our crates. Out of
all the vendors from the great days of djobbing, only Elmire
and Mam Elo were left, the last women to have known us as
powerful master-djobbers, surrounded by our faithful country
clients. The new vendors transported their vegetables in plastic bins. They turned up on Saturday mornings at the entrance
to the market in small vans, which their menfolk helped them
unload. They sold their few wares at impossible prices to
those who could afford such extras, and disappeared for the
rest of the week. We never saw the bush-medicine women anymore – there were so many pharmacies! Their stalls were now
used to sell souvenir carafes, knick-knacks made-in-etc., and
stock close-outs from warehouses frequented by somewhat
sleazy secondhand dealers. When the season for sweet mangoes, green mangoes, or Spanish limes was at its peak, a few
girls would show up, sitting impatiently behind their baskets,
bringing a spark of life back to the sidewalks alongside the
railings. They ignored us too, however. You'd have thought we

were there but not really. We'd look at one another in disbelief, often aghast to catch our outlines getting hazy: we seemed quite simply to be fading away, victims of an invisible eraser. Elmire was the only one who noticed. It was a fate she recognized, and so the former voyager stammered out a daily threnody.

Weep, she said,
        for the Yaka of Cape Horn
        stricken with transparence,
        the Xeta of Brazil,   .
        memories with no future.

Weep, for the Yora of Bolivia,
        the enigmatic Fulah,
        the Tubus,
        the Tuareg of the Sahara, said to be
        like water holes shrinking in the dry season,
ah weep, for the Bushmen of the Kalahari sands.

Weep, for those spewed out of Africa,
        the Malinke of Senegal,
        the Yoruba of Dahomey,
        the Pygmies of Gabon besieged by falling trees,
        the Yamu of Kenya whose huts stand deserted.

Fall weeping to the ground
        for the Ainus of Hokkaido
        whose elders alone still speak their memory.
        Weep, for the Saramaccas of the Guianas,
        the Kanakas of the South Seas,
        the last of the Caribbees.
Alas weep for these butchered promises
hurtling pell-mell into senseless oblivion,

your misfortune scattered like seeds!

Aside from this litany, Elmire did not have much to say. She often fell asleep, gorged with heat and silence. All around our sinkhole there were other miseries stirring. Fort-de-France echoed with street violence and the thud of tear-gas grenades. One rumor spoke of murderous gendarmes rampaging up in the mornes, gunning down those who worked in the failing factories and the seas of sugarcane. Only habit brought us back our joy at Christmas and Carnival time. Within us and around us things were guttering out like old torches. The zombi-peddlers gradually stopped coming, but when they did appear, no one was drawn anymore to this dizzying mirage of dreams, and even the courtyard at City Hall, where Aimé Césaire regularly distilled the fine liquor of his voice, no longer felt our footsteps. We had reached the end of a track that was petering out, with no horizon, where the country was slipping even farther beyond our grasp. Sometimes, in a stupor of loss, we envied Bidjoule, who had planted himself in the land like a yam only to be uprooted at the first sprout – ah, me! – by the migrant-worker doctors at Colson.

Hell-peppers, hot-hot! It was something horrible that reminded us of that marvelous girl's existence: she was in the newspaper! Mam Elo, who was reading it, began moaning some Oh-my-Gods. Dreading grim news about Pipi, we rushed over to her shouting "BLOGODO!" – the only exorcism that works against the blows of destiny.

"Anastase is in prison!" sobbed the impotent Queen.

And as she sounded out each word in the article, the torture that Anastase had suffered, and about which we'd only had our suspicions, was finally revealed. We learned that although Zozor Alcide-Victor had been reasonably attentive to her at first, later on he'd made himself as scarce as a piece of meat in the days of Admiral Robert. The girl had waited fondly, patiently, leaning against a window corner, idly kneading some pastry dough. Impelled by relentless cramps, the seducer would suddenly appear – only to ball her on the kitchen table among the egg shells and smears of flour, and then vanish just as promptly, without giving her any idea where he was off to or when he might be back. Weeks could pass like that without the dusty hallway resounding to his springy step. Anastase took on a permanent load of heartache and the withered-coconut look that had so astonished us before. Throwing off her torpor, she would lose herself in baking cakes, hypnotizing herself with the endless stirring of sweet-making. Now, candying green papayas does not demand the concentration of a watchmaker, but the obsessively finicky rituals she performed over her saucepans soothed her distress. Her days began to copy one another: anxious vigils near the window, selling sweets at the school gates, the ejaculatory apparitions of Zozor Alcide-Victor, who mounted her without a word. Thursday evenings, she would slip on red shoes with white flowers to go take the night air in La Savane, drugging herself on the tart odor of fallen tamarind pods or loitering near the sacrificial tree favored by the master of her heart.

Soon she began living as a recluse, without the desire or courage to appear in the light of day. Her shutters stayed closed. Her hair came out in handfuls. Her lovely star-apple skin grew muddy, like the peel of avocados picked in the rain. Dust lived undisturbed in her home, and the candies she made out of habit piled up in corners for the flies and ants, smelling of rancid sugar. Her life now went on in her head, with a Zozor Alcide-Victor who was always at her side, and certainly most loving. That's why she talked to herself in such a soft voice and smiled so often when brushed by the wing of an inner joy. The poor woman's collapse did not stir Zozor Alcide-Victor to the least bit of pity. A recent adept in strange delights, he was now smoking cannabis from Guiana and indulging the special taste of sodomy, laying Anastase in brutal ways that filled her with shame. The worst thing was that her beloved's new whims kept her face shoved into the sugary stickum of the kitchen table or the grubby sheets on the *paillasse*, which meant she couldn't see his handsome features smoking with the sacred pleasure she was giving him. It was this frustration, by the way, that sealed the Syrian bastard's fate, so true is it that you can play around with a monkey, but you'd better not go too far.

One day, when Zozor Alcide-Victor had been gone so long the sun inside her had drowned in ugly rain, Anastase hid a kitchen knife in her blouse when she heard the sombitch coming down the hall. He, as always, burst into the room, flung his love-slave down onto her stomach, and ploughed right into her. He came quickly, reciting his usual Arab poem between spasms. Sitting on the bed while Anastase tidied herself up, he complacently smoked that cigarette with which he passed the time until he felt up to a second assault. Smugly savoring his sense of relaxation, he never noticed Anastase's staring eyes or her mechanical movements as she approached him. When she reached out toward him, he thought she was eager for another humping, and he pushed her away with one hand: Whoa Anastase hang on, can't you wait one little minute here? . . . The first blow thrust the knife behind the left clavicle. The second raked a few ribs and punctured a lung. The third severed his carotid artery. When the fourth blow disemboweled him, he was dead, at least that's what the forensic pathologist claimed in the report submitted later on at the trial.

She was locked up in the women's section of the main prison. The police had found her curled up lovingly on the bastard's body, softly serenading him with the Creole lullabies old women sing to sick children. Anastase was alone in the women's section, with a female guard in a white uniform to keep an eye on her. The guard knitted place mats and napkins she sold to her friends to earn a bit of extra money. The prisoner learned how to weave Carib baskets, a lost art nowadays. The empty cells and small, deserted courtyard edged their voices with an eerie echo. The guard on the night shift arrived at seven o'clock. The two women would have supper alone by the light of a single bulb in the tiny dining hall. Anastase must be there still, or if she isn't, what does it matter? When Mam Elo went to see her on a visitor's pass, she found her quite calm, and understood that this woman once enslaved by love was finally at peace. This was the first and last time that news of her coaxed a smile from us. (Adieu, Anastase; in hearts burned to ashes the embers still glow.)

Back in those days, young people caught up in politics were clashing with the police. Our student revolutionary, once so full of fire, kept her distance from such things. "A revolution isn't just running riot!" she'd shout. To her great despair, we weren't moved by what was going on. Hemmed in by ants and rats, surrounded by vendors who'd forgotten all about us, plagued by the thought of our king languishing in a clearing, eddying in a stream of impossibilities and free-floating time, we had long since tumbled off the gourd-tree of life. Dried out, we offered the useless readiness of empty calabash-*couis*. So when madness unhinged the city, and we had something solid to cart around, no one – from here to the far horizon – blazed up more desperately than we did.

It all started with the visit of an official from France said to be minister over the seas or something. Reinforced by soldiers of the Foreign Legion and other nasty killers, riot police invaded the streets, clubbing a crowd of young French-flag-burners. This time, alas, they left behind in the wreckage a body with a bashed-in skull. It was Emile, the son of Mam Joge (Bidjoule's forgetful mother) and Ti-Joge the mailman. *Oh the hatred that stirred in us then!* The young man's corpse was paraded around the city by a delirious procession, and we joined in. That night there was an invocation of disaster. We shattered store windows, trashed the glass of fourteen hundred cars. We cut through pipes, the metal shutters of shops, and the wooden shutters of houses. We overturned fire hydrants, phone booths, traffic lights, and electricity poles. Skulking through the shadows like rats, sprinting across open areas, we flowed through the streets like rainwater on a stormy night. The city seemed alive only with flashing weapons and martial uniforms. We streaked through the night with the great strides of our youth and the long-forgotten zest of our big Saturday djobs. As tipsy as a flight of butterflies, or like a horde escaped from some sinister cage, we hurled conch shells and bottle shards at soldiers and gendarmes. How shameful it is today to know we could be so cruel! . . .

Sun-up found a city blinking with smoking cinders. Bouquets of uniforms rustled nervously at intersections. Our adversaries were impressive in the daylight: thundering boots, swarms of helicopters, jeeps with antennas, all this deadly skill that recalled ancestral fears to life in us. The Syrians hadn't rolled up their shutters. The only vendors who braved the market were oldsters or women too down on their luck to fear anything. That night had rather shaken up our poor lives, we were laughing like children, hooting and hollering. This bright spot quickly faded away. As the city settled back to normal, our listless stagnation sat waiting for us amid the rats, the ants, and the few anxious vendors: our outburst had simply been a tantrum by hooligans, as we heard from a radio spewing official threats in all directions.

For Mam Joge, this final period was hell. She had already lost Bidjoule, who'd died mama-less in a cell at Colson, and she had to wait for a long time before she could recover the body of her murdered son. His corpse had become a kind of exhibit A of who knows what, and the authorities had handed it over to an army of forensic pathologists who were trying to explain his death by some cardiac conundrum or arterial affliction. Mam Joge was still waiting when she had to face another tragedy with us: the fire at Chinotte's bar and the death of Ti-Joge. Here's the how of it . . .

The events of that famous night in the city had exhilarated Chinotte: "We're fighting back!" she shouted, "we're fighting back . . ." She was so excited she almost toppled off her throne of ledgers. In celebration of something or other, she brought her hi-fi down from upstairs. It was so marvelous you had to cross yourself at the sight of it. Sitting on the bar, the beast blared revolutionary hymns from Cuba and songs of an unknown America in an unfamiliar tongue. This individual little Carnival had reached our ears, and we'd left our crates to go listen to the Adventuress inscribe her voice so perfectly in these foreign harmonies. It was a moment of heartfelt gaiety during which Chinotte treated us to a few bottles. Some glasses got broken. A few sugar bowls took flight. We left the bistro at the hour when the market bestirs itself for the sale of the evening-soup vegetables. It was simply a reflex: those djobs had all vanished as well. Standing at the door next to her barmaid, Chinotte kept waving goodbye to us, as though despite all her till *tomorrows* she had a premonition we'd never see her again.

That same afternoon, the fateful sailors entered Chez Chinotte on the stroke of four. There were twenty of them. They'd had a hard day: angry students were holding meetings just about everywhere. The men had been assigned to guard the hospital where the pathologists were laboring over Emile's body, and at that hour, the sailors were certainly either out on patrol or off on a spree. Chinotte was still deep in her inexplicable gala mood. The tables were covered with fresh cloths. The window blinds sparkled. The room smelled of bleach and hibiscus. Before the sailors arrived, if we're to believe the number of tibias found amid the ashes, a few rummies at loose ends must have drifted in. Chinotte welcomed them by turning up the volume on her hi-fi. When the sailors all piled in, she received them just as warmly, pouring them brimming drinks without thinking twice about it. The sailors struck up their guardroom songs and started chasing one another around the tables. They stood there, each holding his neighbor's hose, and pissed on the tablecloths. And as often happens during such guzzles, they vented their spleen against the niggers present and this fucking shithole of a rotten island! . . . Was it Chinotte who fell on them, throwing chairs and bottles right and left? Was it a rumhound who pounded those pompoms[56] flat with a table leg, our weapon of choice in such brawls? Chinotte was of a size to disperse a regiment of drunks. We'd already seen her let fly in similar circumstances. So what happened must have been one of those unbudgeable rocks that trip up destinies, the sort of fatality that means life will always, always, end badly.

The sailors tore the bistro apart. The sailors smashed the bar and all the tables. The sailors smithereened the hi-fi and must, as they fled, have tossed a lighted cigarette butt into the flood of alcohol from the broken bottles. Colossal flames shot up, swallowing the ceiling, the apartment above, and the roof of rusted sheet metal. They must have strained against the walls before blowing out the doors and windows. The neighborhood shuddered when they reached the storeroom of bottles in reserve, which they gulped down with a deafening smack.

The market folk were there well before the firemen. Pin-Pon rushed into the blaze and emerged with singed hair, yelling for someone to get him a wet blanket. Wrapped in this laughable protection, he plunged back into that oven alive with cries of agony. The flames reflected the variety of Chinotte's rum reserves. The delicate blue came from Maniba rum. The ocher flashes from Depaz rum. The yellowish swirls were Neisson rum. Saint-Etienne gave off a dazzling red. Among the metallic greens of La Mauny flashed blinding streaks of Favorite, Old

Nick, Trois-Rivières, and Duquesne. Pin-Pon reappeared beneath the burning blanket, flailing about like a Guianese macaque. One vendor doused him with water, another smothered the flames by throwing a tarp over him.

"Yo andidan, an tann yo hélé!" (There's people inside, I heard screams!)

He would have raced back in again if the firemen, who'd finally arrived, hadn't pushed everyone behind the barriers that had sprung up in a flash. It was pure sadness, waiting helplessly like that, staring at the blaze. The water streaming into it seemed to have no effect. Some *quimboiseuses*, cronies of Chinotte's, called down skin-crawling curses on that conflagration. Two firemen fell from their ladder, sending up showers of sparks before they crash-landed. A few others, fuddled by the fumes of alcohol roiling from the fire, staggered with the hoses. The inferno seemed invincible. The firemen wet down the neighboring houses to discourage the beast from getting its claws into them. Night brought its winds, and the calamity fed on them heartily. At sunrise, the flames lost some of their arrogance. The colors of the rum had paled, then vanished. The pine boards of the building now nourished a less spectacular fire, which gave fresh energy to the firemen. Before noon, the dragon was vanquished.

Steam rose from the sodden, blackened skeleton of the bistro. Tibias and brainpans were dredged from the debris. But what they mostly found was melted glass, set in artistic contortions by the water. The bones were collected in a canvas, where a doctor sorted them according to incomprehensible criteria. Concluding this meticulous work, he announced that there were seven men and two women in this ossuary. To the market, it was clear: there were Chinotte of course, the barmaid, and seven old soaks for whose anonymous send-off down the other road of fate we shed fat tears. That's when Mam Joge came panting up: "Where's Ti-Joge? Have you seen Ti-Joge?" Taking advantage of the unrest in the city, the retired mailman had stolen away from his bed.

"HE MUST BE IN THERE!" she shrieked, pointing at the sinister harvest on the canvas.

"You don't know for sure . . . not for sure . . ." we protested, by way of consolation. "Maybe he's off strolling around La Savane . . ." But knowing that a rummy never leaves his bed save for the sanctuary of rum Masses, we were hardly surprised when a *quimboiseur* in the crowd, bending over the bone-heap at Mam Joge's request, selected without fuss or hesitation his tibias, three of his ribs, a dice-throw of vertebrae, and half his pelvis. (Ti-Joge, ho! It's an enviable thing to die in a tafia bonfire!)

Mam Joge emerged from this infernal time when the prefect himself came to return her son's body. He offered his official condolences: the pathologists had found nothing with their knives but the specific effects of police blackjacks. The prefect also said, which was reassuring, that an investigation was under way, that her son's killer would be punished and the sailors tracked down. Mam Joge buried her son, and her husband's bones, in the poor people's cemetery amid a cacophony of ritual Latin and anticolonialist slogans. I must confess that after all this happened we lost touch with her. Her daughter Pauline had gotten married and worked in a government office. People say Mam Joge spent an old age full of boredom in her apartment, which slowly fell to pieces around her. They also say she took to cooking up christening feasts for herself, and that every evening she fed the contents of her saucepans to the pigs penned illegally in the washtubs of the courtyard. Lastly they say that, although the sweetness had gone from her eyes, she never lost the astonishing strength in her arms. So, well, it pleases us, in the void where we are today, to imagine her still stoutly carrying on somewhere in life, indestructible, waging a battle she might win against death and all the rest.

A heart on fire with a woman of the night. Every day, at the deserted hour of macadam, Mam Elo would tell us what we needed to know about Pipi. Without him noticing, she used to spy though the bushes on his entrenchment in the haunted clearing. Things had gone from bad to worse: the former master-djobber seemed to have fallen prey to another evil spell . . .

Beneath a one o'clock moon, after a bit of babbling with Afoukal, Pipi was letting his gaze roam freely through a starry sky to soothe his rage. A-ah! There was an unusual rustling over at the other end of the clearing. Pipi's cat-eyes peered into the shadows. He could make out nothing, but sensed almost physically a presence that was shifting the direction of the wind, spreading silence, and creating a chill like a refrigerator door opened at noon. His hair standing on end, for the first time Pipi felt uneasy in that clearing.

"Afoukal, Afoukal, wha's that over there?"

The zombi-slave was mum. His hour had passed, and the jar had already sunk back into the earth some minutes before. Pipi tried to stand up, but his legs failed him. A few yards away, the presence was as striking as a gathering of clouds in a clear sky. That's when Pipi felt its attractive power. Swept away by the urge to let himself flow like a river, he crawled on all fours toward a shape that was emerging from the gloom, rippling like a delicate veil. And jumping Jehoshaphat, the most charming of *matadoras* this side of beauty now appeared. She had eyes like a forest pool glittering with moonbeams. She had skin the rich, dark color of fertile soil welcoming the dew. Wow wow wow wow she had the thick hair of carefree *câpresses*. She had the supple body of *coulies* and jungle vines, along with the voluptuous curves of *chabines* in their thirties. She had, she had, she had, and she had still more. Pipi felt love move right into his breast with its cyclone bluster, its stopped-up-gutter fever, its parade of desires.

"And how are you, *ti-mâle?*" [57]

The creature spoke gently, yet imperiously. Her melting voice soaked into the earth and the bark of the cashew trees, dissolving among the leaves with a song like rain. It made Pipi shiver. Desire for this woman was riding him hard. He seemed to sense her own longing for him. Damn, she loved him already. He had to go to her. Touch her. Talk to her. Pipi began to wriggle toward her with the grotesque inelegance of a drowning swimmer cast up on a beach. The distance between him and this beauty, however, always remained the same. Pipi didn't notice this until he'd dragged himself, according to Mam Elo, almost nine miles. Torn by gnarled roots, mimosa thorns, and spikes of deadwood, his body broke the spell through a plethora of pains. He found himself alone in unfamiliar forest dimly lit by the sun's first rays, howling like a dog at a full moon because of his shredded skin and beaten-up heart. He wandered a full four days in this trackless wilder- ness before stumbling into Afoukal's clearing as limp as an empty bag.

"What's happened to you now, my son?"

Perking up at the zombi-slave's voice, Pipi scrabbled eagerly towards the jar.

"Hey Afoukal my frien', if you only knew, oh lalala, what a woman! Like honey-syrup! The best kind of punch with a ma-dou[58] chaser! . . ."

"Watch out for pretty women after midnight . . ."

Afoukal's advice was lost in the exaltation of love possessing Pipi. Awakening to a hunger forgotten until that moment, he devoured green mangoes, hog plums, the hearts of young coconut palms, tufts of sweet grasses. He clambered down into the nearest ravine to fling himself into a shallow river where he spent hours washing himself. He smoothed the hairs curling on his cheeks, raked the mop on his head with his fingers, washed his clothes and put them on still damp. He perfumed his armpits with lemon balm, then returned to the clearing looking vaguely human. His wait wasn't a long one, but he felt its endless passing with every beat of his heart. A thickening of the night. A windy chill in stilly air. Something clouding his perception of the world. He whipped around – flap! – and saw the one he loved. (How to tell you about Pipi, his life taking on new meaning and stepping out into the sunshine? Oh that devastating rum-punch of love! Even tosspots lose their heads to it . . .) Pipi stood there before her like an anoli stunned by the heat, with fleeting impressions of seeing Anastase again. While words fluttered around inside his skull, he tried to find some French and only came up with Creole, which left him drop-jawed, swaying mutely in the mysterious gaze of the receding beauty. The victim of a come-hither spell, he covered eleven and a half miles without reaching that inaccessible woman. This time, dawn's rosy fingers (frightening thousands of red crabs) surprised him in a mangrove swamp. Bitter, somewhat disoriented, he didn't return to the clearing until midafternoon. Waiting for nightfall was cruel. That woman loved him to death, he knew it, he felt it. But something incomprehensible was blocking her desire for him. What oh whatever could that be?

The answer to that question came to him abruptly along about midnight, when the earth trembled at the melody of the jar.

"Afoukal, she thinks I'm on-the-street! Gold, give me gold! Bring up the gold so she can see what a moneybags I am! . . ."

He'd had a sudden relapse of gold fever. Frightened by Afoukal's silence, Pipi clawed furiously at the ground, flaying his fingertips, flinging dark clods of dirt over his shoulders in a shower of grass and tiny roots. Despite his fever, he could hear the tender swishing of the jar's departure. Sobbing, he called to Afoukal, "Nooo stay here, pa fè mwen sa [don't do this to me], nooo don't go, don't go . . ." He sensed his beloved's presence once again. He literally bounded toward her, but remained the same distance away as before.

"Anni lô, I've got gold, you understand? You mustn't think I'm a beggar . . . I've got a jar of gold! Afoukal's going to give it to me . . ."

Arms outstretched, he advanced toward the phantom.

"You've got gold, ti-mâle?"

"Lots! I've heaps of gold . . . you'll see . . . but wait . . . stay here . . . don't go . . ."

The strange pursuit began again. The miles went by beneath Pipi's staggering steps and the eerie floating glide of the creature, lovely oo lovely. Dawn dissolved her, leaving Pipi bang in the middle of a flock of sheep, bleeding all over but suffering only from his loneliness.

It seemed obvious to us, and Mam Elo was right: Pipi was the victim of a fresh batch of black magic! Instead of taking refuge in the mournful lethargy that had kept her company since the onset of this gold fever, she put away her cooking pots and announced point-blank: "I'm going to find his father so he can put a stop to this business . . ." Jesus-and-Mary! Getting help from a dorlis! Mam Elo had definitely reached a kind of limit beyond which we, by our prudent silence, refused to go along. But there again, she was right: who better to deal with black magic than a black magician! Mam Elo traveled back to Vert-Pré, where she hadn't set foot since her flight years before. The Queen had herself dropped off at the entrance to the cemetery. She knelt in front of the gravestone of her father, Félix Soleil, searched without success for the tomb of her mother, Fanotte, then approached the grim shack of the gravedigger and the *dorlis*. Black Phosphore, the only immortal in those parts, appeared in his doorway, alone. Stony-faced, Mam Elo asked him in a low voice, "But where's Anatole-Anatole, the father of my son?"

"Dead, my daughter," sobbed the gravedigger.

Without another word, he returned to the gloom of his hut. Flummoxed, Mam Elo fell back on the priest, who, in the dim light of the confessional, whispered to her religiously the long version of the story . . .

(*The tragic fate of the* dorlis. Anatole-Anatole had come to a real bad end some time before. When he'd returned from Fort-de-France, after appearing in the daylight at the market, he'd gone back to his cemetery and his father's company. It seems that the sight of his son Pipi had filled him with a happiness that resulted mainly in a vigorous surge in his sexual appetite and nocturnal visits to unsuspecting women, when he would wallow shamelessly in diabolical pleasures. His father, black Phosphore, did not approve of this. He had taught his son the Method, he often said, so that he might assuage his passion for the girl Héloïse Soleil, not indulge in such vagabondagery.

"Watch out," he also told him, "the *dorlis* has his weak points, and there are those who know about them . . ."

But the young *engagé* didn't give a spit. It must be said that he had considerably improved upon his father's system. To stop him now, you needed not just one but two pairs of black panties worn backwards, plus a pair of scissors open in a cross and placed beneath the pillow. Since very few women met these requirements, his love life was of a richness that would have been the envy of every lady-killer in Fort-de-France and Anywhere-Else. But, ladies and gentlemen, as we've already seen, fate keeps many a nasty trick handy for those who simply don't know when to stop.

One night, Anatole-Anatole had just entered the bedroom of a sleeping beauty, and his mouth was watering as he listened to the breathing of a female-off-in-dreamland when . . . he felt all frosted over with cold. An unfamiliar sensation. The master-*dorlis* went on the alert, ready to parry a countercharm. Minutes passed. Nothing happened. The beauty was still sleeping. Anatole-Anatole smelled the exciting odor of her body, warmed by the bedclothes. He waited a little bit more, then, unable to restrain himself, the magic formula on his lips, he covered the beauty with his icy body, chilled by the power of the evil spell. The *dorlis* had already been hard at work for a few minutes, attentive only to the voluptuous tingling of his nerves, when he felt his victim's warm and supple flesh suddenly take on the glacial rigidity of a body possessed. Anatole-Anatole understood instantly: the beauty was also the *engagée* of an occult force! He tried desperately to withdraw his member, to fling his whole self backward, to get free of the sheets that seemed to have come alive and the bed now in the throes of devilish undulations. A grinding sound rasped from the throat of the possessed woman, whose eyelids sprang open to reveal the pupils of a cat. Our Father in Heaven, forgive us for describing such horror, but folks should know that Anatole-Anatole was aghast to feel a polar chill emanating from the body of his victim and sucking up his flesh with a cold fire as all-consuming as live coals. The *dorlis* was literally freezing. As the water in his body solidified, it was shredding every fiber of his being. He was convulsed with pain. His ears, lips, sex collapsed into gelid crumbs. No one knows how he managed to get out of there. By the power of his own evil spell? Was he released by his victim? Be that as it may, the corpse they found was bleached as white as a tourist, castrated, flayed all down its front, and wearing the expression of indescribable agony that comes over the damned poised on the edge of that abyss. The forensic pathologist, poorly informed about the mysteries of life, diagnosed skin cancer and death by coronary thrombosis . . . Lord, I am not worthy to receive you, but speak only one word and I will be healed. Let me pray.)

The jar comes to light. Mam Elo shed no tears over the sad end of the *dorlis*, of course, and we (who had vaguely dreaded seeing her reappear with the Monster) were relieved to learn of it. We sat down with her, near her tarnished cooking pots, beneath a blanket of still air. The wonderful smell of fruits had gone a little sour, and discarded leaves littered the aisles. The first hint of a night wind breezed through the silences gathered around stalls that gleamed like tombstones. Mam Elo's eyes said there was just nothing more to try. That hurt us like a sudden free-fall, the snapping open of a predatory chasm hard on our heels. We went off to collapse on those crates we would never leave again: from that moment on, Pipi would have to carry out his quest alone, and polish off his fate.

He returned to the clearing at twilight with a cutlass and a shovel he'd swiped along the way. Nothing, no nothing was going to prevent him now from tearing that gold out of the earth. His ferocious determination didn't even waver at the thought of confronting Afoukal. Ready to dig, Pipi watched impatiently, shovel in hand, for the rising of the jar. When the ground shook, when he heard the familiar swooshing sound, Pipi began delving away hell hard.

"Pipi my son, what are you doing?"

Incredulous, menacing, Afoukal's voice burst out as clearly as an underground spring.

"Give me the gold, Afoukal, give me the gold!"

The spade sliced through soft roots, clanged against stones. Abruptly, it hit a pile of very white, very hard sticks. THE BONES! AFOUKAL'S BONES! Pipi stopped dead. An old fear iced up his skin. He expected the shovel to explode in flames, checked himself for the torments foreseen by the legend. But nothing happened. Beneath the blade, the bones lay quiet.

A masonry of silence held everything still. Pipi closed his eyes, partly to keep out rivulets of sweat, but mostly from dread of seeing the horrific things he was imagining. Those so-familiar surroundings suddenly took on new dimensions, which swept him aside as though he were a wisp of froth on troubled waters.

"Pipi my son, what have you done?"

Strangely gentle, Afoukal's voice filled the clearing. It enveloped Pipi like delicate silk before disintegrating with a crystalline hum in the dark fleece of the thickets. In despair, Pipi repeated to his other self, his confidant, master, and friend, that he wanted the gold, that it was the only way for him to win his beloved, that he'd waited a long time and that the hour had come. Afoukal remained silent, as though stabbed in some place among his last bones. Finally, his voice rose through the carpet of dark grass.

"Well then my son, behold . . ."

Pipi felt the ground ripple beneath his feet. A powerful beast seemed to be awakening below. The edges of the clearing appeared to collapse while its center swelled like the hump on a hunchback. Knocked down, the former king of the djobbers observed the miraculous opening of the earth, which gracefully unfolded exactly like the corolla of a hibiscus, wreathed in swirls of mist and the acrid odor of hot clay. A brief silence was followed by the pop of a cork shooting free. Thrust from its matrix, chalky and ethereal, steaming like the breast of a panting water buffalo, the jar floated above a muddy crater. Endowed with a magical aura, it was as elegant as a dragonfly hovering motionless in the wind. It swayed over the crater, riding smoothly on a puff of wind, then waltzed around the clearing in slow arabesques. When it alighted in front of him at last like a docile bird, Pipi was petrified. This jar, this treasure so many stuck-in-hard-luck-niggers had dreamed about, was sitting submissively before him.

"Afoukal, can I touch it?"

"What are you looking for?"

"Gold . . ."

"Well then, take a look at what you've found . . ."

Suddenly free to move, Pipi pounced on the jar. Tearing off the cover of string and rotting burlap, he clutched the rounded edge and tried to lean over the opening. The jar fell to pieces beneath his weight in a whirlwind of suffocating dust, at which Pipi flailed away in vain. Falling to his knees, he raked through the ruins of the jar with his fingers, pinching every nubbin, seeking in the slightest shape the curve of a coin, the chasing of precious metal. His hands closed only on formless things as fleeting as dry sand. When the dust had settled, Pipi lay sprawled in the debris, feverishly sifting through a rancid-smelling mass of ashes. A half hour went by before he was willing to admit the absolute absence of gold. Another went by before he realized there had never been any at all.

What had once been the essential part of his life now lay at his feet, a heap of bone splinters, potsherds, unrecognizable trash. Pipi staggered in desolation.

"But Afoukal, Afoukal, where's the gold, where's the gold I'm asking you, where, where . . ."

His cries were answered by that whistling sigh of a soul breaking free, a sound familiar to habitués of wakes from that moment when the deceased pockets the small change of a vanished life. The former king of the djobbers understood at once that Afoukal was poised to begin the great voyage, the only lasting peace completely outside of time. The zombi's voice was already fading away when it reached him: "Yes, that's how it is my son, no gold, no jewels, the oldtimers around here still believe every jar stashed in the ground is full of treasure . . . They're right, but they forget that not all riches are gold: there is memory . . ."

This revelation might have crushed Pipi. But it was lost in the euphoria he felt at the sudden apparition of the mysterious *matadora*, who seemed disturbed by the devastation of the clearing. She gave an eye-sweep, her lashes fluttering wildly.

"You're a *quimboiseur, ti-mâle?*"

Pipi was troubled by her strange manner, in which he detected a cautious reserve, an imperceptible retreat that undermined the imperial self-assurance of the previous nights. Without really knowing why, our man decided to exploit this misapprehension.

"Why do you want to know that, my *câpresse?*"

He was using the bantering tone that had been so effective on young market women when it was time to pay for a djob.

"It was you who made the earth sing and freed the ancient soul of the jar?"

The creature had drawn back, curiously on her guard. All gentleness was gone from those uh-oh eyes. Two hard and icy marbles stared at Pipi.

"I'm the one, madame, the very one! And I can do more than that," he boasted.

"Then you know who I am!"

Her voice was as dry, cutting, and harsh as the crack of snapping bamboo. Pipi couldn't believe his ears. He gawped at that dreamy creature who was now radiating the savagery of a pack of mad dogs. The beauty was prancing with rage. Dull thuds trampled the ground, raising clouds of dirt around her white dress. When she came rushing at him, he glimpsed the ghastly hooves below her ankles. When she seized him, he saw the pupils of fire and the thousand-year-old wrinkles, the fright wig of yellow string, the gleaming fangs and the sickening drool. When he went cold through and through and all that was left in his dead flesh was the crazed thumping of his heartbeats, he realized that Mam Zabyme – our most deadly *jablesse*, the one who roasts your heart with a love-spell before eating it for real, bellowing with pleasure over your gaping chest – had just done for him. (Saint Zalive, pray for us!)

No trace was found of the grand master of wheelbarrows, the *dorlis*'s son, the king of us djobbers. Hearsay had it that he'd hauled up the jar of gold, set Afoukal free, but hadn't been wary enough of Mam Zabyme. The old treasure hunters, who'd advised Pipi at the beginning of his quest, broke off their stagnant waiting to visit the clearing and collect dust from the jar in little gourds. Mam Elo went there too, and with the help of Marguerite Jupiter's children, she combed the surrounding undergrowth, pleading for the reappearance of her son. Her sadness soaked into the low-hanging leaves of that accursed forest for twenty years. She went back to Vert-Pré without even stopping by the market, leaving all her cooking pots behind. She returned, it seems, to the house of her childhood, where Félix Soleil had wept over his flock of girl-chicks. Some people claim she took up the discreet ways of her mother, so diligently that in her wide-open, all-lit-up house, no vigilance can hear her living.

As for us, Didon, Sirop, Pin-Pon, Sifilon, Lapochodé, we're being devoured by another sort of *jablesse*. Worn out on our crates, huddled together to ward off a piercing chill, we say these words over and over again, these memories of life, certain that we must disappear. Giving you this version has done us a bit of good, and if you come by tomorrow you'll get a different one, more cheerful, perhaps – what does it matter? This much is known, now: History only counts through what remains when the story's done. There's nothing left at the end of this one, except us, and that's not much. When Pipi vanished, pain bunched us all together, as we are now, incapable of saying I or you, or telling one from another, lumped in a collective and diffuse survival without rhyme or reason. We still thrill to the music of the market's opening, to the creaking of baskets unloaded without us, to the mingling fragrances of a few fruits . . . Oh sweet absinthe.

Elmire was the last one who could still notice us among the crates: she'd seen so much! But she has abandoned her Caribbean basket to take a trip in a coffin. Now no one sees us anymore, or looks for us, although it would take only a memory, like someone calling for a djobber . . . but who among these women could do so? Which one of them knew us when? And what would they want of us? These vendors bring so little to sell! Besides, the municipal guardian packed our wheelbarrows off in the garbage truck, embittered, perhaps, by thoughts of us living the fine life in France, where those who vanish from here fetch up, and – ladies and gentlemen good night – it's a real pleasure for us not to set him straight.

Appendix

ETHNOGRAPHER'S NOTE:
Today, not a single djobber is left in the markets of Fort-de-France. Not a single wheelbarrow. Their memory has ceased to exist. Its final vessel, the aging metal of the railings, was not made to last. This is just to tell you, friends, to take good care of yourselves. Settle your arguments with a friendly glass and stay alert: only the ethnographer mourns trifling ethnocides.

Nine Months for the Reconstruction of the Central Market of Fort-de-France

City Hall has decided: although the historical value of the central market on Rue Saint-Louis might have argued the case for restoration, the building will be completely reconstructed instead.

It has been several weeks since vendors vacated the building to move to "headquarters" in Pointe-Simon that offer fewer conveniences, in their opinion, and as is widely known, this transfer has not been an entirely peaceful one. But there's no arguing necessity . . . In any case, moving the site of the market is the first step in an operation that should be concluded in nine months: the reconstruction of the building.

Reconstruction instead of renovation? The question is worth addressing, because there is no doubt that the structure which has housed the vendors until now has distinct historical significance, architecturally speaking, and might even be considered without too much exaggeration as belonging to the patrimony of Fort-de-France. All this is certainly true. But according to the municipal authorities, when the quality of the original metal in a particular case precludes a full guarantee that any repairs will prove lasting, restoration would be a waste of effort. So the market will be rebuilt, but exactly as it was before, we are assured. The construction units that will later be assembled here are currently being produced in Canada by the same company from which the city of Fort-de-France purchased the Grand Carbet[59] of the Parc Floral.

To help defray the cost of this project, which amounts to 14 million francs, the state is contributing the sum of 560,000 F and the Regional Council has authorized a grant of 1.4 million francs.

Article in the newspaper *France-Antilles*

Djobbers' Cries

Kwililik-kwililik!	Sirop's personal cry, which announces the djobber's presence at a market and informs his regular vendors that he has arrived.
Blokotoblo!	Bidjoule's personal cry.
Kot kot kot kodek!	Didon's personal cry.
Krignak krignak!	Pipi's personal cry.
Émile Bertin!	Lapochodé's personal cry.
Djaka!	Sifilon's personal cry.
Kia-kia-kia!	Pin-Pon's personal cry.
Mach!	When the obstacle is a dog or a known enemy. This cry is also used when we feel like fighting with the obstacle.
Blo!	[Boom!] When the wheelbarrow has bumped into someone or something or is about to do so. This cry means: It's an accident, 'scuse me, it's not on purpose . . .
Blogodo!	[Boomity-boom!] When the wheelbarrow tips over, this cry accompanies its fall with the intention of magically limiting the damage.
Wouabap!	Signals the end of a djob: the merchandise has arrived safely at its destination and it's time to pay up.
Woy woy woy!	Vents the djobber's irritation when obstacles aren't moving properly out of the way. It means he's letting the wheelbarrow take over some of the driving and clear its own path.

Pinlomlimpe!	Intended to disperse the obstacle when it's a group of people.
Cho cho cho!	[Look out!] When the maneuver is a delicate one: a slalom between cars or passersby. This wards off mistakes.
Doudou darling!	[Oh sweetheart!] When an accident has just barely been avoided.
Bay lê! Bay lê!	[Gangway! Move it!] Cry repeated constantly when the djobber is moving swiftly and risks not being able to avoid every obstacle.
Pin pon! Pin pon!	[Sound of French emergency siren] Signals that the djobber feels he has priority: get out of the way, or you'll get hurt.
Chou!	[Shoo!] When there is a single obstacle: a staggering rummy, a gawking dummy, a sidewalk poet, or a gossip deep in chitchat.

Hé mérilo hé mérilo
saki vayan lévé lanmin
saki vayan tonbé si mwen

Manman ban mwen dé fey maho
idi mwen pasé simtyè
anké touvé twa ti serkèy
prèmyéé tonm-la sé an kongo
dézyèm tonm-la sé an kouli
twazièm tonm-la sé an chinwa

anké janbé sé ti tonm-la
anké kriyé woy mérilo
saki vayan lévé lanmin
saki vayan ranté an sèk-la
saki vayan tonbé si mwen

anja pasé trantdé komin
trantdé komin de matinik
toujou plié janmin tonbé
si an tonbé an lizin krasé
si an tonbé latè tranblé
si an tonbé lémô lévé

adan an komin pa ni dé mè
si ni an mè sé mwen ki mè
hé mérilo hé mérilo

Hey merrylo hey merrylo
if ya brave put up ya hand
if ya brave come and get me

Mama gimme two mahoe leaf
she say pass by de cemetery
t'ree lil' coffin ah go find
fust grave be fa Kongo
second grave be fa Couli
t'ird grave be fa Chinee

ah go cross dem lil' grave
ah go cry woy merrylo
if ya brave put up ya hand
if ya brave jump in de circle
if ya brave come and get me

ah already pass t'rough tutty-two commune
tutty-two commune in Martinique
always bendin' never fallin'
if ah fall de fact'ry go down
if ah fall de eart' go shake
if ah fall de dead go rise

in a commune dey ain't two mayor
if dey have one den it be me
hey merrylo hey merrylo

[Only the Creole version of Kouli's
Song was published in the French
edition of this novel, but the
author has graciously allowed me
to prepare this translation.]

Djobbers' Voices

These texts served as "breathers" in the original manuscript. Here, the djobbers were speaking directly to the reader and keeping track of the day-by-day life of the market, while the story, tagging along after biographies and going around twists and turns, was wandering far afield. The initial complexity of the manuscript was intended to suggest the normal workings of memory, which never functions in a linear fashion, but constantly shifts time and place and mood and manner. These poems, grounded in the market, were little pivots scattered evenly around to serve as markers and to remind readers of the main point of reference, like beacons and buoys in the tempest's roil. When the narrative was clarified and tightened up, these poems dropped out almost by themselves.

P C

Djobbing was
    desperately perfecting
    the indispensable creation
    of the wheelbarrow

Every vendor had her regular djobber

The djob was a mark above all
of preference
and the delicate pepper sauces of feeling

Djobbing was then
    the last rampart of the down and out.
   *

Market geography

The familiar corner of crockery and brooms
the languid curve of bush medicines
and occult phials

In the center
the imposing encampment of fruits and vegetables
(forest of subtle colorations and every kind of green)

Then came the medley, hodgepodge,
and even the surprising finds of sundry stalls
at the inviting gates

Hubbub wove everything together
and drove our bitter silences
riding the wheelbarrows at the frothy fringe of it all.
   *

The air dried out
the aisles went white

Green leaves grew muddy
Each flower flagged

Iron roofs seemed
to shrivel up

To move was to die
as the asphalt sagged

adamantine light
withering all glances, ah me
crackling with dreams of cool moss
and droplets somewhere in shade

Oo not a back wasn't bent
              like a dog dragging its tongue

Smells
lost their balance
bakoua-frond fans
and every hankie limp
black skins knew how to glisten

the metal of margarine tins
flaked off its paint
and made warm water seethe
No way of knowing
if it was dry season
or heat at its height

Quiet there when the quicklime sun goes by
        *
Here's pure pleasure: enjoying *macadam*.
We got ours at the stall by the main gate
where Mam Elo held court, queen of rice with saffron sauce
and codfish simmered with green peppers.

You had to eat that
between swigs of tafia
eyes at half mast

let yourself surrender to each mouthful
eaten so slowly
and the outburst of ecstasy
(and the Queen triumphed again)

Then Pipi would turn on his radio
for the Funeral Announcements Program
and

leaning closer to hear whose luck had run out
we'd probe between our tombstones
for little leftovers of this joy.

*

The Hot Pepper Beguine[60]

I know it's hard to believe
but there were always zouézo-pepper[61] eyes, squinting small as
kiddies' curl papers, that some guy beached on bad luck would
promenade around in the unraveling day

Now the zouézo-pepper's puny
but it packs a powerful punch

So,
in this dish of breadfruit mash, coffee-pepper and Indian-
pepper zipped their zing: a sure sign of that big fat vendor with
the huge hat who was always waving her arms around and
crabbing about her life, stubborn as the seven-court-bouillon
pepper

Now the seven-court-bouillon pepper could heat you up
something fierce, right on the button

Watch out,
do not take the Chinese-lantern pepper for a Chinese lantern:
its only light was the fire of taste, the fire in the belly, a gut-
clearing fire. That's why gendarmes who mistook it felt a
cutlass slice open their skulls, despite the smile and docile air

Now the Chinese-lantern pepper rules
in the blaff de poissons
merciless, my friend

But think of this:
the year needed only one billy-goat pepper: it defied the
municipal guardian, used its noggin like a savage battering
ram, and North-starred your forehead but good
Wow, a Head that hard was a special event!

Now the billy-goat pepper is a stewpan treasure:
the sauce is enriched and the aroma well stitched
Only three fools ever pricked one open with a fork

once it had boiled
Right at home in a migan

All the same:
it's definitely the callipygian Mam Jacques Matador who ladled
out the sweetest memories, you thought you were tupping her
and saw yourself whirligigged in a *souskay* [62] wailing oo-aa, and
wound up weeping, well away into fond heartache

Now the mam-jacques'-butt pepper
was swollen with promise
and quite simply on parade
in macadam

    *

Who can say
now
where she's taken her poor self off to
Théolème la Pierrotine
She beamed her toothful smile
and her laughter sprang leaks in demijohns

But where are you Carmélite
with your cottony-wool hair
your ornery expression
belied your guava roundness
and your sweet star-apple eyes

Tell us of Artémise the Coulie
who creaked like tall bamboo in the wind
And Sans-Souci
blooming with wrinkles before her time
What news of Suzette
who laughed to see *chiens-fer* deballed

Mmmh slim memories
slipping swiftly down from empty days
to pierce us and go off again so laden

                        fragile reality.

    *

Who said this city was ugly
just who who who said that?

And what about her midday canticle
when she clinks and chinks with rum
wears schoolkids in her hair
and a garland of car exhaust, hmm?

And her brow at half past one
when a cooling breeze
redeploys the dust
at the feet of the façades, after all?

And when evening comes along
as lustrous as dice
she's dripping with shop windows
haloed in light? I mean, good heavens!

    *

On Saturdays, the seductive singers came
Songs as light as flies
and lilting mandolins
All the market's branches
came together on the spot
leafy with small coins
and the market women's hearts

Yet the singers didn't have
our fine meaty legs
for break-neck dashes
Or our demijohn shoulders
precisely fitted to the slung curve of heavy sacks
Or even our arms as knotty as gnarled roots

and we denied their banjos
the sumptuous strength of our wheelbarrows
(ungrateful vendors we'd have you know
that a djob well done
is music better by far)

    *

Days shattered in commotion
and bloodshed
panic flooded in
when cutlasses struck

Couteaux-chiens[63] whisked from pockets
Bec-mer[64] razors everywhere

Conch shells sail by
that dreadful sssssst
oo deadly aim

It was all sudden and bewildering
a Babelish disaster awaited the police

Roosters fighting for masters unknown
and invisible gamblers
we tore ourselves to shreds
in cockpit violence.

    *

The last word on Mam Goul

Mam Goul
you had hauled the people of the honey-canes
toward the deepest flowers
and most distant sugars

the cutlass
had made your arm-bones hum
with the song of unstrung mandolins
where drained mangrove swamps receive their death warrants

Oo weeding fields
woman you broke your back there
patiently unlacing the small songs of the soil

it must be said
that your endless misery
deep in the crab hole of sorrow
had left the green gleam of plants in your eye

and that mud
a paltry treasure but treasure all the same
entrusted your skin to the crusty strength
that surrounds magmas
and
to the most perfect of earth's colors.

    *

Let's not forget that other giddiness: we'd ball the vendors
one after another, and figure out among ourselves
our lists of by-blows

Each coming amid sighing (now she knows who's boss!)
fluffed up our foliage with deep-rustling life

(Ti-Joge, you broke the record for cocksmanship,
and that enthroned you in our eyes)

The rest of us, still weak under the heart's thumb
and forced to slink sideways like crabs at Eastertime
Oh wallop of love
(raise a glass to us, rummies)
          *
Bidjoule, you started to slide when your barrow lost a wheel
and snapped its axle. Your Sunday sat perplexed before your
tool box, indecipherable once opened

Some slapped-together repair
Your speechless gaze
And tongue

You began those sudden whip-rounds every ten yards or so,
trying to catch sight like us of that abyss you claimed was
following you

(we'd long before stopped turning our heads for that glance
into the void: right straight ahead.)
          *
(First absinthe and la décolle[65])

Sunday mornings
the djob was all flowers
and the floating wheelbarrow let us wear
fresh linen
spiffy shoes
and a straw hat

The sparkle of brief showers
and sunlight's dappled tattoos: the streets
breathed lungfuls of fresh air

We'd park the beasts
to move in a herd
toward eight o'clock Mass
and refill our flasks of holy water
not going beyond the porch

Hot spicy blood-sausage at eleven
and crunchy macaroons for relaxed strolls
through both cemeteries

Aah High Mass at noon
where rum is our priest
we worked on getting sloshed
four fingers at a time
without lemon or *madou*
but plenty of palaver

And then the return djob
for the leftover flowers
The vendors were lovelier
and wearing their jewelry

After that came
(if famine'd been averted)
Noilly-Prat
chicken fricassee in an airy shack
near a proffered bouquet

A full-belly nap
in the heat

Hey-hey! six o'clock
the moment for slipping off to the tamarind trees
where beneath a nice stiff torch
we'd fondle those two bad dice

(but first absinthe and *la décolle*)
           *
We were already mixing up our nights
into a single insomnia

When it was impossible for us to say
where Monday was

if today was Thursday
or if Saturday came first

A *Quimboiseur* became alarmed at this run-on life and
somewhere someone wrote down two tears

What did we care?
We carried time around
in our toolboxes.

*

At the latest news
Ephermise becomes a tortoise
with big glossy scales
the two wings of a white hen
and a *chien-fer*'s tail

Flap-flap she's in flight
and puzzling dust
vanishes neither up nor down
in the burgeoning echo of iron roofs

(no need to see that, lil' girl,
keep your eyes on those puddles)

Hey-hey! Curious, she nips off to the South
far from the North, so bushy for marooning,
that encloses you protectively
within a thicket of strength

Hey hey! Why cut a tall story down to size
but Ephermise is heading South
        one long parched cry
        where roots are bone-dry

*

An ancient hatred flung us
against the dogs we'd corner
and beat with iron bars in the market's center aisle
beneath the Syrians' marquee
and under trucks
we had no flamboyance of moonlight
or real dawn saluting us
whipped on by something inexplicable

our distress revered forgotten memories
and only the leafless taste
of charred trees
followed the remains.

     *

Little day in the deep of the day
when the after-noon has switched its shadows round

The whole market shudders once
and the railing's stripes draw in

Oo fountain
big copper faucet
spitter of fake waves
make-believe waterfall
you became Papa of a thirsty people

We'd hover, haggard,
around your gluey verdigris
more dazed and flapped out
than those thousand panting vegetables

     *

Pipi's wheelbarrow
became moondust stuck to sidewalk cement
The city's housewives left their brooms there
and the street cleaners
stashed two shovels

Above it
the rain splayed sideways
sunbeams were simply all soaked up
as with really black skins
Adiabatic presence

Tongues showered
this mystery with words

And so
many months flew by
with nary a tear in anyone's eye

     *

The little poet of early December
came looking for purebreds
(é-é! vistas of dirty rats
                and seam-sprung wheelbarrows)

Prophet of fervors and solar winds
he longed to seize hold of monsters
to open eyes
                (a-a! tiny sketches of backs bent
                over half-empty baskets
                gleaming sultry torpor
                invisible malaise
                The railings' shadows add a poignant touch)

He envisioned assagais of bamboo
forests on the move in brawls and affrays
The enemy was driven from the dream
and Dawn inevitable
                (well-now! the consoling sweetness of rum punch
                clink of spoons
                cold cigarette butts and pineapple perfumes
                quiet words
                and eyes gone vacant)

He sought the distant murmur of jungles
in a glassy alchemy of petrified savanna

Little poet, shouted Elmire,
see what you must see
and if it's red ants dancing
on sugary yellow spit-gobs
watch how busily they bustle about

(when Pipi was off living in his clearing,
we introduced the little poet
to the study of the cryptic ripenings
and desperate joys
of peppers and *macadam*)
        *
In the rain
the iron roofs of the market tinkled like Christmas

long tears trickled down
the railings *tchiii gloooo*

Gutters gurgled anew
reflecting damp displays
of vegetables in the best-of-health
and freshened-up fruits *iiste suiii*

In spite of the shelter
water flies tracked our ankles
pouncing huntresses *suitt pitok suii*

Out in front
a dog still wavered
between us and the deluge *gloo wââr*

Darker
cooler
smells faded, listening
to the gossip of rain from the heavens *tchuii glooo.*

*

In praise of Elmire the voyager

Age had battered you
and by that time
no memories of you without that milk-white head

Oo Elmire
Elmire
a hide like the heels of wandering zombies
proof against many a wind
and your eyes seeking the seven wonders
had fetched first from the world the seven sorrows

In the end
by that time
what a crowd around your words!
What commotion for your memory!
The rest of us still in the egg
and you a breaker of shells

You
who had freed your eyes to look upon
lands blue-misting in the distance

you never told us here was small
You yourself
who had seen ardor challenge bullets
and the gaze of peoples
in mangrove swamps gleaming without eclipse
you never said that here was cowardice

Oo you perceived a great complexity in
the *raziés* of misfortune
thickets uncombed for centuries

Bending over us you steadied yourself
without courting tornadoes
from quaking flesh
and
planted like a totem
you kept words warm for us
brooding a resonant hoard of eternal promise.

*

It was Sirop [66] a vendor insulted
calling him black
as Béhanzin

We refused then and there to djob
her baskets

Only Sirop would accept on the spot
to do her errands
he worked wonders for her
in traffic jams and sprinkled water
on all her fragile vegetables in the blazing sun
            enraptured by the insult.

*

The rats took over
the stalls, the sacks of beans, and the
cardboard boxes where the scales were sleeping

They so filled up the night
they overflowed into the day
among the first footsteps, fresh sweetsops,
the taro sprouts and neat bundles of herbs

After our panic
we got used to that weaving braid of dirty fur

Rôôô the darkness of crab holes and lost culverts
plagued by love-sickness
and without fear of the sun
had fixed her North to the navel of our night
and that busybody had come out to meet us

        (everything's just fine, thank you).

    *

De profundis

No one was surprised
when the funeral notices took six hours
and a half We chocked our wheelbarrows
in a most chilling distress, backs
bowing beneath each announcement of bad luck

Odibert heard her name
in the second quarter-hour Her eyes had lost all life
for the longest time already
and her only smell was pepper perfume
Clinging to her nun's habit were flakes
from the one-way trip to the land of quicklime

She didn't flinch
Neither did we

In the bin of fruitless errands
and yellowed vegetables in lovelorn baskets
worse than the mystery of the tools
ripened the daily horror
of the death that precedes death

(sister mine, for you as for us all
the Announcements came a little late).

Your last reflex was that handful
of earth held to your myopic eyes
in which no enigma was resolved
no indifference returned to caring

You remained a stranger in this
strange world

and
evanescing like too fine a mist
on a sizzling stone
you left behind a useless grave
(even in death
you were afraid of roots).

 *

There were vegetables that we no longer saw
and herbs gone missing without a trace

No *razié* offered up wild fruits
and fifteen hundred flowers had run out
of sun

Half-filled
the vendors' baskets left
our wheelbarrows lightheaded
and our eyes lackluster
the mornes weren't coming into town anymore
and out there oblivion was hard at work

Oo vendors without vocation
Country girls cast up here by mean old life
foolish women forgetful of the ancient names
we have ourselves neglected

   do you know that
   nothing will remain of us
   not even a who's that

mango-season doomed to barrenness.

 *

Sometimes our sleepless nights surprised
the swish of somnambulistic cars
rolling aimlessly and driverless
down WRONG WAY streets

 *

Think of a really sad day. Sad because the night before's *serbi*
had bled your dice dry, or because you'd danced your bones
achy at a *zouc*,[67] or because the vendors had brought fresh news
from the hills about murderous gendarmes. The sun made us
as drowsy as anolis, the stark shadows from the iron railings

sliced up the market, the vendors sagged over between their
spread-apart knees, the tiles of the stalls washed the silence
white: a straying night wind swept the aisles clean.

*

When at six o'clock
the lights flared up
(fruits of fire on iron coconut trees)
We dragged our shadows along
like convicts' Cayenne[68] chains

The sweet smells of fruits
had somewhat soured
and discarded leaves
mussed up the aisles

Drying the day's sweat
the first evening wind breezed through the silences

Ah, the market women moved so slowly
packing up

Their early-morning oomph had burned right out

The advancing twilight never honored
any promise from the dawn
Nyah-nyah gnats and mosquitoes
nourished each light bulb
with a speckled skim milk

The creaking of loaded baskets
Stalls gleaming like tombs
darkness besieged the five patches of light
and life softly left
hounded by the brooms of municipal zombies
floating down the damp aisles

We left the premises
like and with the garbage.

*

Now, at night, all the tiles
were swabbed down with creosol

This blue milk dispersed the life
left behind by the day

Oo that lingering murmur by the stalls
the hunt is on
for lost voices
and hopeless fruits
gone begging there

the market lived without us
a disinfected night

    *

At the song of the pippiree
a wheelbarrow stampede
we hurtled toward the vendors
coming in from the countryside

The streets were deserted
and the city was naked

We looked modestly down
on the worthy widow's bowed head
dignified despite the insults lobbed
by flocks of poets

Tough field to clear ooo

We're new muscles
and we know how to lend-a-hand

FROM THE CHRONICLE

Four years of writing. A kind of obsession: scribbled sentences, words, remarks. An idea of writing you get into your head without really knowing what you'll do with it. Characters who appear, evolve, falter, and leave the story. Emotions, smells, sensations brought back from who knows where, that seem good and true, and that drop like autumn leaves. So many genocides for a simple novel, such slaughter for a shadow.

P C

Only patience was of the essence.

*

Then there were useless words about a mystery at some water's edge where every drop is pregnant with a fish.

*

Beneath the open roof of the market, sickened, we waited for that night in May when twenty-two scattered fears would demolish this jungle for us.

*

Oh, bewilderment of falling.

*

Every smile pulled to pieces.

*

When the mild rains came, you calmed down. Macadam forgotten, you risked marooning without torches in your own night. Who could have known, Pipi, that you were untangling nets of colors, greenwood birds with plant-sap plumage, the hotheads of a grassy clearing?

*

All grades-and-models of dead flesh.

*

He remembered the Alma fountainhead: its living spring is a plant form, unfinished in a lost gurgling of lacy fragility.

*

Ah, the dream-merchants quite simply cracked open our indehiscent lives with a vomitory leading to forgotten doors.

*

Ephermise had been coming to the market for two years now. She sold bunches of scrawny carrots, callaloo greens, and sometimes the odd yam. The guardian had given her a niche near the brooms, right on the center aisle, and no step, no glance could help but find her. She paid for her djobs with a generous hand. Eyes of rain sparkling with a captive sunbeam, a coulie's wiry body, dugs flat from suckling fourteen children. Eight of them surrounded her basket in a constant cacophony of blackbirds. Sirop, who knew how to set them laughing, won the coulie's heart, and spent three Sundays in her shack in

Ajoupa-Bouillon: to get down to business, he shook the brats off somewhere in town.

*

About Sirop, tell her these three memories: darkness, blood, death. And, without beating about the bush, let her know that armed with dreams the man was a dreamer, always a dreamer, a ferocious dreamer.

*

Here, botched dreams shattered against one another without a single spark. Stubborn regrets, much withered, encircled imaginary springs. There was massive ennui, standing quite straight in a passel of pleats and puckers: Marie-Julie's eyes turned empty when she was about fifteen.

*

Here, all passions spent, the unbelievable no longer amazes the impossible.

*

We had repainted your wheelbarrow, scrubbed the wheels with vinegar and salt, lined the bottom with linoleum, tightened the bell, and touched up the gilt trim. As dazzling as in your finest hour and parked in her place, she spoke of you every day. Only, here's the thing, Pipi: sun, wind, and rain led her such a dance that we could see her drooping before our eyes like those lonely anolis under long-lost trees. Oh, nothing's budding here, the perfect profession for a man adrift, end-of-the-century djobbers squeezed right out of life.

*

To tell the truth, the cyclone made us feel young again. All in a tizzy, Fort-de-France was lapping the mud from our ankles: what endless carting around for all the Syrians! They even talked about us on the radio! And for a few heady days our calamity was real . . .

*

Every day some word would spin out of our language and plummet to oblivion, where it didn't push up flowers. Or even leave petrified remains out on the savanna. A flight without survival in the wild.

*

Madame Carmélite you hotfooted it off to the airport, abandoning your basket, and even your head scarf. Your silence increased the silence of the market in the merciless leprosy of spots going bare.

*

Elmire, one day, she bowled us over with other kinds of Creoles. The words were relatives and strangers. We were wandering in a familiar town with round-the-corner surprises in a few new neighborhoods. We perceived ancient things that troubled our tongues, a dense *razié* without any clearing, and abrupt tufts of wildflowers that seemed to know us. Dazzled by a real opacity in which we spied everything. Elmire laughed at our excitement. We listened to her, fascinated to learn we were blustering all over this region and in no way washed out to sea by the waves on our shores. Elmire wanted us to have true glimpses of the blue lands on the horizon, and pointed out to us invisibly hidden things.

*

Famine was paying calls we didn't know how to refuse. She got a foothold, for an hour, in Didon's wheelbarrow: with that opening, rum settled his hash – but fast.

*

Jugged rat[69]: when we caught the she-rat, Bidjoule had the bad idea of popping her inside a demijohn where the first day she zipped around in anguished circles, the second she went backwards, the third she gave up squealing, the fourth she lost three memories and the fifth all color from her eyes.

Her sixth day staggered us: the scoundrel seemed just like us.

*

Leaning against the railings, one foot up on the wheelbarrows, we'd watch the ladies who shopped like sheep at the made-in-France stores stop by for a few things on Saturday. Not one vendor's basket wasn't haggled over! No fruits were indisputably splendid, no yams or sweet potatoes escaped re-weighing: there every last drop of sweat was bargained for – and all life as well.

*

"Marie-Julie," Mam Goul would say, "the Syrians have changed a lot, the ones I knew, let me tell you, those beggarly fellows behind their barrows of rags we bought out of pity to see them tramping the country like homeless dogs. Now just look at those shop windows, those lights, those marble counters. Not for them anymore our kerosene lamps, our small wooden shanties. It's satin lies next to their skin, and it's tiles they walk on, and they don't come with us any longer, round midnight, to bring out their night soil." This was the only fairy tale for that little vendor who was sadder than the rest.

*

Anaïse, how could I say nothing about your unexpected ruin? Draped in white, you floured your black skin and huffed ether non-stop. Your gray silhouette was a laughingstock, and your dream of easy achromasia made you a pushover for thirteen sex fiends. When you up and vanished, we harvested a smidgen of flour near the Crédit Agricole Bank: like the unblinking stare of a cloudy-eyed blind man, oh, it summed up your misfortune whitely.

*

All Saints' Day bloomed in our barrows of flowers and planted a garden like a wreath for the market. We put in hours on djobs for the poor in Trabaut or for rich folks in their own cemetery, as painters of whitewash, virtuosos of gilding, scourges of weeds and candle-poops. With the first shadows (they were violet) a thousand domestic stars winked out our regrets (in oily yellow), a heart of conflagration for Fort-de-France in the November of graves (on a red horizon), and the ambience made an incomparable backdrop for serbi (streaked by the dirty comets of our dice).

*

The pineapple vendors from Morne-Rouge brought us the news from Colson, that ship of mists in the woods of Balata, barely glimpsed through a rent in the bamboo curtains. No rains weathered it. Oh, Colson, you damned dogged hunter, sole banker of the great serbi, you left us the going since you had the coming, chien-fer thriving on our twists and turns . . .

*

Mam Sidore's patient wait gave her the glazed eyes of bonitos on ice, and the shadows of the railings sliced up equal portions. Round about, dented trucks unloaded late-arriving hampers:

Yélélés greeted outbursts of *Mi mwen!* [Here I am!] Two listless dogs came sniffing the baskets of verbena despite shouts of rage. Near the main gate, the *macadam* rice was washed, and the salt cod was soaking. The aisles were caught in a milky web of dried creosol. A few flavescent leaves, shed during delivery, fell to weaving the carpet that would be finished by nightfall. A *chabin* toddler wobbled about near a basket of mangoes. The fragrance of ripe fruit was on the rise. Racked on the railings, madras cloths and Syrian rugs blocked out the sun. The municipal guardian stood on the fountain, counting his flock, tracking down those unaccounted-for with an accusatory eye. In the center: the startling red of tomatoes and the lively exchange of curses between two warring vendors. The iron roofs started sending down heat that spread tepidly on the tired wind from the canal. The muffled screaks of our wheelbarrows rose or fell over by the gates. The tone of our voices kept pace with the heat. Scales fumbled their way into balance. Knives puzzled out the hearts of roots, flowers were married in garish bouquets, and the vendors, their legs set at ten-to-two, elbows on knees, faces looming like halos over their wares, assumed for the duration of the day the worried gaze of hooked garfish.

*

Despite the sanitation department's nightly rounds, the culvert had snagged a dutty dog dispatched by a vicious blow. It was patchy with scummy froth. The morning's mandarin-orange leaves planted a fake lawn on its belly. The first wave of heat tormented it with distant shudders. The *Blokotoblos* of Bidjoule, who alone would go near it the whole blessed day, kept it a company nowhere near as palatable as a tasty bowl of arrowroot.

*

Sacks of coal marked his domain with a periodic cloud of swiftly dispersed night. Out in front, Solibo[70] reigned like the pope of a whole heap of big-blacks, while wickedly famished red roaches and *clakclak kakos*[71] skittered around a calamity they never even suspected.

*

Tell of the bastard yam, a rare dish, spiky with tiny hairs. The bamboche, permanent porter of a faint bitterness. Oo, the white yam, Pipi would say, with dreamy eyes: light and crumbly, salted with tears of joy. Our yellow yam, long black African fingers, answering promptly to its name. The fat-head, horse's-hoof, and the *ador*. Oh mama, the *bocodji*, so juicy you have to bite into it from below. Not forgetting the cush-cush, daughter of the Other America, that opens up into a melting white mousse: around here everyone just pounces on that . . .

To reassure ourselves, each day we would read these earthy heaps in their bulging baskets. Mam Goul monitored the Word.

We wept over the rusted *raziés* of factories, but Elmire bemoaned the stooping wretches in the steel mirrors of Europe, the grease of American gears, the stench and ropes of smoke from the clanking factories far away.

We wept over the concrete, gobbler of fertile soils, but Elmire sobbed over the muddy beggary of fields, the agricultural tortures of the Other America, across the way from us.

We wept over the downfall of yawls on scowling waves, but Elmire the Voyager said she knew the shadow corroding the squinting men that float in monsters, on the fringe of carpets of fish, on the high seas.

Why don't you weep, she shouted, for Gogo instead, the bird who saw fit to drown himself right here, when his throat felt a touch dry.

*

In Saint-Joseph, four fiery *chabines* char pepper shrubs by turning up their heat.

*

Little poet, Elmire would say, don't invent a song saga when it's moss that chews up iron.

*

Down the deepest slopes within, we braided, bloodless, the roots of absence.

*

Your final face, Sirop, gleamed with the moist slickness of half-past noon, when your gaze became a shipwreck on the red horizon of rum's old acquaintance. We knew, ho, the stiffness of your neck and the too-blue color of your lips from your last Mélia cigarette. This sickness was a bitch, without master or heart, we quailed before it, true victims of a storm, as on that day freshly painted in glory when a Rasta de-baptized the city.

*

Oh new giddiness of liberties obscene!

*

Then came the time when her favorite voyage was silence.

*

He saw there a whole geography of shadows where vast births could be committed.

*

A strange feeling called her name to the beating of his heart.

*

With a sour fervor that overcame his lassitude, Afoukal promised his memory audience in its sacred madness.

*

Up on the Gueydon Bridge, he saw himself in the water: the only possible mishap in the reflection.

*

For Amélia, service was impossible: she hauled a hidden sorrow along the stalls. Oo djobbing her own heart . . .

*

Bonne-Mama was left deranged by her husband's death. Her hair shaved off, she slept on the square in front of the church, letting dust and spiders invade the bistro. The Loony now did nothing more than open the doors and take cover behind the grimy bar to wait for clients who never came, for it cut our thirst off cold to see her so. Chinotte acquired the place with a shining gold piece that Bonne-Mama tucked too quickly over her heart, like a communion wafer to be treasured. Barely had the bill of sale been signed, it's said, than that coin brought her an unhealthy joy. Possessed by unquenchable laughter, she haunted the market for several days, spooking the tourists, the municipal guardian, and even the dogs that overran the place

at night. The gendarmes who arrived to put a stop to this business could cart her off no fuss no bother. The dement followed
them obediently into the jeep, singing her lungs out, waving
greetings like the popes and De Gaulle. She died in a room in
Colson, the victim of a hoarse cough with no horizon.

Afterword

PATRICK CHAMOISEAU has written eloquently and extensively about the bilingual heritage of the French Caribbean and his personal sense of mission as a Creole writer. The literature of Martinique, he points out, did not evolve smoothly from a native oral tradition of linguistic creativity but sprang instead from a fundamental discontinuity: the gap between the orality of Creole, a language born – of cruel necessity – in the days of slavery, and French, the language of a colonial power that proudly, ruthlessly, and efficiently discredited almost all Creole culture in the name of *la civilisation française.* And so it is only the reenergizing contact between orality and literature that can assure the authenticity of Creole writing, insists Chamoiseau, turning for his model to the figure of the Creole storyteller, who even back in the dark heart of the slave plantations spoke words of life to ward off the spiritual poisons of colonialism.

In Chamoiseau's essay *Que faire de la Parole?* [What to do with the spoken word?], he says that the Creole writer must try to speak for an audience "of downtrodden souls who look to him for wonder, distraction, escape, laughter, hope, excitement, the key to resistance and endurance, an audience drawn from all over the world" and newly conscious of its diversity. In searching for his voice as a writer, Chamoiseau has sought to give voice to the powerless, to those who have been marginalized in Martinican society, so that they may question this *otherness* that has been imposed on them. While it is true of any society that the identification of the strong and the weak begins with language and is perfected through education, this is particularly true of those former colonial outposts where a crippling self-loathing is still too often taught in the classroom along with a foreign "mother tongue." And yet, as Chamoiseau describes in his moving memoir *School Days,* he learned as a child "bent over his notebook [to trace], without fully realizing it, an inky lifeline of survival . . ."

For Chamoiseau, the Creole writer, writes in French. Like many authors in our postcolonial world – in India, Africa,

South America, the Caribbean – he has taken the fight to the enemy, so to speak, and made the empire strike back. In the introduction to his *Creole Folktales*, he describes how the slave storyteller must outwit the master, "must take care to use language that is opaque, devious – its significance broken up into a thousand sibylline fragments. His narrative turns around long digressions that are humorous, erotic, often even esoteric." The captors' History becomes the captives' histories and subversive stories. How discreetly Chamoiseau refers in *Chronicle* to America's stranglehold on Martinique during World War II, and how fancifully he embroiders his anecdotes of deprivation, modestly reclaiming the island's reality – its *locality* – from the limbo of a footnote in the epic of Western Civ. The corrosive power of colonialism is perhaps nowhere more telling than in the amnesia of a people deprived of collective memory by an ancient wound, a wound the writer must reopen to shock his Martinican audience into a new awareness of itself. "For history is not only absence for us," writes Glissant, "it is vertigo." The vertigo of a community expelled from Eden, transported from Africa, separated from France – despite departmentalization – by a distance even greater than the Middle Passage itself.

What Glissant refers to as magical realism in Chamoiseau is another storyteller's ruse: not merely the escapism that imagines slaves' souls winging home to the Great-Country at last, but a kind of defiance of "rational" civilization on behalf of those who are considered hopeless riffraff because they remain unconvinced that the heroic fathers of their country – those slave traders, merchants, and plantation owners of the good old days – were anything but vampires. Pipi may hang with a zombi, but he's no fool: "Gentlemen, they're still here!" The real zombies are those who move through their world with minds that are culturally dispossessed, who spurn the market's island bounty for mealy supermarket apples from France. Afoukal, that master storyteller, must literally raise a concealed world to the level of consciousness, for who else will break the silence and tell the people of Martinique *who they are*? The little black boy in *School Days* opens his history book and reads, "Our ancestors, the Gauls . . ." Now there's an exercise in genuine magical realism that beggars anything Chamoiseau could ever dream up.

That little Creole boy learned French, and with a vengeance: Chamoiseau writes in a French that has been "Chamoisified," to borrow a term from Milan Kundera. In this *Chronicle*, Chamoiseau tries out for the first time the relaxed yet elegant style so suited to his enterprise, which is – to talk to us. He does not pretend with his narrator to mimic the speech of "real" djobbers (no market porter in Martinique ever spoke as Chamoiseau writes), but playfully, yet with the utmost seriousness and the confidence of a superb technician, he puts classical French through some tropical paces. It is no secret that French is a touch more stuffy than English about allowing liberties to be taken, but Chamoiseau gently tweaks that French *hauteur* with casual charm. His attitude is a generous one: anything goes, if it gets the job done. "My use of French," he writes in his instructions to his translators, "is all-encompassing. For me there are no obsolete, antiquated, uncommon, out-of-bounds words." Chamoiseau is a free-range writer who tries to keep his language "open" so that readers will feel its humble, questing flexibility, a kind of remarkable mongrelism that proves perfect for the task at hand: presenting a deftly self-conscious form of Creoleness in this chronicle of "mouth-memory" telling stories to a word scratcher.

And of course, Chamoiseau uses Creole. He employs Creole turns of phrase and images and occasionally tosses in sound bites of Creole speech (his translations appear within parentheses, mine within brackets). The Creole words for various plants, fruits, vegetables, animals, and so on that pop up throughout the original French text are to a great extent retained in this translation and are either explained by the author himself, easily understood in their context, clarified by me with a descriptive word or two, twinned with their English meanings when they first appear (*manicou*-possum, for example), or explained in the notes I have provided. Some Creole words, particularly those for a host of native plants with medicinal properties, have simply been translated into English. With the author's permission, I moved the material in his original footnotes either into the text itself (when it fit in gracefully) or to the notes (where it is marked with an asterisk).

Chamoiseau is not fond of glossaries and believes that the "Creole dimension" of his work should be safeguarded against the alienating ideal of "transparency." I have tried to respect the author's desire not to see what he calls "shadow areas" whited out by the rude glare of translation – while not leaving the reader floundering in the dark, either. If every last linguistic blip on Chamoiseau's screen were explained, the addenda might explode the novel. (When I looked up Zouti's name, for example, I found it meant: 1. nettle 2. weapon 3. tool 4. penis 5. an extraordinary man.) I like to think that the items in Chronicle's notes are little pages out of Chamoiseau's own book, for are they not "sibylline fragments" in their own right, tiny tales that might open up into who-knows-what? How about Auguste Cybaris, tossed into jail for drunkenness one fatal night in Saint Pierre, sole survivor of the nuée ardente from Mt. Pelée, who spent the rest of his life with the Barnum Circus performing in a replica of his cell? And what of marronnage, that shaping force on Caribbean culture, the armed flight and rebellion of such legendary figures as Mackandal, Cudjoe, Quaco, Accompong, Cuffee – and the woman maroon Nanny, one of Jamaica's national heroes? Like the amorous sign language of the famous madras turban, the least little detail of Chamoiseau's narrative may be a cipher that leads to great things . . .

Chamoiseau's appendix of outtakes from his novel is a kind of glossary in its own right, where texts call out like cheeky répondeurs, at times almost speaking in tongues, commenting out of the blue on the Chronicle we have just read. The appendix is particularly rich in that opacity so dear to Chamoiseau (echoes of incidents reported in local newspapers, cryptic references to hitherto unheard-of characters, what the author refers to as "impossible" turns of phrase) and offers a tantalizing jumble through which the reader may wander at will, like the young Pierre Philomène in the entrancing marketplace of Fort-de-France.

As Édouard Glissant observes in his Caribbean Discourse, "for us it is a question of reconciling, in the end, the values of the culture of writing and the long-repressed traditions of orality." It is in this spirit that Chamoiseau brings to the printed page the mysterious dimension, the irreducible chaos, of the voice. And here is the last of Chamoiseau's personal rules of writing: "I sacrifice everything to the music of the words."

Linda Coverdale

Notes

Notes that appeared in the original are marked with an asterisk; the others have been added by the translator.

1. *Geste* means both "gesture" and "heroic act," as in the *chanson de geste*, an Old French epic tale in verse organized around a single figure.

2. A *marqueur de paroles* is a "word scratcher": in Martinican French, this neologism means a "writer" or "novelist," but Chamoiseau has made clear that to him the term means someone who seeks out and attempts to pass along the rich oral traditions of *Créolité*.

3. *Oiseau de Cham* – "bird of Ham" (the son Noah cursed as the father of a race of slaves) – is a play on the author's name, as is *Chamgibier*, which may be read phonetically as "fieldgame" (game in the sense of wild birds or animals).

4. Dub poetry, which emerged in the early 1970s in Jamaica and England, is a form of popular poetry in the vernacular or patois and is influenced by the rhythms of reggae music. The term was first applied to the improvised rapping of Jamaican deejays declaiming over instrumental "dub" tracks.

5. From the French *marmaille* [children, kids], *manmaye* can also mean epithets such as "guys" or "folks." *Manmaye ho!* is this storyteller's invitation to listen up.

6. The Creole for *Madame* is actually *Man* – which, for obvious reasons, became *Mam* in this translation, with the author's consent.

7. A steep hill or small mountain of volcanic origin.

8. The prefix *ti* means *petit* [little]; *ti-nains* [lil' dwarfs] are small bananas that are still green.

9.* No fooling around, friend: use only this term to refer to a snake . . . [The extremely venomous *trigonocéphale* or fer-de-lance probably reached Martinique on timber floating down the Orinoco from the Venezuelan hinterland. It lurks in long grass or lies along tree branches, darting at its prey like a javelin. "It haunts our subconscious," according to Édouard Glissant. "The countrypeople say: the enemy, the long beast. They even call it (to avoid saying the word 'snake') *la cravate*, the necktie." – Trans.]

10. Silk-cotton trees are highly valued by sorcerers for their magical properties. The x-ray eyes of a jablesse cannot see through silk cotton, for example, so a man may protect himself from a she-devil's wiles by carrying a crucifix wrapped in this elastic fiber.

11. An incubus of Martinican folklore.

12.* A *béké* is a white Creole whose family has lived in Martinique for generations. The word is said to derive either from the French *becqué* [beaked, "beaky"] or from the early colonists' repeated exclamation *Eh bien quoi?* or *Eh ben que?* [And so what?].

13. After the abolition of slavery in the French Antilles, people from many different parts of the world were brought in to work on the sugar plantations. The immigrants from India, or *coulis*, were the largest group of indentured laborers. Two other groups of new arrivals were the Chinese, who tended to enter small shopkeeping, and the Syrian or Lebanese (present-day Lebanon was at that time part of Syria), who specialized in retailing cloth, clothes, and household goods.

14.* In Creole, the term *engagé(e)* referred to those who indentured themselves: the servants of *boucaniers*; poor whites; Indian immigrants; blacks after the Emancipation. These bondsmen were *aux gages* [pledged, "forfeited" to their employer], so blindly did one obey the orders of the colonists in those days. The term is now applied to "dealers," those who are thought to have put themselves in thrall to the Devil in return for receiving special powers. [*Mukem*, the Tupi word for a wooden framework on which meat was smoked or barbecued over a fire, became the French *boucan*; the name *boucanier* or *buccaneer* was given first in St. Domingo to French hunters of wild cattle and later to the pirates who preyed on Spanish-American ships and settlements in the seventeenth and eighteenth centuries.]

15. St. Anthony of Padua, Patron of the Poor, is popularly invoked for luck and for help in finding lost objects.

16. *Bakoua* refers to the screw pine and also to the conical, wide-brimmed straw hat woven from its fronds.

17. *Chabin(e)*: someone of mixed race with "high yellow"

coloring: light skin; sometimes green, blue, or gray eyes; and often wavy or curly reddish or blond hair.

18. La Trace was originally a track cut through the mountainous interior by Jesuits in the seventeenth century, the first road from Fort-de-France to Saint Pierre. Today it offers a drive though dense rainforest.

19. The word *quimbois/kenbwa* comes from French instructions given when remedies were dispensed: "Tiens, bois" [Here, drink]. *Quimbois* magic can be black or white; a *quimboiseur/quimboiseuse* is a seer or healer. The prefix "papa" or "mama" is an intensifier, so a *papa-quimboiseur* is a powerful sorcerer.

20. The daughter of a mulatto and a black person is a *câpresse*.

21. I added an *a* to Chamoiseau's *matador*, which in Creole usage means a strong, authoritative woman with a certain haughty elegance.

22. In his novel *Texaco* (1992), Chamoiseau tells the story of a scam by *békés* who toured Martinique with a statue of the Virgin, collecting money and jewels from the populace, and then vanished with the loot. The plaster statue was later found abandoned in a chapel in the Jossaud Quarter of Fort-de-France.

23. *Pacotille* originally referred to the goods taken aboard ship by seamen or passengers for private sale. Elmire is a "merchant-adventuress" who sells trinkets. The *pacotilleuses* who peddle craft items in Fort-de-France sometimes go to Haiti to purchase their stock.

24. Henri Philippe Pétain, Marshal of France, chief of state in the Vichy government, convicted of treason in 1945.

25.* The djobbers are referring to Admiral Georges Robert, High Commissioner of the French Antilles (1939) during World War II.

26. Mulatto, mulattress: the offspring of a black and a white; popularly, any person of mixed black and white ancestry. Ti-Joge, for example, is a quadroon, but Chamoiseau refers to him as a mulatto.

27. A *vidé* is a boisterous mixture of singing, parading, and

racing around that takes place during Carnival, after elections, or at the end of a dance.

28. One of the most characteristic dishes of the West Indies, a *blaff* is a spicy fish stew named, it is said, from the sound the fish makes when popped into the kettle.

29. Once the cultural and commercial heart of Martinique, Saint-Pierre is the oldest town on the island and one of the prettiest in the Caribbean, protected from the Atlantic trade winds by Mt. Pelée (Bald Mountain), which erupted on May 8, 1902, killing more than 30,000 people within two minutes. Although it had been the administrative center of the island since 1681, Fort-de-France was a sleepy and unhealthy backwater town until this disaster, when it rose, so to speak, from the ashes of its former rival.

30. *Gwo-ka* [big drum] is the traditional drum and vocal music of the hills. The largest drum is played with the hands by two drummers; a *gwo-ka* ensemble may include various *ka*-drums of different sizes, and players may also strike large sections of bamboo called *ti-bwa* [lil' wood].

31. Vetiver, from the Tamil *vettivēru* [root that is dug up], is a tropical grass whose roots yield a fragrant oil, prized for perfumes, and fibers for making screens, mats, and so on. When used for scrubbing floors, vetiver keeps away insects and leaves a pleasant scent.

32. *Bois-bandé* [hard-on wood]: *Roupala montana*, the "male" remedy taken to help induce and sustain an erection.

33. Mt. Hillaby is in the north of this pear-shaped island; its parishes are named after saints.

34. The calenda originated in the kingdom of Arada on the Guinea coast, according to Father Jean-Baptiste Labat, a Dominican missionary who at the end of the seventeenth century provided one of the earliest accounts of the life of slaves in the Antilles. To the beat of drums, a line of women and a line of men would repeatedly advance toward one another and retreat, leaping and pirouetting with "lascivious" gestures and improvised songs. "Their passion for this dance," wrote Père Labat, "is beyond the imagination."

35. The *collier-choux* is a necklace of several rows of large, hollow gold beads worn with the national costume of the island.

36. The *gros-sirop* [heavy syrup] necklace of double-linked chain is one of the traditional pieces of Martinican gold jewelry. "Dahlias," "sweetsops," "negress-nipples," and "wasp's-nests" are made from tiny flowers, balls, and petals of gold arranged in distinctive designs and worn as earrings, brooches, and so on. The *chenille* is made by twisting together three strands that are themselves formed by twisted gold threads; this "caterpillar" can be used as a necklace, brooch, or other jewelry. Earrings and brooches *à clous* are a very old design featuring golden cylinders with golden balls at each end; the *clous* are supposedly modeled on the rollers that crushed sugarcane in the old sugar mills.

37. This Antichrist is a *monstre*, which in Martinican folklore is a creature born from a hen's egg that is incubated in a person's armpit all through Lent. The manikin that hatches on Easter has magical powers, including that of bestowing riches, and is sometimes invisible to all but its master.

38.* See the list of djobber's cries in the appendix.

39.* *Échappé(e)-couli(e)*: a person of black and East Indian parentage.

40. *Laghia*, which resembles the *capoeira* of Brazil, is a form of dance-combat supposedly developed by African slaves who trained in secret to fight.

41.* The entire song appears in the appendix.

42. The French *marron* is an abbreviation from the Spanish *cimarrón*, meaning wild and unruly, from *cima* [mountaintop]. A maroon was originally a fugitive black slave living on a West Indian island or in Dutch Guiana; the term is now used for the descendants of such slaves.

43. A rhythmic exchange between the Creole storyteller and audience. "É kri?" calls out the teller, demanding attention; "É kra!" respond the listeners, proving their vigilance. The English version is: "Crick-crack?" "Pommerac!" ("Monkey break 'e back on a rotten pommerac!")

44. La Savane is Fort-de-France's twelve-acre park of lawn, shade trees, walks, benches, playing fields, and towering royal palms. Martinicans come to "promenade" here in the evenings.

45.* The djobbers are referring to Statute Number 46–51 of March 19, 1946, which granted "the status of overseas départements to Guadeloupe, Martinique, Réunion, and French Guiana."

46.* *Haute-taille*: a dance during which couples must follow a constant flow of directions sung by a caller.

47. An almost hairless dog with grayish skin; according to Chamoiseau, the *chien-fer* is the most detested dog in the Creole imagination.

48. In *The Memoirs of Père Labat*, 1693–1705, yellow fever is referred to as *le mal de Siam*.

49. Columbus visited "Martinica" and found it charming, but the Caribs had their "Madinina" essentially to themselves until 1635, when the first Frenchmen arrived. After twenty-five years of hostilities, the French signed a treaty, agreeing to stay on the leeward coastline and leave the Atlantic side to the Caribs, who were soon exterminated nevertheless. Sauteurs [Leapers] on Grenada commemorates the last stand of that island's Caribs, who hurled themselves into the sea from the top of a steep morne rather than be massacred.

50.* Rastafarianism [from Ras ("Prince") Tafari, the given name of Haile Selassie]. A utopian religious, political, and cultural movement from Jamaica that has attracted many young Martinicans. [Rastas believe that the last emperor of Ethiopia was a black messiah whose call for an end to racism presaged the time when God will lead black people out of oppression and back to the promised land. The spiritual and political concerns of the movement have influenced the often cryptic lyrics of reggae music.]

51. *Cochon-planche* [plank pig]: a particular breed of Creole pig that is as thin as a board.

52. The *bois-canon* (trumpetwood) is a tropical American member of the mulberry family with a hollow stem and branches that are used for wind instruments. In *The Traveller's Tree*, Patrick Leigh Fermor describes the *Cecropia peltata*, which he admired while tramping through the forests of Dominica. "[It] is a beautiful and delicate thing with thin silver boughs all curling up from the stem at the identically spaced points in semicircles like the branches of Jewish candelabra, ending in sparsely growing leaves the same shape as those of the fig tree, but much larger; grey green on one side and on the other, silver

white. In Créole it is called Bois Canon, because, according to one porter, its trunk, when broken, makes a report like a gun firing. The second said it was because it explodes if it is used as fuel, while the third maintained that it owes its name merely to its hollowness, which suggests the barrel of a cannon. This botanic argument carried us for an hour or two through the awe-inspiring high woods."

53. Migan: a soup, cream, or purée; a migan fruyapin, for example, would be a dish of mashed breadfruit.

54. The Martinican court-bouillon is not the classic French poaching liquid, but a dish of fish in sauce with herbs and spices.

55. Aimé Césaire, the great Martinican poet, is a leader of the French black consciousness literary movement Négritude and a former representative of Martinique in the French National Assembly. He has been the mayor of Fort-de-France since 1945. André Aliker was the secretary of the Communist Party of Martinique; he was planning to denounce the big planters for tax fraud but "committed suicide" instead. His corpse washed ashore tied to a piece of sheet metal. . .

56. French sailors wear berets with a red pompom.

57. A ti-mâle is the young hero of a film or any young fellow or pal.

58. Madou: a sweet fruit-juice backup for a shot of rum.

59. The Caribs lived in high, roomy longhouses of woven rush, bamboo, or palm called carbets, and the Grand Carbet is an auditorium for special events in the Parc Floral Sermac in Fort-de-France.

60. The biguine, which Édouard Glissant has called the "true voice of Martinique," began evolving several hundred years ago, first as guitar or banjo music with added percussion, later incorporating clarinets or violins. Biguine dances were based on Africanized French ballroom steps. Martinicans sent to France to fight in the First World War brought their Creole music with them, which sparked a biguine craze in Europe in the 1920s and 30s.

61. "Bird-peppers," tiny scarlet triangles shaped like a bird's tongue.

62. Souskay/souscaille resembles the mango chutneys brought

to Martinique by East Indian field workers. It is usually made from the coarse-fleshed *mangot vert*; in the following recipe, any type of mango may be used as long as it is green and unripe. Peel and slice green mangoes, then marinate the slices for at least ten minutes in a hot sauce made of these ingredients mixed together: 1 cup cold water, ¼ cup fresh green lime juice, several crushed garlic cloves, ½ teaspoon salt, freshly ground pepper, and 1 or more fresh hot green peppers, chopped fine. Eat with the fingers.

63. A common knife with a dog trademark on the handle.

64. The "sea-beak" is the tip of the swordfish's long upper jaw, filed for use as a weapon.

65. *La décolle* [the blast-off]: the first rum of the day, sometimes taken on an empty stomach for maximum punch.

66. *Sirop de batterie* is molasses, and a *nèg gros-sirop* is someone with very black skin, a country bumpkin.

67. *Zouk* is a Creole word that used to mean "party," but when sound systems – also called *zouks* – replaced live music in the 1960s in the French Antilles, the Caribbean's first high-tech dance music was born in a blend of American funk, Caribbean pop, and African rhythms. *Zouk* is emblematic of the crossbreeding that now characterizes much of the international pop scene: the global presence of creolization set to music.

68. A penal colony in French Guiana.

69. A play on words in the French: *scellée rate* [sealed rat] sounds like *scélérate* [scoundrel].

70. Solibo is the exuberant bard of Creole storytelling who enlivens the market of Fort-de-France in *Solibo Magnifique* (1988), Chamoiseau's second novel, and who – in witness to the passing of his way of life, overwhelmed by the "progress" of Western mass culture – drops dead after one last all-night recitation, his throat cut by an exploding word.

71. Big cocoa-colored cockroaches.